D0422465

DEADLY REUNION

Recent Titles by Geraldine Evans from Severn House

The Rafferty and Llewellyn Mysteries

DYING FOR YOU
ABSOLUTE POISON
BAD BLOOD
LOVE LIES BLEEDING
BLOOD ON THE BONES
A THRUST TO THE VITALS
DEATH DUES
ALL THE LONELY PEOPLE
DEATH DANCE
DEADLY REUNION

The Casey and Catt Mysteries

UP IN FLAMES
A KILLING KARMA

DEADLY REUNION

A Rafferty & Llewellyn crime novel

Geraldine Evans

This first world edition published 2011
in Great Britain and the USA by
SEVERN HOUSE PUBLISHERS LTD of
9–15 High Street, Sutton, Surrey, England, SM1 1DF.
Trade paperback edition first published
in Great Britain and the USA 2011 by
SEVERN HOUSE PUBLISHERS LTD.

British Library Cataloguing in Publication Data

Evans, Geraldine.
Deadly reunion. – (A Rafferty and Llewellyn mystery)
1. Rafferty, Joseph (Fictitious character)–Fiction.
2. Llewellyn, Sergeant (Fictitious character)–Fiction.
3. Police–Great Britain–Fiction. 4. Class reunions–
Fiction. 5. Detective and mystery stories.
I. Title II. Series
823.9'14-dc22

ISBN-13: 978-0-7278-8016-1 (cased)
ISBN-13: 978-1-84751-337-3 (trade paper)

All Severn House titles are printed on acid-free paper.

Severn House Publishers support The Forest Stewardship Council [FSC],
the leading international forest certification organisation. All our titles that
are printed on Greenpeace-approved FSC-certified paper carry the FSC logo.

Typeset by Palimpsest Book Production Ltd.,
Falkirk, Stirlingshire, Scotland.
Printed and bound in Great Britain by
MPG Books Ltd., Bodmin, Cornwall.

ONE

'Poisoned? Are you sure?' Detective Inspector Joseph Rafferty regretted his rash query as soon as it left his mouth. For Dr Sam Dally let him have it with both barrels.

'Of course I'm sure. Would I be telling you the man was poisoned if I wasn't? I never question *your* professional judgement –' which was an out and out lie – 'so I'd thank you not to question mine. *Conium Maculatum* was what killed him. Or, to your uneducated ear, hemlock.'

'Hemlock?'

'That's right. A very old-fashioned poison. Goes back to the ancient Greeks, so I believe. Maybe even further back. Now, is there anything else you'd like to question while you're at it?'

'All right, Sam. Keep your hair on,' said Rafferty. Which, given Sam's rapidly balding pate, was another unfortunate slip of the tongue.

But this time it brought nothing more than the testy, 'Well? Is there anything else you'd like to question my judgement about?'

Rafferty felt – given his mounting foot-in-mouth episode – that a simple 'no' would suffice.

'Hmph.' Dally sounded disappointed as if he was just in the right frame of mind to have another go. 'Ainsley had been dead between fourteen and sixteen hours before he was discovered. The first symptoms would have started after around half an hour. He'd have experienced a gradual weakening of muscles, then extreme pain and paralysis from the *coniine* in hemlock, the effects of which are much like *curare*. It's probable he went blind, but his mind would have remained clear till the end.'

'Christ. What a horrible way to go.'

'Yes. Death would be around three hours later from paralysis of the heart.'

'Is the poison likely to be self-inflicted?'

'Well, it wouldn't be my choice.'

Nor mine, thought Rafferty. He couldn't believe that a sportsman like Adam Ainsley would choose such a way to go.

'But figuring that out's your job, Rafferty. I suggest you get on with it.'

Bang went the phone. Or it would have done but for the frustrations caused by modern technology, which didn't allow anything so satisfying.

'Sam and Mary must have had a domestic this morning,' Rafferty said to Sergeant Dafyd Llewellyn as he leaned back in the now shabby executive chair that Superintendent Bradley had decreed was the appropriate seating for his detectives. 'He just bawled me out something chronic.'

Llewellyn, who had never been known to make an ill-advised remark, gave a gentle sigh. 'Dr Dally has never appreciated having his professional conclusions questioned.' It was a gentle reproof, but a reproof nonetheless. 'You were talking about the body found in the woods, I presume?'

Rafferty nodded. Adam Ainsley had been found in Elmhurst's Dedman Wood around eight in the morning two days ago by a local woman walking her dog. There had been no visible signs of injury and it had been assumed the man had had a heart attack while out for too energetic a run; the tracksuit and trainers had suggested the possibility. Ainsley had been attending a reunion at Griffin School, an exclusive, fee-paying establishment for eleven to eighteen year olds situated two miles outside the Essex market town of Elmhurst, where Rafferty's station was located.

'Did I hear you mention hemlock?'

Rafferty nodded. 'I thought that would make you prick up your ears. That's what Sam reckons killed him. Said it goes back to your pals, the ancient Greeks.'

'Yes. According to Plato it's what Socrates used to kill himself after he was sentenced to death. He drained the cup containing the poison and walked about until his legs felt heavy. Then he lay down and, after a while, the drug had numbed his whole body, creeping up until it had reached his heart.'

'Yeah, Sam said it was paralysis of the heart muscle that would have killed him. Sounds like hanging would have been quicker, even without an Albert Pierrepoint to work out the drop required. Anyway, enough of this classical Greek morbidity. We'd better get over to the school,' said Rafferty. 'Can you get some uniforms organized, Dafyd? I'll go and tell Long-Pockets what Sam said and meet you downstairs.'

'Long-Pockets', otherwise known as Superintendent Bradley,

was obsessed with the budget, in Rafferty's opinion, hence the nickname. As far as he was concerned, crimes took what they took, in time, money and manpower.

The uniforms were quickly mobilized by the simple expedient of roistering those on refreshment breaks out of the canteen. After Rafferty had gone to see Bradley, he returned to his office and rang the school to let Jeremy Paxton, the headmaster, know the results of the toxicology tests and that they were on their way; that done, he went down to reception to meet up with Llewellyn and the woodentops and headed out to the car park.

The August day was gloriously fresh and bright, just as a summer day should be, with a light breeze, to stop it getting too hot, and a deep blue sky without a cloud in sight. Rafferty, Llewellyn and two of the constables, Timothy Smales and Lizzie Green, piled reluctantly into the car, which was as hot as Lucifer's crotch as it had been standing in the sun. Rafferty, not a lover of air conditioning, which, anyway, would barely have started to work by the time they got to the school, wound his window right down and stuck his head out to catch the breeze.

The run out to Griffin School was a pretty one, past lush farmland, via roads overhung with trees whose leaves formed a soft green bower over the tarmac. On days like this, it felt good to be alive, though this latest suspicious death lowered his spirits a little. Winter was a more fitting season for death.

Adam Ainsley had been staying at Griffin for a school reunion. Unusually, the reunees had opted to get back together for an entire week rather than the more usual one evening and, conveniently for Rafferty, were still put up in the school's dormitories. He wondered if they were regretting it now. Being cooped up beyond one's desire with old enemies, as well as old friends, was a recipe for rising antagonisms that could be helpful to their investigation. There was nothing like spite for encouraging gossipy revelations.

Griffin House was an imposing building, dating back to the late 1500s. It had been recently featured in the local paper, the Elmhurst Echo, as part of a series on Essex's historic houses and Rafferty, keen on history and old buildings, had kept a cutting. The school was approached by a long, straight drive with mature trees and shrubberies either side of the road. It was built of red brick that had mellowed over the years to a deep rose and it had the tall, twisted chimneys so typical of the Elizabethan age. Like a lot of the houses of the period, it was constructed in the form of a letter E, in tribute to the virgin queen. It had once been the main home of the mad Carews, a family of aristocrats who had gambled and fought and wenched their fortune away. It had gone through various metamorphoses over the years, including being a bawdy house and the county lunatic asylum, but had been a private school since the 1880s.

They found the headmaster, Jeremy Paxton, waiting for them outside the huge grey oak door of the school's main entrance. Paxton was a tall, gangly man who seemed to be all elbows and knees. The headmaster was a surprise to Rafferty. He'd expected an older, donnish type, with a gown and mortarboard in keeping with the school's venerable status. But Paxton could be barely forty and seemed to have adopted an eccentric mode of dress comprised of a cream silk cravat and a scarlet waistcoat reminiscent of some Regency rake. To Rafferty it seemed as if he was trying to mitigate for his youth by adopting the fashion popular during the Carew family's last dying days.

Paxton led them to his study. Considering the school was a prestigious establishment with fees to match, the headmaster's study was not even shabby-chic. Yes, he had the obligatory computer and other high-tech gadgetry on his desk, but the oak-panelled walls with their scabby varnish looked as if they had some unfortunate disease and the furniture appeared to have stood here since the school was founded in the late nineteenth century. And while the mahogany desk was large and inlaid, its leather surface was scuffed and stained with ink blotches. There were several ill-assorted heavy Victorian chairs in front of the desk and Paxton invited them to sit down.

Paxton had a foppish manner to go with his dandy clothing. He tended to wave his arms about a good deal and generally gave off an air of being like an escapee from a St Trinian's farce. But, in spite of the clothing and mannerisms, he must have been considered suitably qualified for the post. Perhaps the parents expected an eccentric character given some of the post's past incumbents, one of whom had been a scientist in the mould of Dr Jekyll, who, instead of using himself, had used his pupils as guinea pigs for his outlandish experiments. If Rafferty remembered his local history correctly a couple of the pupils had died and the headmaster had been removed from his post and just escaped a murder charge.

Rafferty had explained about the situation with Ainsley over the phone and now Jeremy Paxton displayed an efficiency entirely at odds with the foppish appearance, He gave Rafferty a list of the school's old boys and girls who were currently staying at the school as well as a detailed map showing the school's sprawling buildings, which dated over several centuries.

'You said over the phone that Mr Ainsley would have died within two or three hours of ingesting the poison. That being the case, I've taken the liberty of inviting those who shared his table at lunch that day to wait for you in the Senior Common Room.' Paxton paused, then added, 'You'll need somewhere to interview the reunees, I imagine. There's a room opposite the Senior Common Room which is empty and which has a desk, chairs and a phone. I hope it suits you.'

Rafferty thanked him. 'You've been very thorough. If you could show us to the Senior Common Room, we'll get started.'

'Of course.' Paxton stood up. 'Please come with me.'

Rafferty and Llewellyn followed him along several dark, art-strewn corridors and up a flight of massive stairs to the first floor. Paxton opened the door of the Senior Common Room. It was large and surprisingly airy with an array of well-worn mismatched settees, a large plasma TV and the usual technological gizmos deemed essential by today's youth. The occupants of the room were as ill assorted as the settees; all seven looked to be in their early thirties, but that was where any similarity ended. They wore anything from ripped jeans to City suits and everything in between.

Paxton introduced them to the group and vice versa, then left them to it, saying he'd have coffee sent up to their new office across the way. The group comprised four men and three women, and while their hairstyles and clothing might be widely dissimilar, they all had a wary look in their eyes. Jeremy Paxton had told them that he had explained the situation to the reunees, who had all received the best education money could provide, so would be under no illusion that – if, as seemed likely, given the dreadful symptoms the poison produced, the dead man *had* been murdered – they were all suspects.

That being the case, Rafferty had expected the group to call up their briefs, pronto, but there was no sign of any legal types in the room protesting their clients' innocence and demanding they be allowed to leave immediately. One man seemed to have appointed himself spokesman of the group. He was one of the City 'suits' and, happily for Rafferty's memory, repeated his name. Giles Harmsworth.

Everything about the man was just so, from his well-groomed brown hair to his well-polished black shoes. He had an extremely self-confident manner that Rafferty put down to a mix of an excellent education, plenty of money and possibly the cocaine that was endemic in the City. Sharp intelligence flashed in his eyes as soon as he spoke.

'You'll want to interview us all individually, Inspector. Has Jeremy suggested that the room across the corridor should meet your needs perfectly?'

Rafferty nodded. Clearly, Harmsworth was an organizing type and Rafferty was happy to let him get on with it. It saved him the trouble.

The torn-jeaned one who sported a shock of fair hair à la Boris Johnson, London's mayor, that looked, to Rafferty to have had assistance from the peroxide bottle, drawled from one of the settees from where he lay sprawled. 'Still doing your Head Boy routine Harmsworth? Can't you lay off and let the police organize themselves?' Sebastian Kennedy cast a sneering glance in their direction and added, 'I'm sure even the pigs are capable of doing that.'

'Shut up, Kennedy. And if we're all suspects as I assume, it might be a good idea to dispense with the rebellious teen routine for the duration. It's about time you acted your age. I'd have thought the ripped jeans could have been left behind with the student demos when you reached thirty.'

Sebastian Kennedy's only response to this was another sneer.

Harmsworth turned to Rafferty, who was pleased to note that, as he'd hoped, the reunion seemed to be fraying at the edges. It might just help his inquiries. 'You must excuse Kennedy, Inspector. He's the resident 'bad boy' and has always liked to cock a snook at authority. He doesn't have the brains to realize that at his age, the rebellious youth act is extremely tiresome and had worn thin some years ago.'

'Authority?' Kennedy drawled. 'Who deputed you to be boss man, I'd like to know.'

'Oh, put a sock in it, you two. You seem to have forgotten that poor Adam is dead, probably murdered. Can't you stop your bickering for a moment?' This was from a bespectacled young woman in a baggy grey jumper and faded jeans. Victoria Something, Rafferty thought.

'Brains is quite right, Kennedy,' said Harmsworth. 'Can't you behave yourself for once and lay off being the naughty boy? I don't imagine the inspector's impressed.'

Sebastian Kennedy's full upper lip curled, but he said nothing more and simply resumed gulping the lager that he had been drinking since Rafferty and Llewellyn had entered the room. Rafferty took the intermission in skirmishes to get the ball rolling.

'As you said, Mr Harmsworth, we'd like to interview you all individually. Perhaps we can start with you? If you'd like to accompany us across the way.'

Harmsworth nodded. He cast one last, 'behave yourself' look at the thirty-something naughty boy before he followed the two policemen out of the room.

Rafferty paused long enough to station Lizzie Green just inside the door. Lizzie was one of his more intelligent officers. She knew what was required and would report on any unwise disclosures the reunees happened to make. He paused to inhale the scent of the old-fashioned lily of the valley talcum power she favoured, briefly closing his eyes before shutting the door.

Sebastian Kennedy's final riposte floated after them through the cracks in the warped oak door. 'You'd better not go grassing anyone up, Harmsworth. We'll all know it was you if you do. Old habits die hard.'

Harmsworth acted as if he hadn't heard and merely opened the door across the landing and gestured them inside, with a smile as if he was a host encouraging guests of the shy and retiring sort. Rafferty, playing up to his allotted role in the hope it would loosen any guard Harmsworth had on his tongue, hesitated for a few seconds, like a wallflower who couldn't believe her luck at finally being chosen, before he, too, crossed the threshold.

'Now, Mr Harmsworth,' Rafferty began once they were settled in the small office that Jeremy Paxton had let them use. He was glad to see that the headmaster had already organized a pot of coffee. By the time he'd finished questioning the seven reunees who'd lunched with Adam Ainsley before he'd gone off on the run from which he had never returned, he'd be parched. 'Perhaps you can begin by describing what happened on the day Mr Ainsley went missing? Start at your arrival at the school and go on till after lunch, when I believe Mr Ainsley set off alone for a run.'

'It was a day much like the reunions have been in previous years. I come every year,' he added. 'I noticed Adam was quiet at lunch, as though he had something on his mind. But he's always tended to be a bit moody, so I didn't take any notice. He set off on his run straight after lunch and the rest of us just lounged around the common room getting reacquainted until lunch had been digested. I'd brought my laptop with me, so I was able to get on with some work. I think Victoria and Alice had a game of tennis around three and Gary – Asgar – Sadiq went swimming in the school's pool. Kennedy seemed to be happy to just lounge around, listening to music and drinking that never-ending supply of lager he brought with him.'

'Was there a lot of milling around during lunch?'

'Not during lunch, no.' He smiled, showing perfect teeth. 'It was the rule, when we were at school, that once we were seated, we stayed put, apart from the servers. And we all seemed to continue the tradition even though there's no Mr Barmforth any more to glower and yell out, 'You, boy!' The gleaming smile faded. 'I imagine that means that the only suspects for this crime are the seven of us that were seated at Adam's table.'

'If what you say is correct, yes, it would seem so. And nothing out of the ordinary happened? No arguments, for instance?'

Harmsworth smiled again. 'I don't know as I'd call arguments unusual, Inspector. I've had spats with Kennedy off and on since we got here. He always did like winding people up. But other than that, no, I can't think of anything.'

'Can you tell me who used to be particular friends with the dead man and whether they're still friends?'

'Adam had his own clique – the other sporty types. And they all attracted the girls. None of them have attended this year, though usually two or three come to the reunion. I suppose I could be called the school swot, along with Victoria and Alice, so we weren't as popular with the opposite sex. I always thought Adam was very obvious, with his muscles and so on, but it seemed to appeal to the girls. I recall that both Sophie and Alice had a crush on him at one time.'

Rafferty nodded. 'And what about enemies? Did Mr Ainsley have any that you know of?'

Harmsworth frowned, then shrugged. 'No one that I can recall. Certainly nothing serious. There were the usual spats at school and Adam had his share, but that's all.'

And so it went on. The other six reunees said much the same as the late afternoon wore into evening and the remaining coffee went cold.

The call from Sam Dally had been the second unwelcome phone call of the afternoon for Rafferty. His ma had been on earlier and had told him to get one of his spare bedrooms ready.

Rafferty had been expecting this. It had only been a matter of time, he told himself. His ma still liked to poke her nose into his life and since his June marriage to Abra, she must be consumed with curiosity to see for herself how wedded bliss was going; staying with them over several days was the only way to indulge this curiosity that would fully satisfy Ma. Rafferty, facing what couldn't be avoided, had given a tiny sigh and said, 'That's all right, Ma. When do you want to come and stay?'

But it seemed he'd misjudged his woman. His ma wasn't requisitioning one of his bedrooms for herself after all, as she was quick to tell him.

'Don't be stupid, Joseph. Sure and why would I want to come and stay with you when I've got a perfectly good house of my own not half-a-mile away from you?'

'What do you want it for then, Ma?' he had asked in his innocence. 'Do you want to store a pile of Bring and Buy stuff for Father Kelly?' As long as it wasn't his ma's illicit 'bargains' she wanted him to give houseroom to. He'd draw the line at that.

'No.' She paused and Rafferty wondered what was coming.

For once, Ma seemed a trifle diffident. It was unlike her. His ma was nothing if not forthright.

'The thing is son, you know I've got some long-lost cousins coming to stay?'

'Yes.' His ma had first mentioned this a month ago. But he couldn't see that it would affect him. Beyond a courtesy meal out with them, it was unlikely, between his new wife and this new case, that he'd see much of them. But now, as his ma explained, he learned that this family reunion had snowballed. His ma had been on the internet – not so much a 'silver surfer' as a dyed brown one – and it turned out that she'd unearthed not only the known-about Irish and American cousins and their wives or husbands, but also Canadian, Antipodean and South African ones. The Aussies, no doubt, being Raffertys, would have descended from family who had got there via an 'assisted' passage courtesy of the Crown.

Rafferty was dismayed as he guessed, rightly, what was coming. He hated having people to stay. He never felt his home was his own with others in the house. And the couple his ma wanted to foist on him – for all that they were family – were total strangers to him. The thought of sharing a bathroom with people whose habits were an unknown quantity was unnerving.

'Sure and most of them are pensioners like meself,' she told him in wheedling tones. 'Can't afford fancy hotels.'

'They don't have to be fancy, do they? Bed and breakfast would do, surely? Or the YMCA these days has nice rooms as cheap as you'll find anywhere.'

'And haven't I told you,' a faintly cross tone entered his ma's voice, 'they haven't the money for hotels of any description. The air fare's enough for most of them. And then, they'll need spending money. And they're family, Joseph. Family I've not seen for a long time.'

'Can't one of the girls put them up?' This was a rearguard action and not one he expected to hold the tide. But he had a plentiful supply of siblings and he thought that, between them, his two brothers and three sisters should be able to accommodate several cousins, especially if they farmed their kids out at their friends' houses.

'The girls have no room, you know that. Besides, even if they were able to foist the kids on someone for the duration, Maggie and Neeve are in the middle of decorating.'

His sisters could be as crafty as all their sex. Rafferty wished he was up to his eyelashes in magnolia emulsion. It would give him the excuse he needed. But once back from their honeymoon after their move to the semi from Rafferty's flat, he'd delayed making a start on doing the place up and had made excuse after excuse to Abra when she suggested he pulled his finger out and got on with it. But he'd never suspected that his ma's invitation to her American cousins would snowball to the extent of the fifty guests that she casually mentioned she was now expecting over for the family reunion party that had been born out of the small get-together originally planned. How could he have anticipated that the casually stated and half-heard idea that his ma was expecting four guests would expand to fit his two spare rooms and more? Because he doubted that Ma would stop at liberating just one of his spare bedrooms, even though there was only a bed in one of them. She'd find a bed for the other from somewhere and would then expect him and Mickey and Patrick Sean to lug it around to his house and up the stairs.

'It's only for two weeks, son,' she said, wheedlingly. 'You'll hardly know they're there.'

Two weeks! To Rafferty, it seemed like eternity stretching before him. He hadn't inherited his ma's sociable gene and while he enjoyed a good craic as much as the rest of the family, he preferred to keep his home to himself. So he hadn't said 'yes'. But then, he hadn't said 'no', either and that was all the encouragement Ma needed. Still, he had consoled himself as he prepared to set off for Griffin School, this murder would keep him busy and out of the way and these cousins that his ma had saddled him with were likely to be out doing the sights for most of the time. Between his work and their sightseeing, it was unlikely their paths would cross much.

The Senior Common Room was at the front of the house and their borrowed office was at the back. From where he stood, Rafferty could see cricket and rugby pitches stretching to the middle distance. At the edge of his vision was what looked like tennis courts and Jeremy Paxton had mentioned they had a swimming pool in one of the outbuildings. All in all, they seemed to do very well for themselves.

They had interviewed all the reunees and they had all said much the same. Even the ever-rebellious pig-hater, Sebastian Kennedy hadn't strayed from the general line, which was that nothing out of the ordinary had happened on the day that Adam Ainsley had gone for a run and never come back.

When questioned as to why nobody had commented on his absence at dinner, they had all claimed they had assumed the dead man had either gone to his room or decided to eat in the town. According to Giles Harmsworth, and the others had said the same, Adam Ainsley had been in a funny mood all morning and – considering this was a reunion – had been pretty unsociable towards most of the group. And when Rafferty had commented on this, Harmsworth and the rest had claimed the dead man had never been any different.

'Always got in a humour on the slightest pretext', had been Harmsworth's take on this. 'We thought nothing of it.'

'So none of you went to see where he was when he didn't show up for dinner that evening?' Rafferty persisted.

'No. We had no reason to.'

The school's dormitories, for the older pupils at least, were made up of two-bed rooms. The dead man had been sharing with Sebastian Kennedy, but as Kennedy had been steadily depleting the school's wine cellars during the evening, he had – or so he claimed – failed to notice that Ainsley was still not in their room at midnight, which was the time Kennedy had finally staggered off to bed.

'What do you think, Dafyd?' Rafferty asked once they were finally alone. 'Do you reckon they're colluding for some reason?'

Llewellyn shook his thinly handsome face. 'No. They're too disparate a group. I can't see that Giles Harmsworth or Victoria Watson would agree to conceal a crime.'

'Unless they did it,' Rafferty chipped in.

'There's always that possibility, of course. But we have no evidence as yet that this was anything other than a suicide.'

'Come on! How likely is it that anyone of sound mind would choose such a method?'

'We don't know that he was of sound mind – we found antidepressants in his room. And maybe he didn't know what symptoms the poison would cause and thought he would just go to sleep. As I said, we've no evidence that he didn't kill himself.'

'We've no evidence that he did, either. And given that he must have been a well-educated man seeing as he attended Griffin School, would he really not have taken the trouble to find out what the poison did to the body before he did the business? And, taking that into consideration, if he did kill himself, hemlock seems a particularly peculiar method to choose, given that it paralyzes the limbs and Ainsley used to be a professional sportsman. Why not just use pills and whiskey?'

Llewellyn gave a tiny shrug. Rafferty was pleased to see that, for once, his educated sergeant had no arguments against his theories. They had been through the dead man's things and there had been nothing – apart from the anti-depressants – to indicate that suicide was a possibility, though he got Llewellyn to make a note to check with the dead man's doctor. No one had said that he seemed other than they remembered him from the days when they had been cooped up together for weeks at a time and got to know one another intimately. No suicide note or suspicious substances had been found. Though, on the other hand, as Rafferty regretfully acknowledged, neither had there been anything to indicate that Ainsley felt he had reason to fear for his life from one of his fellow reunees. Why would he have attended the reunion if that had been the case?

They had found nothing of any interest at all. Yet it must be one or the other as accidental death was surely out of the question.

Adam Ainsley had, after a career as a professional rugby player, studied to become a sports coach and was now employed as a Physical Education teacher at another private school; this much he had learned from the other reunees. He had been twice divorced and at the time of his death had been single, with no known romantic entanglements. From the various comments from his former classmates, the dead man had been a popular boy with the girls at the school and had cut a swathe through most of them. His moody, Byronesque manner clearly finding favour with the fair sex. And, given his sporting prowess, he had been equally popular with the boys.

To listen to the surviving reunees, the wonder was that anyone should have wanted to do away with such a popular young man. But someone had. Rafferty was convinced of that, in spite of Llewellyn's mention of suicide. And he would find out which of them it was, no matter how many expensive legal types they conjured up between them.

TWO

Given that Dr Sam 'Dilly' Dally had performed the post mortem late on Tuesday and the toxicology reports hadn't come through until the afternoon of the next day, it was eight in the evening by the time Rafferty and Llewellyn finished questioning the seven suspects amongst the reunees. They had also questioned the cook, Mrs Benton, who had got on her high horse when Rafferty had asked her if she had any idea how hemlock might have found its way into either Ainsley's vichyssoise soup or his chicken salad.

'That food was perfectly all right when it left my kitchen,' she had insisted, bosom and grey curls bouncing indignantly. 'Has anyone else died or been taken ill? No,' she answered her own question. 'Of course they haven't. It's that lot out there you need to interrogate.' She stabbed her right index finger in the direction of the dining hall where the seven suspects had been joined by the other reunees for their evening meal. To judge from the racket going on beyond the serving hatch, the news of the day was still being avidly discussed, but Rafferty noticed that the seven were being given a wide berth. As though conscious of their leper status, they huddled together for warmth. Even the oh-so-confident Giles Harmsworth and the bad boy, Sebastian Kennedy, seemed subdued and kept their heads bent over their melon and Parma ham starter.

Mrs Benton reclaimed Rafferty's attention. 'Thirty years I've worked at this school and some of that lot were vicious thugs back then; it seems they're no better now. Yes, it's them what you want to question, Mr Detective, not me. I've always been a good, honest woman, never done anything wrong in me life, not like that lot. That Giles – the one who's now 'something in the City', he's not as holier than thou as he'd have you believe. Teacher's pet and a snitch is what he always was. I don't suppose he's changed much and it won't be long before he's confiding something to you. It just better not be about me, that's all or I'll fetch him a clout round the ear, big and self-important as he is, that he won't forget in a hurry. And that Kennedy boy, he was always a troublemaker. Lives on a trust fund, or so I gather. The saying that the Devil finds mischief for idle hands is true enough. And another thing. You want to ask yourselves why it was that too handsome for his own good bloke, Adam Ainsley, was the one who was poisoned. He always had the girls after him. You mark my words, this'll be one of them crimes of passion that the Froggies go in for. I always thought he'd come to a sticky end.'

Rafferty had, in spite of her unhidden antagonism, questioned the cook thoroughly, though she'd inadvertently told them as much about several of the suspects as any snitch.

He thought he could discount Mrs Benton and Tom Harrison, the groundsman cum caretaker, from the list of suspects, as even though Mrs Benton had admitted little liking for the dead man or a number of his fellow reunees and had prepared Ainsley's last meal on this earth, he couldn't see how she could have poisoned him without taking out some of the rest of the table; each table's soup was served up in a tureen from which it was ladled out into the individual dishes at the table. The same applied to the salad. The lemon sponge that they'd had for pudding would have given no opportunity for doctoring. And, however chippy her personality, he didn't have Mrs Benton tagged as a psycho. Harrison, the groundsman, had been in the kitchen earlier in the day, for his elevenses, and could have added hemlock to the ingredients for the meal. But again, like Mrs Benton, he would have had to have no qualms about taking out whoever was unfortunate enough to share Ainsley's table.

Mrs Benton had explained that one person at each of the dining hall's eight-seater tables would come to her hatch and collect each course. For the suspects' table, it had been the Senior Common Room peacemaker, Victoria 'Brains' Watson, who had collected the food and dished it out. This would then be passed along the row, first on one side and then on the other. Adam Ainsley had been sitting at the far end of the table on the opposite side from Victoria. From this, Rafferty had concluded that any one of four people would have had the best opportunity to slip something in Adam Ainsley's food. There was Victoria 'Brains' Watson, who had served up each portion; Giles Harmsworth; the over-serious Alice Douglas; and Simon Fairweather, the quiet young man who, beyond mentioning that he was a civil servant at the Home Office, had had little to say for himself, even at the interview. This left the other three as less than prime suspects: Sebastian Kennedy, Sophie Diaz and Asgar Sadiq. It seemed unlikely but possible that either Kennedy, Ainsley's left-hand neighbour, or Gary Sadiq, Ainsley's neighbour across the table from him, might also have had a chance to slip a foreign substance in his food. Anyway, they would all remain on the suspects' list for the present.

Rafferty had brought in some more uniforms to help question the other hundred reunees. Although it didn't seem they would have had the opportunity to poison Ainsley, Rafferty had the feeling that the cause of this murder – if murder it was, as it might turn out that Llewellyn was right and they could still be labouring over a suicide – lay deep in the past when they had all been teenagers together. So they might well have useful information. The motive for murder was, he thought, going to take some digging out. But at least, for now, he was more than happy to simply burrow into the surface memories of each of them. Any deeper digging would have to wait until they'd separated those who'd been amongst Adam Ainsley's intimates, whom Rafferty and Llewellyn would question more deeply, and the rest.

Paxton, beyond supplying them with their room, the map of the school and the list of the reunion's attendees and their home addresses, had been able to provide them with little other information. Of course, he had been in post for less than a year. Rafferty made a mental note to find out the name and current address of the school's previous headmaster, who had, according to Paxton, been *in situ* for several decades and who had certainly been in his post when the current reunees had attended the school.

They returned to the station and while Llewellyn typed up the interviews of the seven suspects, Rafferty sat and made a list of chores for the next day. If he was to find out about possible vendettas, soured love affairs and the like, he would need to go and see Adam Ainsley's parents, who lived in Suffolk. And he would need to send somebody to question Adam Ainsley's two ex-wives. For that he thought a woman's touch was called for and Mary Carmody, the motherly, thirty-something, sergeant sprang immediately to mind. People confided in her; even Superintendent Bradley tended to seek her out in the canteen and bend her ear over budgetary worries and insubordinate inferiors – not that Mary had betrayed his confidence – but Bradley's earnest stance over the tea cups and Mary's motherly, head on one side air, had given it away. That, and the fact that, even when he was whispering, Long-Pockets Bradley had something of a booming voice. Quietness wasn't in the man. Yes, he'd despatch Mary with Llewellyn, who was diffident with women, to one ex, and he'd take the other himself.

As for the suspects, the number of these was thankfully small, as after speaking to the cook and the seven reunees, he couldn't see that anyone else but those on the same table as Adam Ainsley would have been able to administer the hemlock. Coffee and biscuits had been served on the reunees' arrival on that first morning, but that was all. Their first – and only, as it turned out – meal all together had been the lunch. And he thought it almost certain that the hemlock must have been administered that Tuesday lunchtime in Ainsley's meal, as it was too far-fetched to imagine he would accept any part of the plant from anyone. What possible reason could be given for proffering such a thing? No. It was the not-so-magnificent seven who were in the frame.

Rafferty yawned and glanced at the clock on the wall. It was ten o'clock. It had been a long day and tomorrow would probably be longer. 'You get off home,' he told Llewellyn once he had typed up the statements from the seven suspects. 'We'll make an early start in the morning.'

After Llewellyn had said goodnight and left, Rafferty spent some time wondering how he was going to explain to Abra that they were about to have some unexpected houseguests. She wouldn't be any more pleased than he was himself, especially as she still had hopes of persuading him to get started on the decorating, which the presence of guests would make impossible.

How to break it to her, though? Could he perhaps claim that Ma was celebrating a special birthday that required the attendance of the wider Rafferty and Kelly families? He shook his head. No. Abra was the one who remembered all the family birthdays; he hadn't had to trouble since they'd started living together. She'd know that Ma wasn't anywhere near a particularly special birthday.

No, there was nothing for it but to break it to her straight and wait for the fallout.

As it happened, when Rafferty got home, he found he didn't need to break the news to Abra after all as his ma hadn't wasted any time after staking her claim on his spare rooms that morning and had used her key to ensconce the visitors in Rafferty's home. And he'd been right, there were four of them. Never one to waste an amenity, she had made the unilateral decision that his second spare bedroom was just the thing.

Abra was forced to employ only a fierce whisper to berate him as she dished up the hastily organized home delivery meal that evening.

'You knew about this and you didn't tell me?' she accused as she spooned up the Balti Chicken.

'No I didn't,' Rafferty whispered back. 'Ma sprung it on me out of the blue this morning. But she never mentioned that she was bringing them over today. And, until today, I was under the impression that she was only expecting two cousins and their partners, whom *she* was going to put up. She never mentioned any more. What, do you mean they all just turned up and you found them here when you got home?'

'No,' she conceded. 'Your ma rang me at work to let me know. Kind of her.' She dished out the rice with a vicious chop of the serving spoon. The metal on earthenware clang reverberated around the kitchen. Rafferty hoped their guests couldn't hear it.

'I think it came as something of a surprise to her, too,' Rafferty said in an attempt to placate her. 'I think the reunion just snowballed once she got on the internet and discovered more family than even *she* knew we had.'

Abra wasn't to be placated. 'How would you like it if *my* mother dumped two brace of *my* relatives on us?'

Rafferty gave an uneasy grin as if to demonstrate that he'd have been happy to accommodate them. It wasn't true, of course, as Abra well knew. He had had little chance to say anything other than a surprised 'hello' to their guests since he'd got in. Abra had been forced to entertain them since six o'clock when she'd got home from work. She'd even had to make up the beds as, not expecting any guests, they hadn't bothered to make up the one spare room that was furnished since they'd come back off honeymoon at the beginning of July. His ma had, apparently, even sent the other spare bed over with his two brothers, who had spent two hours sweating over it before he came home as they tried to get it assembled.

In spite of having little love for guests of any sort, Rafferty found himself suppressing a grin. He supposed they'd have to feed his brothers as well. He hoped Abra had ordered enough food for them all.

It was now half-past ten. He'd had a long day and would have liked nothing more after his meal than a hot bath and an early night. But that wasn't on the cards. One of their guests had a touch of the Bradleys about him and spoke in a loud voice as if he was addressing a meeting *sans* microphone –

Rafferty could hear his Southern twang from here. Cyrus Rafferty had been holding forth ever since he'd got home. It didn't bode well for his chances of retiring before midnight.

Rafferty glanced at the clock as the bedside radio switched itself on that Thursday morning and groaned before his head slumped back on the pillow. He reached out an arm and turned off a way-too-chirpy Chris Evans. How could anyone be that full of beans *before* breakfast? It was unnatural.

Cyrus Rafferty had indulged in a monologue till midnight and beyond on what appeared to be his favourite subject – the lax morals of the modern generation. Wait till he found out about his teenage niece, Gemma, and her illegitimate little boy, was Rafferty's thought.

It turned out Cyrus was a lay preacher from America's Bible Belt and was inclined to climb into the pulpit with no encouragement whatsoever. Rafferty, sober as a judge after four large ones, had hunted in vain for a topic of conversation that didn't set him off again. But after he'd made inroads into Rafferty's best Irish whiskey, Cyrus had been nigh on unstoppable. His wife, Wendy, had tried to restrain him, but even she had fared no better and Rafferty had been forced from politeness, to resign himself to listen to the never-ending sermon. It had been like being a kid again and forced to endure Father Kelly's at St Boniface, without benefit of the sly humour that Father Kelly would interweave into his words of reproach for the parish ne'er-do-wells.

He braced himself and lifted his head again. It was thumping and he had little white lights dancing about in his eyes. He blinked, but they were still there.

He levered himself out of bed, considered hunting for his one dressing gown and thought 'Oh, sod it', and went to the kitchen in search of tea in his boxers. He was dismayed to find Cyrus there before him.

'See here, Joe,' he said in his pulpit voice. 'Ah know how you Brits love your tea. Wendy said Ah had to make some for you and Abra', and he thrust two mugs full of weak cat's piss towards him.

Rafferty managed a sickly smile. He hated weak tea. So did Abra. He supposed this meant he'd be on the receiving end of more verbals when he gave it to her. Perhaps he'd be able to sneak down in five minutes and make fresh cups.

'What's this?' a sleepy Abra asked as he handed her the mug.

'Morning tea,' he told her. 'Courtesy of Cyrus.'

'Yuk. Does the man not even know how to make a decent cuppa? I thought he had Irish blood in his veins.'

'Fair dos, Abra. He's drinking it himself. It was meant well. Still, it's no wonder Americans marvel at our British love of tea. If we drank this swill for pleasure, I'd marvel at it as well. Give it here. I'll chuck it out the window. I'll give it five minutes for the coast to clear and then I'll make some fresh.'

Once again, Rafferty made it down to the kitchen, creeping past Cyrus and Wendy's room, only to find Cyrus still in the kitchen, emptying the dishwasher. He insisted on making him and Abra a second cup. Rafferty accepted them with forced politeness and returned upstairs to get showered and dressed. He thought better of presenting Abra with another cup of cat's piss and deposited it down the bathroom sink.

He had a little chuckle at the thought that Cyrus and Wendy as well as Angel and Louis, their other two guests, must be dying for a decent cup of American coffee. He could see that he would not only have to get a decent brew in, but that he would also have to train Cyrus up in the gentle art of tea-making, or this could go on for the entire fortnight.

Rafferty left early for the station, not stopping for breakfast in case Cyrus appeared again and decided to play the helpful guest and make him yet a third cup of undrinkable tea. He arrived before Llewellyn, which wasn't something that happened too often – usually only when he'd felt glad to leave the house to escape a domestic.

He got himself a builder's brew from the canteen, put Llewellyn's on his desk in expectation of his imminent appearance and started to read through the statements that uniform had taken from the other hundred school reunees. The first half-dozen were very short and circumspect, as though those interviewed had felt it unwise to confide youthful school indiscretions in which they or the rest had been involved. But then he started to read the seventh statement and realized he must have reached the school gossip, for here was food in plenty for a suspicious policeman.

'Adam was always a girl magnet,' confided someone called Trudy Teller. By God, that wasn't a misnomer, as he discovered.

'Most of the sixth form were smitten with him as well as plenty of the fourth and fifth formers. Even mousy little Alice Douglas used to give him the moon eyes. Not that he'd have looked at that little swot once, never mind twice. Sophie Diaz was mad about him, too and they had a sizzling affair all that last summer, right under old Barmpot's nose.' 'Barmpot' was their endearing nickname for the then headmaster, Cedric Barmforth. He was someone else he must make time to interview, along with Ainsley's parents. Uniform had already broken the news to them, of course, as his death had originally been thought to be a natural one, but he felt he ought to go along too and let them know what little he had discovered as well as find out what they might be able to tell them about their only son. He was glad he was able to say that their son had been a popular boy; maybe they'd known that already, but it would bear repetition. It might be some comfort to them.

He put Trudy Teller's gushing confidences aside as someone worth a second interview just as Llewellyn appeared and did a double-take to see his superior in the office so early.

'Not another domestic with Abra?' the Welshman asked. 'You've only been back from your honeymoon a month.'

'No, though if I'd have stayed we might have,' said Rafferty. He explained about his visitors and wasn't surprised to see the Welshman's thin lips curl faintly upwards. He was just recounting about Cyrus and the tea when Superintendent Bradley popped his head round the door.

'You still here, Rafferty? Should have thought you'd be back up at Griffin School, but. Some very influential people on the Board of Governors there, you know. I want you to give the case tip-top attention and clear it up asap.'

'Plenty of overtime, then, Super,' Rafferty said deadpan as he suppressed a grin. 'That's good.'

Bradley's lardy face fell into lines of anguish at this mention of Rafferty's possible inroads into his precious budget. But he recovered admirably, to tell Rafferty, 'I shall want daily reports on this one. There's a cabinet minister's son at that school, so I don't want it getting round that we're less than efficient as a force.'

Rafferty's lips itched to tell him that one of the suspects was a civil servant in the Home Office. That would be likely to turn him purple and foaming at the mouth. But he really didn't fancy risking having to give mouth-to-mouth. Not on Cyrus's cat's piss tea. Once Bradley had slammed his way back out, Rafferty spent a few seconds wondering again why the superintendent had assigned him to the case, given his less than princely confidence in him. Maybe it was Bradley trying to play both sides against the middle again. He'd done this before – sending him into posh environments, presumably hoping he'd make such a cock-up that, after the ensuing inquiry, he'd be either demoted or fired. Rafferty suspected the super would have gladly risked a poor showing on the crime statistics if it meant he could get rid of *him*.

He split the rest of the statements in half and handed Llewellyn his share. 'Never mind Bradley. It's my case and I'll decide what gets done when. We'll get these read and see who needs a second interview before we head back to the school. But before we go there, I think we ought to take a drive to Suffolk and speak to Ainsley's parents. We might learn something useful from them.'

Two hours later, Rafferty had a little pile of statements put aside, their authors worthy of a second grilling. He finished his fourth cup of tea of the morning and stretched. 'Right. We'll head off for Suffolk. Maybe, by the time we get back, our witnesses might have remembered another tasty morsel or two for our delectation.'

The ride out to Adam Ainsley's parents' home in Suffolk took around an hour. They lived in a pretty village a few miles from Ipswich in which the thatched roofs vied with the black and whites for the title of most picturesque home. There was even a duck pond that seemed to be home to a particularly territorial swan, because as they parked and got out of the car, he came rushing across to them, wings flapping threateningly and emitting the most horrendous row.

Rafferty beat a hasty retreat, waving his arms and uttering placating noises as he went. He hurried to put the car and Llewellyn between it and himself.

'God,' he said. 'The wildlife around here's none too friendly. If I'd have known I'd have brought some bread to distract him.'

Thankfully, baulked by the width of the car from getting his beak into his intended victim, the swan decided to seek less mobile prey and approached an elderly woman who was hobbling along with a stick. But she must have been a local because she was well able to deal with the beast and shook her stick at it, whereby it beat its own hasty retreat.

Mr and Mrs Ainsley were older than Rafferty had expected. Well into their seventies, and clearly crushed by the loss of their son. There was a photograph of Adam with his parents on the mantelpiece. He looked around the mid-thirties in it so it must have been pretty recent, and the change in his parents was striking. They looked quite sprightly in the photograph, but now they seemed ten years older and weighed down by their grief. They were inconsolable at the loss of their son. It was clear they'd doted on Adam, clear, too, that he was an only child from the lack of photos of other offspring – no wonder he'd thought so much of himself, was Rafferty's rather unkind thought. Must have been a Change baby and all the more precious for that.

There were pictures of him on every surface; every tiny achievement was recorded on film. Even the loss of his first baby tooth had been the occasion of a photo opportunity. Rafferty felt like a murderer himself, especially as the couple were likely to learn a few unwelcome things about their only son during the course of the investigation.

The visit brought no additional information about the dead man. Mrs Ainsley seemed able to do little more than clasp a photo of her son to her bosom and moan, 'My son, my son', over and over again and Mr Ainsley wasn't a lot better. He insisted on dragging them up to Adam's boyhood bedroom and proudly showed off all his cups and medals and rosettes.

'Excelled at everything.' Andrew Ainsley's eyes filled with tears. 'I don't know where he got it from as my wife and I were never the sporty type. It seemed to come effortlessly to him. And friends. There were always friends in the house, lots of them. Used to eat us out of house and home during the holidays from Griffin. Though we wouldn't have had it any other way. It was wonderful to see how well liked he was.'

'When did you last see your son, Mr Ainsley?' Rafferty asked him as Ainsley stood polishing one of his son's many prize cups on his handkerchief.

Andrew Ainsley shuffled a little on the thick carpet before he answered. 'It's . . . it's a little while now. I can't quite remember. But he was such a busy person, always, taking boys abroad for schoolboy championships for this and that. He was never still for a moment. My wife will tell you.'

His carefully controlled grief was painful to see and Rafferty was as glad as Llewellyn to escape the claustrophobic cottage and get out into the fresh summer air. Rafferty looked around nervously in case the swan decided to come back with reinforcements, but there was no sign of the bird and they reached the sanctuary of the car safely.

'Back to the station, sir?' asked Llewellyn.

'No. Not just yet. I know a nice little pub just up here. We'll have a meal. They'll only be having lunch back at Griffin School, so we might as well. Besides, I didn't have any breakfast. I thought I'd better get out of the kitchen before Cyrus appeared and made me another cup of tea. We can kill two birds with one stone, as we might bump into one or two people who knew Adam Ainsley when he was young. We might learn something unsavoury that his parents wouldn't tell us.'

Starving, Rafferty was glad to get outside of a portion of cottage pie and chips. Replete, he sat back and basked in the sunshine streaming into the pub's garden. The weather was a little warmer, but still not oppressive and he soaked it up. 'This is the life, hey, Dafyd. Roll on retirement.'

'We've both got a way to go before then,' said Llewellyn. 'And a lot more cases to solve.'

'Don't remind me. And the way the government keeps upping the retirement age, I'll be getting my telegram from Prince William before I qualify for a state pension. The only retirement that would give me greater pleasure than my own is Bradley's. Do you think he'll go early?'

'I doubt it. He likes his position too much.'

'Mmm. All that hobnobbing he goes in for; Mr Mayor this, and Lord and Lady that. You're right. I can't see him being willing to give that up in a hurry.' He swallowed the rest of his Adnam's bitter and got up for replenishments. 'We don't want to go in mob-handed. Gently, gently, catchee monkey, and all that. I'll ask the landlord if any long-resident locals are in the bar. If so, I'll have a little chat with them so don't expect me back for a while. What can I fetch you?'

But Llewellyn still had half a glass of his mineral water and he said he was all right.

Back in the bar, Rafferty ordered another half pint of Adnam's and buttonholed the landlord. 'I'm investigating the death of Mr Adam Ainsley, the rugby player, who lived in the village as a boy. I wondered was there anything you could tell me about him.'

The landlord, a large, red-faced man, who, to judge from his beer belly, was over-fond of his own ale, clutched his chin thoughtfully. After a few seconds of pondering, he told Rafferty, 'I can't tell you anything about his youth. I've only been here two years. But he used to come in with his parents very occasionally. On Mother's Day and Christmas and the like. He wasn't ever what you'd call a regular.'

'What did you think of him?'

The landlord pulled a face. 'Bit of a loudmouth. Seemed to take over the entire bar when he was here, talking loudly and boasting about his triumphs when he played professional rugby. Never made it to the England team, though, I always thought. I said it to him one day when I'd got out of bed the wrong side. He didn't take it too well. Thought he was going to thump me. No. I didn't like him. If you want to know what he was like when he was young, you want to speak to Harold over there in the corner.' The landlord nodded to an old boy who looked to be around eighty and whose chin and cheeks sported the stubbly look favoured by footballers and actors, though Rafferty thought it likely that Harold had favoured the look long before either of them. 'Lived in the village all his life. He'll be able to tell you a lot more than me.'

'Thanks. What does he drink?'

'When he's paying, he has half a mild. But if you're buying, he'll have a large scotch.'

Drink duly bought, Rafferty approached Harold and introduced himself. 'The landlord told me you used to know Adam Ainsley and his parents,' he began as he placed the whisky down on the beer mat.

'Oh. You're here about that, are you? Copper, you said?'

Rafferty nodded.

'I've had some dos with coppers in my time,' Harold complained. 'Why should I help you now?'

'There's another drink in it.'

'Never was one to hold a grudge, me.' Harold picked up his scotch glass and drained it in one go, smacking his lips afterwards to be sure he didn't miss any. 'I'm ready for that next one you promised me.'

Rafferty picked up the glass and made for the bar. But he didn't even have to order as the landlord clearly knew his customers and had anticipated Harold's demand. Another large one was on the bar and the landlord took Rafferty's money and retreated, laughing into his double chin.

'So, what can you tell me?' Rafferty asked as he placed the glass in front of Harold.

'Not a nice lad that Adam. Parents spoiled him. The missus used to wait on him hand and foot. When I complained to them about his blasted cricket ball coming over the hedge again and landing in my vegetable patch all they said was that their boy had to play. Said they were sorry and all that, but they never stopped him playing cricket. Used to give me a mouthful, he did, the boy, when I told him off. Not a nice kid. Got Mandy Dobbs in the family way. Pretty girl, but a bit simple. Denied it was his, of course. So did his parents. Loves that kid, she do, Mandy. But he never came near nor by to see his son, even after he admitted he was the father. Selfish to the core, that lad. The way he treated people, I'm not surprised that someone's done for him.'

Rafferty gave a slow nod. 'Thank you. You've been very helpful.'

Harold said nothing, but gave his once more empty glass a significant glance.

Rafferty grinned, walked to the bar and told the landlord to give Harold another drink. He handed over a note and went back into the garden to collect Llewellyn.

'I suppose we'd better get back,' he told him, after he'd given Llewellyn the gist of what Harold had confided. 'We've a lot to do.'

Rafferty's pile of statements from witnesses who required a second interview had been added to by Llewellyn before they'd left for Suffolk. He gave them a quick glance when they got back, noted down the names, handed the rest to Llewellyn to distribute amongst the team and headed out to the car park. He also wanted to question the two ex-Mrs Ainsleys to see what revelations they might come up with, though that might have to wait till tomorrow. Llewellyn appeared, so Rafferty turned the key in the ignition.

Lunch was clearly over by the time they got back to Griffin

School. The dining hall was deserted and so were all the corridors. From an open window Rafferty heard the thud, thud, thud of a tennis ball on the hard court. The scent of newly cut grass wafted in and reminded Rafferty of his own schooldays. They hadn't had the facilities that the Griffin pupils enjoyed, but they'd all been trooped along to the town green and allowed to waft a yellow buttercup under the chin of Mary Ellis, the prettiest girl in the class, and tell her that she liked butter. When that palled, there was always kiss and chase and when Mary hadn't wanted to play ball, it had been the perfect place to bunk off from. Many an afternoon he'd spent in the town's one arcade.

Rafferty, with Llewellyn in tow, went in search of their prey. As expected, they found the usual suspects in the Senior Common Room. Sophie Diaz was curled up in the corner of one of the settees painting her nails and waved her fingers at the two policemen. On the far side of the room, Sebastian Kennedy lounged on the same settee as before as if he'd never left it. The warm day had clearly brought on a thirst for a little pile of lager cans nestled on the floor beside him, dribbling on to the varnished wooden floor. For once Kennedy didn't have a lot to say for himself and seemed far more inclined to shut his eyes and take a snooze rather than answer their questions. But Rafferty persisted. He sat in an armchair beside him and gestured for Llewellyn to do the same.

'Tell me, Mr Kennedy,' he said quietly, determined not to be ignored and happy to needle the insolent rent-a-mouth. 'How did you get on with Adam? I gather you were never very sporty so you must have been in awe of him.'

This made Kennedy open his eyes. 'You've got to be joking. In awe of that muscle-bound moron?'

'You sound as if you didn't like him very much.'

Kennedy shrugged, not to be drawn.

'I hear he was something of a girl-magnet. That must have caused a bit of jealousy amongst the other boys.'

Kennedy swung his legs around and sat up. 'He wasn't the only one that was a girl-magnet. Some of the girls were more discerning and went for something other than over-developed pecs.'

'Oh? Liked the rebel without a cause, did they?'

'I had my causes, Inspector, don't think I didn't. At least I had more in my head than Popeye, who was only interested in seeing how far the school spinach would enable him to flex his muscles for the girls. You should have seen him when we had double maths. He wasn't such a hero then.'

'And you were . . .?'

'Always good at maths, me. But then I have a brain.'

'I understand you don't work. Have no career. It seems a shame.' It was a roundabout way of voicing the opinion that it was a shame he hadn't done anything with his brain, without actually coming out and saying it.

Kennedy gave a lazy smile. 'Jealous, Inspector?'

'No. I'd far rather be occupied.' Especially with Cyrus and his other visitors at home. 'What do you do with your days? I must say, I didn't think a school reunion would be your thing.'

'It wouldn't be, normally. But I was at a loose end this week and decided to come along at the last minute, sure Paxton would be able to find a room for me. Besides, I've reached the age where I'm curious to see how some of the others have turned out. And I wanted to see if some of the babes still merited babe status.' He pulled a face and spared a glance at Sophie, who was absorbed in her nail painting and clearly oblivious to them. 'Only none of them has come. Just Brains and little Alice and the been-around-the block school bike, Sophie Diaz. Even Ainsley dumped her after a while, when it dawned on him that she wasn't the catch he thought. Dropped her knickers for most of the sixth form. The hero came at the end of a very long list. I was surprised she bothered, as his parents aren't wealthy and she always liked a boy to be able to get his hands on a nice bundle of money. She married a banker, after all.'

'Did you like any of your school-friends? Or did you despise them all?'

This brought a genuine laugh from Kennedy. 'One or two were all right. Even Simon Fairweather's OK once you get beyond his quietness.'

This surprised Rafferty. He wouldn't have thought that the Home Office man, Simon Fairweather, was Kennedy's type. He changed the subject. 'Where is everybody? Not gone home, I hope?'

'No. I think most of them have gone into town. You'll find our resident book-worm in the library.'

'Alice, you mean?'

'Yeah. Could never drag her out of the place when we were

in school. No wonder she got in to Cambridge. The rest are sunning themselves in the grounds – they'll have Harrison the harpy after them, if they're not careful.'

'Where did you go to university, sir?'

'Me? I didn't go to university. I couldn't see the point. I didn't want to be levered into a career and do the whole middle-class bit. Nice little semi, two point four children and the rest. I bummed around Europe for a year or two. Did the Grand Tour. Picked up a few things I never picked up at Griffin.'

'Oh yes? Like what?

'Never mind, Inspector. Probably better you don't know.'

Rafferty just stopped himself from snorting. Besides, he thought he could guess. Drugs – what else did dropouts like Kennedy go in for? Drugs and an easy life, which he thought would be just about Sebastian Kennedy's mark, though he'd have thought his trust fund would keep him in beer, skittles and cocaine without the need to turn to drug running.

Rafferty and Llewellyn turned left out of the Senior Common Room. Rafferty consulted the map of the school that Paxton had given him and made confidently for the library.

Sebastian Kennedy had been right. Alice was there, books spread on the table in front of her and her head bent in the pose of the perennial student. She didn't seem to have heard them come in as she didn't raise her head.

As was only fitting in a school as prestigious as Griffin, the library was a large, well-stocked room and took up a fair percentage of the first floor. There were a dozen large tables spread out in neat lines and bookshelves from floor to ceiling as well as jutting out into the room at right angles. There was an oil portrait of a man whom Rafferty took to be the founder of the school. He walked up to it and peered closely. *Josiah Griffin*, he read, *1882 – 1940*. He'd lived long enough to see scores of old boys join up for the killing fields of the First World War as well as the Second. Rafferty had seen the names of old Griffinites killed in action etched on the walls either side of the Griffin emblem outside the headmaster's study. He'd counted them; there were ninety-two – young men who were destined never to fulfil the promise that their education at Griffin had bestowed. But, Rafferty thought, at least they were honoured, which was more than had happened to those from his old school who had entered the services and died in action.

Rafferty sat himself down at the table opposite Alice Douglas and cleared his throat. She looked up with a frown. 'I thought you'd be outside getting some air on such a lovely day, Miss Douglas.'

'No. I prefer the library. I always did. It's quiet and I knew I'd have the place to myself. Or I thought I would.'

He smiled. 'Sorry to disturb your peace, but like you, I have work to do. Tell me what you remember about Adam.'

'Adam? I really never had much to do with him. I wasn't his type.'

'Was he yours? I gather he was popular with the school's ladies.'

She sat up straight. 'No. Of course not. We were far apart in our outlook, interests, everything. Adam spent all his time on the sports field or in the gym, places that held little appeal for me.'

'Always the last to be picked, were you? I was the same,' he fibbed. But his attempt at stirring a fellow feeling could have fallen on Vincent van Gogh's shell like as she copped a deaf 'un. A silence descended. Alice Douglas seemed as disinclined to talk as Sebastian Kennedy had at first been, and Rafferty couldn't help wondering whether she was just reserved, like a lot of bookish people, or whether she had something to hide.

THREE

Rafferty, although he felt a heel for doing it and leaving Abra to cope with their guests on her own, felt he had no choice but to wait for the other reunees to return for their evening meal. He had a list of those he needed to question again. He wanted to catch them before the dinner gong sounded or he'd be here half the night.

Fortunately, the reunees who had gone into town returned two by two in plenty of time for dinner and Rafferty stationed Timothy Smales at the school's main door to catch the rest as they returned and point them in his direction. Young Timmy looked dissatisfied at being given the job. Where had that wet-behind-the-ears innocent gone? Rafferty wondered. Little Timmy Smales was getting as hard-bitten as a ten-year man.

'Into each life a little rain must fall, Timothy. It could be worse. You could work in Traffic and have a multiple pile-up to disentangle.'

'Yes, sir,' Timothy intoned sullenly.

Rafferty grinned to himself and left him to it.

Trudy Teller proved the most informative of the reunees worth a second interview. She was as gushing in real life as she was in her statement. She was a chubby girl and unlikely to be one of Adam Ainsley's chosen conquests if she had been the same way when she was younger. This seemed to rankle a little.

'Tell me about Adam,' Rafferty invited. 'What was he like?'

'God I don't know what he was like. I never had much to do with him. He was only interested in the pretty ones. Why don't you ask Sophie? She was with him all the time during that last summer.'

'Yes, so I gather. But you must have got some impression of him. Was he studious?'

'God no. If he could escape from the classroom he did. And he had plenty of opportunity, unlike the rest of us, being in just about every sports team the school had. Most of us had to sit of a summer's afternoon and listen to Mr Brown droning on during double bloody maths. I ask you, what's the point of algebra or geometry? I've never used either of them from that day to this.'

Neither had Rafferty. 'Oh? And what do you do?'

'As little as possible.' Trudy's chubby face split in a smile that revealed two rather fetching dimples. 'I'm that rare breed, a housewife who doesn't work. I was never academic, never terribly ambitious. I left that to Alice and Vicky.'

'Did you like Adam? As a classmate?'

'He was all right. Could act a bit superior. Apart from that, I've nothing against him. We never palled around together. He had his own friends and I had mine.'

'Were there any antagonisms at school?'

'Gosh, yes. Both Giles and Sebastian, for all that they'd now protest that it wasn't true, were jealous of Adam in their own ways. Sebastian was always on the scrawny side, though the beer has helped him to fill out now he's got older, and Giles always felt he should be the most popular boy in the school.

God knows why. He was always such a swot and nobody likes a swot, least of all Adam.'

'And what about his girlfriends? Did any of them take being dumped very badly?'

Trudy nodded and leaned forward eagerly. 'Sophie Diaz didn't take it too well. She started bad-mouthing him. Said he was a piss poor lay – and she should know, the way she put it about! Mind, he was always so full of himself, I thought she was probably right. No one as full of self-love as Adam was is likely to take the trouble to make sure the woman enjoys herself during lovemaking. From what Sophie said he was all show and nothing special between the sheets. Or the sports pavilion, which, I gather, was his preferred trysting place.'

'What about other girl friends? Did anyone else take being dumped badly?'

'One or two. But they're not at the reunion. Sophie's the only one of his old lays that troubled to attend.'

'Is there anything else that you can tell us?'

'Not that I can think of. I'll let you know if I remember anything.'

He let Trudy go. The rest were waiting in a straggly line outside the door, tutting and looking pointedly at their watches. The dinner hour was fast approaching. Rafferty let the rest go and just kept back the first four. He'd have to speak to the others after dinner.

But although their statements had looked promising of further revelations, none of the four were able to add anything significant. Or so they claimed. When the last one had gone, Rafferty turned to Llewellyn. 'We'll find Sophie Diaz after dinner. See if she won't do a bit of bad-mouthing about Adam to us.'

'Unlikely, I would have thought. Not now he's been murdered. It'll be how fond she was of him and how good it had been to see him again.'

'A bit of optimism wouldn't go amiss.'

'*Ad astra per aspera*. To the stars through difficulties. It's the Griffin School motto. It could have been written for you.'

'I don't want to reach the stars. Only the solution to this case. But I'll try to look on the bright side, if you will.'

'I've always found optimism an over-rated concept. Why set yourself up for a disappointment? Logic and realism have always been the precepts by which I've abided.'

'Don't I know it. Come on. Let's go down to the dining hall. We might just be in time to beg a glass of wine.'

But it seemed that Llewellyn's stance against optimism had been right as Rafferty not only got no wine, but he got no Sophie Diaz to talk to, either. When he asked where she was, no one knew and he learned she hadn't been present at dinner.

Perhaps she'd been renewing acquaintances in the village and had received an invitation to dine. Tomorrow would have to suffice. But, for now, he wanted to get the rest of the second interviews out of the way. He was curious to discover if any of the other people on his short list would expand on what they had already said.

Of the ten witnesses left, to save them waiting in line like schoolchildren, Rafferty asked them to come up to see him at ten minute intervals. Two hours should see the job done.

It wasn't till the last witness that Rafferty learned something useful. Artemis Willoughby was rather a louche character, who sashayed into the room with the gait of a fashion model. Strangely, from the school gossip that he had already heard, Artemis wasn't gay, though he certainly gave a good impression of being so, to Rafferty's eyes. He wasn't surprised to learn that Artemis was an actor.

'Resting.' Artemis tossed fetching golden curls. 'Though I have hopes for the autumn. Piece of Noel Coward's.'

Artemis Willoughby was a good-looking, if fey, young man with the aforementioned curls and a stubble as fashionable as old Harold's from the pub. 'You hinted in your previous statement about some sort of secret society at the school. Perhaps you can tell us more about it?'

'Oh that.' Artemis shrugged. 'Piece of nonsense. It was started by the girls as some sort of tribute to Reynold Ericson, one of our former classmates, who died during the summer holidays after the fifth form in a ghastly car accident. Funnily enough, the girls ended up being shut out of it as it became exclusively male.'

'Were you a member?'

'Not me. Never asked, darling. Not that I'd have joined. Reynold was a pompous prick who took on mythical status after his death. As far as I was concerned, the only difference was that he was a dead prick instead of a live one.' Artemis glanced at his watch and Rafferty took a surreptitious glance at his own. It was gone ten o'clock. Abra wouldn't invite him over to her side of the bed tonight, for sure.

'Called themselves the Sons of Satan or some daft name like that.' Artemis went on. 'Thought they'd be able to call back Reynold's soul. Why anyone would want to is beyond me.'

'Who was a member of this society?'

Artemis swept his carefully styled hair off his forehead; it slid back in the perfect disarray it had been in before. 'A select little band: Adam Ainsley, Sebastian Kennedy, Giles Harmsworth, Gary Sadiq, Noel Hayles, Freddy Jones and Charles Spence.'

Rafferty smiled. 'What did they do? Sacrifice virgins to the Devil in return for Reynold's soul?'

Artemis shrugged. 'Could be. I know it involved the use of the number of the Beast. Six-six-six and all that. Even managed to get the key to the chapel for their devilish ceremonies. Though they can't have been very successful, as I never saw an apparition of Reynold around the school.'

'When would this have been? During the last summer before you left?'

'Yes. But it started right at the beginning of term, in September. Reynold died during the summer holidays after the fifth year. I think during the six weeks' break everyone must have forgotten what an idiot he was. One of the girls painted a portrait of him and turned a corner of her bedroom into a shrine.'

'Which girl?'

'A girl called Annette Manners. She hasn't come to the reunion. I remember she had her nose put out of joint when the boys decided the club was to be an all-male affair and turfed her and the other girls out.'

'Why didn't they want the girls as members?'

'Oh, I think it was one of those macho things. Went in for 'my dick's bigger than your dick' games. At first, that is. They only got more Devilish during that last summer term.'

'I'm surprised at the members. Several of them don't get on any better now than they apparently did then.'

'You mean Adam and Giles and Seb, I suppose?'

'Mmm. I wouldn't have thought any of them would be keen to belong to a club that the others were members of.'

'They were always in competition. I suppose they thought

they might as well compete in the land of the dick and the Devil as about anything else. I'll tell you who would have won the former contest every time. Adam. He wasn't a girl magnet just because of his muscles.'

Artemis sashayed his way out a few minutes later, leaving Rafferty bemused.

'Did you ever belong to a society dedicated to calling up the Devil?' he asked Llewellyn, who had also gone to a fee-paying school, though one lower down the social and educational pecking order than Griffin.

'No.'

'Nor me. Must be an upper class thing. All those classics lessons and myths about snake-headed monsters and the like must have turned their pubescent brains.' He stood up and stretched. 'Time we turned *our* brains for home. Not to mention the rest of us. Abra'll be spitting fire. I bet Cyrus has been holding forth again about modern youth and how much they need religion. Abra's inclined to take it personally.'

'What about writing up the reports? We should do it tonight.'

'Don't be my conscience, Daff. I've a perfectly good one of my own. Tomorrow morning will do. As long as we beat Long Pockets in by an hour, he won't be any the wiser about our backsliding. And at the speed you type, you'll get them done in no time.'

'Even so—' Llewellyn began.

'Even so, nothing. At the moment, I'm more concerned with placating my lovely bride than I am in placating Bradley. At least he's not likely to withhold his favours as I never had them in the first place.'

When Rafferty got home Cyrus told him that Abra had gone to bed with a headache. 'I took her a cup of tea up. That should help.'

Rafferty just managed a taut smile and a 'thank you'. Poor Abra. Not only had she to deal with their four visitors alone, but Cyrus had forced more tea on her. You're going to cop it, Rafferty told himself as he said good night and headed upstairs.

But thankfully, whether or not her sick headache was real, Abra had gone to sleep. He crept about the bedroom, fearful of waking her. He'd have to get up extra early in the morning in order to beat Cyrus to the kitchen. It was too much to expect Abra to put up with Cyrus's morning tea two days running.

The next day was even busier as their interviewees were further afield. They had yet to interview Ainsley's ex-wives. They lived on different sides of the country and Rafferty had already decided to split his forces. He sent Llewellyn and Mary Carmody to see the first wife and he took the second, on the principle that the more recent wife would be likely to bring forth more of a bitter tirade and Llewellyn could be a delicate flower about such things.

Ainsley's second ex-wife, Stella, lived in Somerset. He set off at nine, once Llewellyn had finished typing up the previous evening's interviews and he had seen Bradley to give him his report on the investigation thus far.

In the interim, Bradley had somehow found out that Simon Fairweather was at the Home Office – some arse-licker on the team, no doubt – and he interrogated Rafferty about the man and was far from satisfied with Rafferty's answers, which, seeing as Fairweather was quieter than a whisper, meant there was little to report.

'But he must have said something,' Bradley protested. 'Did he make any complaints, for instance?'

'Not to me, he didn't. I don't think you need worry, sir. He doesn't seem the complaining sort.'

'Not to you, perhaps.' God, thought Rafferty, the old bugger's sniffy today. 'He probably prefers to take his complaints to a higher authority. He could be the sort who make their complaints on paper so they're always on your record.'

And you'd know, was Rafferty's thought.

Bradley seemed to have got himself in a bit of a lather on the subject of Simon Fairweather, though, for the life of him, Rafferty couldn't see what Fairweather could have to complain about. But he was perfectly happy to let Bradley stew about what memoranda might be finding their way back to the brass at Region. If he wasn't such an arse-licker himself, Rafferty might have felt sorry for him. But as it was, he set his mind to thoughts of the coming interview and what questions to ask the ex-Mrs Ainsley.

* * *

He made good time and reached the Somerset town of Carworth just after lunch. Llewellyn, the techno whizz-kid, had set the satnav for him and the computer had directed him faultlessly. It never did that when *he* set the gizmo.

The second ex-Mrs Ainsley turned out to be tall and willowy like her house, though with what Rafferty guessed must be surgical enhancement around the bosom region. They were never natural, he thought. They certainly weren't a matching set with the rest of her.

Stella Ainsley was surprisingly welcoming. He soon learned why. He had been right and the bitter recriminations against her former husband set in within five minutes. It was as if she couldn't wait to let the festering juices out.

'He was like that song, you know? "He had one eye on the mirror and he watched himself go by".'

'Carly Simon.'

'Was it? Anyway, he didn't have much love to spare for a real woman' – well as real as she got, with those bazookas, was Rafferty's irreverent thought. 'He loved himself too much. He used to like to fix the car out front, stripped to the waist, though we had a perfectly good garage. He'd flex his muscles for every passing bimbo. A wife can only take so much of such behaviour. And when I came home and found him in bed with one of our next-door neighbours, it was the last straw. I kicked him out.'

'How long were you married?'

'Five years.'

'You never had children?'

'God no. Adam wasn't father material. He wasn't husband material, either, as I learned.' She bit her lip and hurried on. 'I married him when he was still playing professional rugby and I don't mind admitting that I enjoyed those early days of our marriage. We were feted wherever we went. Adam lapped it up. He got rather depressed when it all ended and he looked round for another sport where he'd get the same adulation. He found one with the bimbo athletics.'

'Did he ever talk about his schooldays?'

'Did he ever. According to Adam, he was always first at everything: rugby, swimming, running. You name it and he won it. I got sick of it in the end when his subjects of conversation came down to little more than boasting or bemoaning his fate that he should have come down from the height of his fame to teaching sport to adolescent boys. Well, I imagine you can guess what it was like?'

Rafferty nodded. He could. Stella Ainsley reminded him of his late wife, Angie. He hadn't been able to do anything right for her. Getting her pregnant and the hasty wedding that followed were the highlights and it all went steadily downhill after that. They hadn't had children, either – the baby she had been carrying had died in the womb very early in the pregnancy. Or so she'd claimed. Rafferty, already caught on the hook, was just as pleased there were no more little hostages to fortune.

Stella Ainsley could recall few names from her late ex-husband's schooldays. Adam had apparently always been the star, the winner, with everyone else as also-rans. All in all, he'd learned little more than he already had, though he suspected there was further information she could give him.

Rafferty rang Llewellyn on his mobile once he got back to the car. 'Any joy?'

'The first Mrs Ainsley was quite forthcoming. She even recalled a few names from the past.'

'More than my one managed. So who did she remember?'

'Giles Harmsworth. She knew him, apparently and several of the others. She went to university with Giles and Asgar Sadiq.'

'Did she now? And did she have anything nasty to say about either of them?'

'She was of the opinion that Giles wouldn't have the nerve to drop hemlock into Adam Ainsley's food and then calmly eat his own lunch as if nothing had happened. She didn't know Mr Sadiq quite as well, but she did say that she checked on the Internet after we rang her and she said that hemlock, apart from being grown in Asia, is also quite commonly used as a poison on that continent.'

'Is that so? Seems Mr Gary Sadiq has moved up the suspect pecking order. Remind me we must have another little chat with him this afternoon. I'll see you back at the cop shop.' Rafferty disconnected and settled down to the long drive home.

Asgar 'Gary' Sadiq was a light-skinned Anglo-Indian, and he had spent most of his life in England as he had undergone all his schooling there.

'A long way from home,' Rafferty commented. 'What did

you do during the holidays? Stay with your English relatives or fly back?'

Sadiq shook his head. 'Neither. My mother's family disowned her when she married my father. And it was too far and too costly to return to India in the holidays. The fees cost all that my parents could spare. No I mostly stayed with school-friends. I stayed with Giles several times and Sebastian. I even stayed with Adam once, though it was an experience that neither of us chose to repeat.'

'Oh? Why was that?'

'I'm quite competitive. Adam had never had occasion to discover this at school, as we weren't competitive in the same things. But at his home we were thrown together more and we played games with his family. I beat him regularly at Scrabble and Trivial Pursuit. He didn't like it. He was barely speaking to me by the end of the holidays. Neither were his parents – they didn't like their wonder boy having his nose put out of joint. Though they were more successful at concealing their antagonism than Adam was.'

'Not a very nice experience. You must have been glad to get back to school.'

Sadiq gave a fatalistic shrug. 'I've had worse.'

Rafferty wondered that Sadiq should choose to confide this little titbit. Admittedly, it could hardly be said to be cause for poisoning Ainsley all of seventeen years later. Unless he was being disingenuous and the rebuff had cut deep. Teenagers could be sensitive souls. Perhaps Asgar had been a particularly tortured teen, with homesickness and racism mixed into the brew. All would have been so much more painful with him so far from home and with little hope of seeing his family. Perhaps he had nursed Adam's rebuff all these years and this reunion had been the first chance he had had to get his revenge?

'Have you been back to your home in India recently, Mr Sadiq?' Rafferty asked, curious to learn if Asgar had had opportunity to consult some Indian wise man about what plant would kill a mortal enemy in the way Adam Ainsley had been killed.

'I live there now. I work in IT and India is a rising star. Rivals Silicone Valley in the States. I just came back here for the school reunion.'

'Long way to come.'

'Yes. But I often have to fly over to Britain on business, so it was little more expense to tag this reunion on the end of a round of meetings.'

'Did Mr Barmforth, the last headmaster, keep you updated on who else would be attending the reunion?'

'Oh yes. He always sent out a round robin email; Jeremy Paxton did the same when he took over. There's an Old Griffinites' club. A number of us meet regularly.'

'What about Adam? Was he a member?'

'No. We have a clubhouse in town, but I never saw him there. Admittedly, I couldn't manage to fly over too often. And this is the first time he's turned up for a reunion. I was surprised when I saw his name on Jeremy's round-robin email as one of the attendees.'

'Did he say why he'd come this time?'

'He just said he was curious about how we'd all got on, though I think, from reading between the lines, that he was bored with what he was doing. You know he worked as a sports instructor after he quit rugby?'

Rafferty nodded.

'I got the impression he missed his life as a professional sportsman, though he didn't say as much. Didn't want to admit it, I suppose. He was always very fit, but he'd let himself get a bit flabby. Sure sign of lack of self-esteem, don't they say?'

Rafferty pulled in his incipient beer belly and said, 'I wouldn't know.' Still, it was interesting that Ainsley seemed to have been letting himself go. He was currently single – neither he, nor the two ex-Mrs Ainsleys had said his love life was as red-hot as it had been when he was the school sporting hero or the professional rugby player.

'I think he came to the reunion in the hope of putting out a few feelers about other work. But most of his peers went into professional careers – banking, lecturing, the medical or legal world. Or, like me, IT. Adam was never academic, so there was no way any of us could have fixed him up with a suitable job. I don't think he found the help he was seeking. He died an unhappy, frustrated man.'

Once Gary Sadiq had gone, Rafferty leaned back and said to Llewellyn, who had been taking notes, 'So Sadiq had been aware that Adam Ainsley would be returning to Griffin. Asgar Sadiq is a Muslim, according to the school records in Paxton's study. Did he nurse a grievance all these years and seize his opportunity to get his own back, perhaps encouraged by Muslim fanatics in his homeland?'

Of course, Llewellyn wasn't slow to remind him that Sadiq hadn't been the only one to receive Paxton's round robin emails, which had listed Adam as an attendee at the reunion. All the reunees would have had them and could have planned accordingly; the hemlock alone indicated that planning had gone into this murder. And murder, Rafferty was convinced, this was, even though Sadiq had tried to paint a picture of a man on the brink of possible suicide. He had found time to have a chat with Ainsley's doctor and he had said that Ainsley hadn't struck him as being a suicide prospect. The anti-depressants had been prescribed as the reflex action of a hard-pressed GP, he admitted. He told them that he had thought Ainsley more frustrated and lacking ego-fuel than depressed. And for all that Adam Ainsley hadn't been academically bright, he had received an excellent education and was as capable of looking up poisons on the Internet as the next person. It seemed unlikely in the extreme that he would have selected the paralyzing hemlock as the means to his own destruction. Everyone they had spoken to had described Ainsley as proud of his physique and his physical abilities. And even if his body had become a bit more lardy than it had been in his youth, Rafferty had seen his corpse and he had still been what his ma would have described as 'a fine figure of a man'. Somehow he doubted that a man prone to such self-love would choose to render himself a blind paraplegic at the end. After such an easy, successful life, he would choose an easy death.

'Let's look at what we've got so far,' Llewellyn suggested. 'We have Asgar Sadiq possibly nursing a grudge all these years after Adam Ainsley had given him the silent treatment. Though why he told us about it, if so . . . He had no need. Mr Ainsley's parents were hardly likely to give him away seeing as to reveal that Adam Ainsley had been piqued to be beaten by Mr Sadiq at Scrabble would have shown their son to be a petulant young man. We have Sophie Diaz whom he dumped when he learned she had slept with most of his classmates. We have Alice Douglas, who is supposed to have made moon eyes at Adam and been ignored. It's not much, is it? What else?'

'Nothing else. Unless we count Mrs Benton, the cook and Harrison the groundsman. The first because Adam perhaps sneaked to the head about her lumpy custard and the latter because Adam had stubbed out one spliff too many on his manicured lawn. Hmm, you're right. We've not got a lot to go on. There must be more. And we'd better find it before the weekend or we're going to be chasing our tails all over the country. They're all due to go home on Sunday and we've not got the evidence to keep hold of any of them.'

After musing on this for a few moments, Rafferty suggested they went in search of lunch in the village before Llewellyn sought out Alice Douglas again. As he told the Welshman, he thought better on a full stomach.

Sebastian Kennedy and Simon Fairweather were in the pub in the village when they got there. When Rafferty and Llewellyn had got their drinks and ordered their lunch, Rafferty asked if they could join them at their table.

'If you must,' said Sebastian Kennedy, the rebellious pig-hater, as he sat back and gave them an insolent, challenging stare.

'Charming as ever, I see,' said Rafferty as he sat down.

'That's the glory of being rich, Inspector. It allows a man to be as rude as he likes and there's no comeback. No one's going to sack you or refuse to employ you. No one's going to tear you off a strip or give you a bad work assessment or try to put you down. And it doesn't much matter if they do. Money's a great comforter.'

'I can imagine,' said Rafferty, as he thought of the super. Bradley specialized in several of the above. 'So what are you doing in here? Fed up of school meals?'

'Something like that,' Kennedy told them. 'Plus the fact they don't serve up my preferred booze at lunch or dinner.' Kennedy had a pint in front of him. 'It's all fine wines from the school's excellent cellar and they're meant to be savoured, not thrown back with gay abandon.'

Rafferty laughed, being something of a gay abandon man himself, and sipped his Adnam's bitter. He gradually brought the conversation round to what Simon Fairweather did at the Home Office – if only to have something with which to appease Superintendent Bradley if the investigation dragged on.

'I'm not a politician,' Fairweather replied to his question. 'I'm a civil servant. An Under-Secretary. I joined the Home Office straight after university.'

'Double First, our Simon,' Kennedy told them. 'They were lucky to get him. But, God, Si, how do you stand all that bureaucracy and paper shuffling?'

Simon Fairweather smiled. He had a particularly engaging smile – it altered his rather solemn face amazingly and gave him a mischievous pixie quality – most unsuitable in a civil servant, was Rafferty's thought, where inscrutability was the norm.

'It's rather more than that, Seb. We deal with day-to-day policing, security for the royal family, combating terrorism. We have rather a wide field of responsibility. I've never regretted joining the civil service as a career. And there's plenty of scope for the ultra-ambitious.'

'My boss has been getting his knickers in a twist about your involvement in the case,' Rafferty revealed, without a blush for any possible disloyalty.

'Why?' Fairweather flashed that impish smile again. 'Has he been fiddling the overtime figures?'

'Not as far as I know.'

'Then he's nothing to worry about. And I've nothing to complain about. So far.'

Rafferty nodded. 'That's good.' He paused, took another sip of his bitter, and then went on. 'Bit awkward for you, this case, isn't it? In your line.'

Fairweather gave another impish smile. 'Certainly, we're not encouraged to get caught up, as a suspect – which I suppose I am – in murder investigations. But I think Griffin School can be regarded by the senior mandarins as being a suitable place for me to socialize. After all, several of my colleagues attended the school and some come back to the reunions. I won't get a black mark on my record.'

'Unless you killed Ainsley,' Kennedy quipped. 'You might get a bit more than a black mark then, even from the mandarins.'

'As far as I'm aware, Sebastian, the killer, whoever he is, aside, you're the nearest the school comes to harbouring a criminal. Though, I have to say that, as an anarchist, you're too lazy to be a very enthusiastic one.'

'That's me put in my place,' Kennedy said. 'Trust a civil servant to get the last word.'

'I rather think you just did that, Seb.'

Their meals arrived then and Rafferty tucked in heartily to

his roast beef and Yorkshires. The beef was melt-in-the-mouth tender and the potatoes were delicious; crunchy on the outside and soft on the inside, just as he liked them. He hadn't expected much from a small village pub, but he made a mental note to put this one in his address book as a possible place to take Abra.

Sebastian Kennedy had started on his fourth pint by the time Rafferty had finished his meal. He gave Llewellyn the nod and a twenty pound note and his sergeant got up to get more drinks. 'Will you boys have one with us?'

Like old Harold previously, Sebastian Kennedy pretended to be horrified. 'What? Drinking with pigs? Go on then, I'll have a large Martel.'

'Are you taking the mick out of a poor Mick pig, Mr Kennedy?'

'Wouldn't dream of it. And call me Sebastian, seeing as we're now drinking buddies. I'm a Mick myself on my father's side. Limerick.'

'Dublin.'

'Not the land of the Sniffy Liffey?'

'The very same.'

'We want to be careful or Si here will have us both investigated for IRA sympathies. I take it you're not a Prod?'

'No. Seriously lapsed Catholic.' Seeing as they were getting so pally, Rafferty decided to ask a straightforward question. 'Tell me, Sebastian, who do *you* think killed Adam Ainsley?'

Kennedy shrugged. 'Don't know. Don't much care, either. As long as I don't get fitted up for it.'

'Don't worry. I don't do fitting-up.'

'Glad to hear it. I'd hate to do jail time for Alki.'

'Alki?'

'One of my other names for Adam Ainsley. AA. Alcoholics' Anonymous.'

'And was he? An alki, I mean?'

'Never used to be. Was always a keep fit fanatic. But he didn't look so hot to me. Running to seed. He was definitely sinking the vino pretty heavily that lunchtime for all his show of going for a run afterwards. Drank the best part of two bottles of wine; good job several others didn't want their share or I might have gone short. I've never been one for keep-fit. I mean, look at Adam. Goes out for a run and dies. Not much of an advert for exercise.'

'He was poisoned, Sebastian, according to the inspector,' Simon Fairweather reminded him. 'He didn't have a heart attack like that middle-aged jogger who died some years ago. His death had nothing whatsoever to do with exercising.'

'What about you, sir?' Rafferty turned to Simon Fairweather before the conversation had a chance to develop into an argument. 'Have you any idea who did it?'

'No. Though don't they say that poisoning's a woman's crime?'

Typical mandarin to pass the buck. 'Yes. But then, that saying might just be taken advantage of by one of a bunch of private-school educated men as a cover for their own misdeed.'

'Ha. I do hope you don't intend to arrest *me* Inspector?'

'No fear, sir. Not unless you did it, that is. Did you?'

'Under the protective auspices of the Home Office, you mean?'

'Something like that.'

'My dear chap. You need have no fears. No one's going to come down on you with a heavy hand if you do arrest me. I'm not that high up the pecking order.'

Rafferty smiled, but he didn't believe him. The Home Office would look after its own. They always did. He'd be the one in the mire, most likely, and it wasn't as if Bradley would do anything to get him out of it. He'd be only too delighted. And if he did manage to climb out of the mire, he'd probably push him back in.

'Oh well,' he said as he stood up and picked up the dirty glasses to return them to the bar. 'Back to it.'

'Are you getting anywhere, Inspector, do you think? asked Fairweather.

'Hard to tell yet, sir. But at least we've been able to whittle down the suspects early in the case, which is always a good thing. We'll get there.'

'Glad to hear it. I didn't particularly like Ainsley, he was something of a bully when we were at school and I don't think he'd changed over the years. But I'm not a believer in people meting out their own justice. That's what the courts are for.'

Rafferty, thinking again of possible motives, asked, 'Do you know who, in particular, he bullied?'

'So you can bully them in turn? No Inspector. I won't give you that information, though I'm sure you can find it out elsewhere. Besides, it was all a very long time ago.'

'That doesn't sound like mandarin-speak. It seems you're a bit of a rebel on the quiet also, sir.'

'I've had my moments. This particular civil servant has never believed in speaking with Sir Humphrey's esoteric brand of the truth. It probably explains why I'm still just an Under Secretary.'

It probably did, at that, Rafferty mused. A readiness for speaking the truth rather than going in for police office politics hadn't done a great deal for *his* career, either. 'Anyway, we'll see you gentlemen later. Come on, Llewellyn.'

'That's the first mention that our Mr Ainsley was a bully,' Rafferty commented when they got outside. 'Find out who his victims were, Daff. Try asking the ladies. I've always found them less inclined to keep mum over such things. But before you do that, find Alice Douglas and Sophie Diaz, the latter, her of the "sizzling" affair, might have something interesting to confide, supposing we can prise it out of her, so I want to speak to her first.'

FOUR

Once back at the school, Llewellyn went off to find Sophie Diaz and Rafferty went in search of tea. Surprisingly, the feisty Mrs Benton proved amenable to stopping her dinner preparations and making him a cup. He took the opportunity of asking her about bullying at the school during the reunees' time there.

'Oh, there was bullying right enough. I nipped it in the bud when I saw it. Nasty little devils, some of them. That Adam was a prime example. He was tall and well built for his age. He'd often start picking on the younger ones when he was in the queue outside my kitchen. I gave him a good smack on the knuckles once with a heavy metal soup ladle when he started bullying that wouldn't-say-boo Simon Fairweather. I didn't put up with bullying in my dining hall, as I told the old headmaster when that Adam complained.'

'What did Adam do when you hit him?'

'Him? Nothing. Looked ashamed of himself for once. A few decent leatherings would have done him the world of good.

My own children got a smack when they deserved it and they've all turned out well.'

'What was the school's attitude to bullying?'

'Mr Barmforth seemed to leave the kids to it to fight their own battles on the principle that that's what they'd have to do in life. I don't hold with such an attitude. If you're *in loco parentis* as the head and teachers are, they should impose a parental discipline. Bullying needs stamping on or it'll get nastier and nastier.'

Rafferty nodded. He agreed with this sentiment. His own younger brother, Mickey, had been bullied at school; he'd been a bit of a runt then. He'd filled out since and his work as a carpenter had given him muscles to spare.

Mrs Benton made him a second cup of tea as well as one for Llewellyn and he took both upstairs to their allocated office. But there was no one there. He poked his head around the door of the Senior Common Room and found Llewellyn. The Welshman was standing in what looked like a very convivial little circle with Victoria Watson, Giles Harmsworth and Sophie Diaz, discussing some play or other that they'd all seen. Llewellyn looked as animated as he'd ever seen him and, in an instant, Rafferty felt again the wave of resentment for his sergeant's superior education that he'd felt when they'd first worked together. Cambridge versus Secondary Modern was no contest. No wonder he always felt inferior in spite of being the *sup*erior.

'Sergeant.' Rafferty's voice was sharp and Llewellyn looked over in surprise.

'Sir?'

'I've been looking for you all over. If you're going to hobnob with Griffin's old boys and girls, I wish you'd let me know.' His sarcasm wasn't lost on Llewellyn, who flushed, though whether from embarrassment or anger wasn't clear. However, he murmured a few words in Sophie Diaz's lavishly gold-encrusted ear and the two of them moved towards the door.

Rafferty sat down behind the desk and sipped his tea. He apologised that he didn't have one for Sophie.

'I don't drink tea.'

'Really? How do you get through the day?'

'I don't regard my day as something to be got through.'

'Lucky lady.' Unsurprising, with a rich banker for a husband, was Rafferty's thought. Probably spent her days in the enjoyable pastime of reducing his wealth.

'Now, Mrs Diaz, I'm sure you can help me get a more rounded portrait of Mr Ainsley. I understand you dated him steadily for several months during your last term at the school.'

Sophie Diaz nodded. 'Yes, we were an item for a while. It was nothing serious, of course, just a fun boy/girl thing.'

'Oh? I understood it was rather more than that.'

Sophie Diaz lowered her gaze and asked, 'Who told you that?'

'It doesn't matter. But I was told that you and Ainsley had a "sizzling" affair that summer term and that he dumped you when he found out you and he weren't quite the love's young dream he thought you were.'

'It's my recollection that it was more of a mutual thing,' she murmured. 'I admit that Adam was a bit upset when he found out I'd slept with one or two of his friends, but our break up was amicable in the end. It was good to see him at the reunion.' A single tear formed in her right eye. 'I couldn't believe it when I learned he was dead. Murdered. Who could want to do such a thing?'

'I was rather hoping you might tell me that.'

'Me? I can't tell you anything, Inspector.'

'I'm sure you can if you just try a little. Adam must have confided things to you during your time together. After all, you were an item for quite a long time in adolescent terms. You must be able to tell me more than, say, Victoria Watson or Alice Douglas, both of whom seem to have been the studious sort during their time at Griffin.'

'Huh, you'd be surprised. Alice wasn't quite the prim and proper little swot by any means.'

'What do you mean?'

'Oh Alice indulged in at least one little love affair during her time here.'

'Really? Who with?'

Sophie's beautifully made up face looked piqued. 'I don't know. She wouldn't tell me. Though she did tell me one thing.'

'Oh, yes? What was that?'

Sophie smiled. 'I wasn't the only naughty girl, Inspector. Alice "the swot" Douglas fell pregnant during the last few weeks of term. She came to me for advice. I told her to get rid of it.'

'And did she?'

'What do you think? With parents like hers she wouldn't have dared do anything else. Oh she got rid of it all right, though God knows where she'd have got the money from as her parents kept her on very short rations. I suppose the boy, whoever he was, paid up in the end, though Alice told me he hadn't wanted to know at first. She said he'd denied the kid was his. But you'd better ask her about that.'

'Oh, I will. You can be sure of it. Any other confidences you should tell us about?'

She stared at him for a moment, as if undecided, but then shook her head.

'Now, Miss Douglas,' Rafferty began, twenty minutes later after Sophie Diaz had been ushered out and Llewellyn had found Alice Douglas and brought her into the office. 'I think you've got something to tell us. Something you failed to mention when we spoke to you before.'

She faced him down. 'I don't know what you mean, Inspector.'

'Really? A little matter of an unwanted pregnancy at the end of your last summer at the school. It's not the sort of thing you're likely to forget. Why didn't you mention it?'

For a moment, he suspected she was going to deny it, but she obviously thought better of this. 'I see Sophie's been sharing.' She paused, settled her long, slim fingers back in her lap, where they lay loosely entwined. 'I didn't see what relevance it had to your investigation.'

'Didn't you? Relevance or otherwise is for me to decide,' he told her. 'So, did you go through with the abortion that Sophie advised?'

She was slow to answer and Rafferty guessed that shame made her reluctant to admit it. But she finally said 'yes'.

'It can't have been easy, what with you brought up as a Catholic.'

'No. Look, do we have to talk about this, Inspector? It was all a very long time ago.'

'Yes, I think so. Is it true that the father didn't want to know?'

'You seem to know all about it, Inspector. What do you think?'

'I'd rather have you tell me.'

'Very well. No, he didn't want to know. Does that answer your question?'

'Yes. Thank you. His refusal to share the burden must have been upsetting.'

'Yes. It was. Of course it was.'

'You never thought of going to the head?'

'Old Barmpot?' She smoothed back her glossy dark hair, which she wore in a practical pageboy. 'What on earth for? What could he have done?'

'Nothing, perhaps, except, maybe, get the father to acknowledge paternity and support you through the abortion. Who was the father, by the way? I understood you were a studious girl and didn't go in much for dating.'

'I'm afraid the identity of the father is my business, Inspector. It really has nothing to do with your current investigation.'

'I'll remind you again, Miss Douglas, that the relevance or otherwise is my province.' He had a sudden brainwave and asked, 'Was Adam Ainsley the baby's father?'

Alice flushed hotly, though whether from shame that he'd hit the nail on the head or anger that he should think the muscle-bound Ainsley the father, Rafferty couldn't guess.

'No. Whatever gave you that idea? He never looked at me at school. He was always surrounded by pretty nymphets.'

'He mightn't have looked at you, but I understood from things one or two of the others said that you had eyes for him. In fact, I understand you had quite a crush on him.'

She attempted to laugh it off. 'That was silly schoolgirl stuff. Most of the girls had a crush on Adam at one time or another. He was the school hunk.'

'So if Adam wasn't your baby's father, who was?'

'I'd rather not say.'

A mulish look had set in and he could see that she wouldn't tell him the identity of the father. Never mind. He could wait. She'd tell him eventually. Or else someone else would. He changed tack. 'What do you do for a living, Miss Douglas?'

'I'm a librarian at the British Library'

'Really? You did well for yourself after school, then?'

'Yes.' She sat back and, seeming to have gained rather than lost confidence during the interview, she asked, quietly, 'You never thought Adam might have killed himself?'

'The possibility has been considered, yes. But so far, no one has mentioned a strong enough reason for him to do such a thing.'

'Perhaps you should consider it a bit more. He missed his fame very much. He had hoped to get a television job of some sort, but more clever retired sportsmen beat him to it. I believe the BBC gave him a trial, but he froze behind the microphone, hence the job as a lowly sports master. It really can't have suited his temperament. He always enjoyed being the star too much to play second fiddle to a bunch of adolescents.'

'How do you know that? Did you keep in contact with him?'

'No. I had no reason to. But Giles Harmsworth has a friend who works at the BBC, and he told him all about it. Giles didn't waste any time in spreading news of Adam's failure to gain a broadcasting career around at the reunion.'

'Nice.'

'Payback time, I believe it's called, Inspector.'

'And what reason did Giles Harmsworth have for wanting payback?'

The shutters went down and she replied pertly, 'Why don't you ask him?'

'Oh I will.' Rafferty finished his now tepid tea. He noticed that Llewellyn hadn't touched his. Probably sulking because of his sharp rebuke before, he thought, irritably.

'May I go now?'

Rafferty nodded. He sat back when Alice Douglas had gone, swivelled his chair round so he didn't have to look at Llewellyn and stared out over the extensive grounds of Griffin School. Paxton had told them the grounds spread to forty-five acres. Thinking of Griffin's grounds and playing fields gave him an idea and he swivelled his chair back again. Llewellyn still had a face to freeze Hell over, but he ignored it and said brusquely, 'Let's go and have a word with Tom Harrison, the groundsman. Like Mrs Benton, he's been here for years. He must have seen a fair few examples of bullying around the school. We might as well find out who Ainsley bullied, apart from Simon Fairweather who the cook mentioned.'

It was a fine, warm day and it was pleasant to walk through the grounds, which looked very lush. Llewellyn's face thawed in the sunshine and Rafferty grinned to himself.

Tom Harrison might be a surly man, but he knew his job. The lawns surrounding the school were verdant green with not a weed in sight and the playing fields looked as smooth as silk and would be the envy of the Wembley that had had a few problems with its own turf.

Rafferty saw a bunch of the reunees lounging on the grass and felt envious of their leisure. But then, Harrison hove into sight round the corner of a shed, on a ride-on mower and he wondered if he had deliberately decided to cut the grass where they were sitting, which already looked pretty well-shorn to Rafferty.

The reunees got hurriedly to their feet as the lawnmower headed straight for them with no sign of stopping. Rafferty saw Sebastian Kennedy give Harrison the finger. In retaliation, he left his ever-present empty lager cans behind to get caught up in the blades. But it seemed Harrison was wise to this trick and he pulled up and removed them, giving Kennedy a nasty look as he did so.

'Happy days,' said Rafferty. In order to avoid standing in front of the murderous mower to gain Harrison's attention, Rafferty hurried across before the groundsman swung himself back on board.

'Mr Harrison. I wanted a word.'

Harrison said nothing, but merely waited for him to go on, Sebastian Kennedy's discarded lager cans clutched in his hands.

'You must see a few things, working all round the school as you do.'

Harrison stuffed the cans under one arm, pulled off his cap and scratched his head before he answered. 'This and that.'

'And does the this and that extend to seeing bullying?'

For a moment, Harrison looked bemused at the question and then he answered bluntly, 'Well, of course it does. It's a school, isn't it?'

'Can you cast your mind back to when these reunees were here as students? You can't have been much older than them at the time.'

'Twenty-five, I was, when I started here.'

'You must have been a target for the girls.'

Harrison's ruggedly handsome face flushed an ugly red. 'Used to torment me something rotten. I went to Mr Barmforth about it but he just told me I was big enough and ugly enough to keep a few teenage girls in line. After that I just ignored them. They soon got tired of the silent treatment.'

'What about the boys?'

Harrison blushed even more hotly. 'What about them?'

'How did you get on with them?'

'I was glad to see the back of them. Worst of the bunch, they were, that year.'

'Oh really? Why? What did they do?'

'Little bastards used to like to sabotage my machinery. Caught that Kennedy boy pouring sugar into my petrol mower once. I gave him a clip round the ear and dragged him off to the headmaster.'

'Get any satisfaction?'

'Oh yes. He knew how to discipline boys, did Mr Barmforth. Took no notice of featherbedding government edicts, didn't Mr B. Not like this new one. Don't like the look of him at all, with his namby-pamby cravats and waistcoats. He's young, too, and will doubtless have been fed all that no smacking horse manure.'

'What about the dead man, Adam Ainsley? Did you see him bullying anyone in particular?'

For some reason, Harrison flushed up again. Then, before Rafferty could say anything, he said, 'Why do you want to know about what happened years ago?'

Why indeed? It would probably turn out to be a waste of time. Was it really likely that the normal bullying that went on in every school could have led to murder over a decade and a half later? But he had little enough to go on and people harboured grudges. Besides, this murder must surely have originated during their schooldays together. It was too much of a coincidence that Adam Ainsley was only murdered when he attended his first ever reunion. 'From little acorns, etc,' he told Harrison. 'Who knows what might have triggered Ainsley's murder? Given this was the first time he'd appeared at a reunion and he winds up dead, it seems likely that the reason for his death is buried in the past.'

Harrison looked unconvinced and laid a hand on his lawnmower as if he couldn't wait to get on with his work. With a frown, he turned back to Rafferty. 'I don't suppose there was a child that was smaller or younger than him that he didn't pick on. Does that answer your question?'

'Not altogether. Who among the reunees did he pick on?'

Harrison sighed heavily as if he was tired of the subject, then he reeled several names off at a rate of knots, climbed back on to his mower and rode away, narrowly missing Rafferty as he did so.

Rafferty felt tempted to emulate Sebastian Kennedy's rude gesture, but it was beneath his dignity. Anyway, Harrison had his back to him and wouldn't see it. Instead, he brushed his jacket free from invisible engine taint and said to Llewellyn, 'I hope you got all those names.'

'Yes. I noticed that Sebastian Kennedy featured in the list. And Simon Fairweather got a second mention.'

'Mmm. No wonder Fairweather fought shy of telling us who it was that Ainsley bullied. The wonder is he mentioned it at all.'

'Probably knew that someone would and thought he'd better mention it first so as to lessen any look of guilt. Not a mandarin for nothing, as you might say.'

Rafferty merely went 'Mmm' again. Then he said, 'This is not likely to please Bradley. Wait till I tell him that our tame mandarin is not only a suspect, but also has a pretty good motive if Ainsley made his schooldays particularly vile. It's his worst nightmare, someone from the Home Office being under suspicion of murder. He'll think I'm putting Fairweather forward as a possible murderer deliberately, just to vex him.'

'And aren't you?'

Rafferty grinned. 'Oh yes. Partly, anyway. You know aggravating Bradley's what I live for. Right, I suppose we'd better question Messrs Fairweather and Kennedy. See what went on in the bogs and behind the bike sheds. They certainly looked as thick as thieves when we saw them in the pub. Maybe they colluded to get rid of Ainsley?'

'Surely, Mr Fairweather at least, given his job, would be too sensible a man to attempt to gain retribution after so long?'

'Don't you believe it. Some of these so-called civil servants hold grudges for decades. If they can do one another down, you'd best get out of their way. I heard one story of a Foreign Office bloke who wanted to get his own back for some slight remembered from university days, who slipped a sheet of internet kiddie porn between the pages of the man's CV when he was going for a job promotion.'

'What happened?'

'The bloke got the job. No. Sick joke. He didn't get the job or any further ones that he applied for. He was lucky not to get the police on his tail, but as I told you, civil servants look after their own.'

'Didn't he suspect who had done this to him?'

'Oh yes. He knew. Got his own back, too. Ran the bloke over and said it was an accident. Crippled him. Got away with it, too. You won't believe it, but they still work together. Still hate one another's guts. Probably still playing evil tricks on one another, too. Depressing thing, human nature. Let's see if Fairweather and Kennedy protest their innocence too strongly.'

Kennedy after being chased off the lawn by Tom Harrison and his lawnmower, had retreated, with his cans of lager, to the Senior Common Room where he was once again stretched out on one of the settees at his ease. Fairweather was nowhere to be seen. And, apart from Kennedy, the room was empty.

'Mr Kennedy.'

'I thought we'd agreed that it's Sebastian, Inspector. Want a can?'

'No thanks. I'm a bitter man. Can't stand lager.'

'Sergeant? What about you?'

'I don't drink, sir. Besides, I'm on duty.'

'You're no fun, you two.' He stretched luxuriously. 'What did you want, anyway?'

'Just something we heard. You remember, in the pub, Simon Fairweather mentioned that Ainsley was a bully?'

'Yeah. So what?'

'I've discovered who he bullied. I gather you were one of his victims, sir.'

Kennedy scrunched up his can and dropped it on the floor. 'Who says so?'

'That's not important, but it was from more than one source.' That wasn't the strict truth, but a little white lie was no lie at all, in Rafferty's book.

'So what are you saying? That I slipped hemlock into his soup because he used to beat me up?'

'That's about the size of it, sir, yes.'

'So where's your evidence? You have got some, I take it, or is this just a fishing expedition?'

'Just call it checking out the possibilities, Mr Kennedy. But it certainly gives you reason to have a down on him.'

'What? For something that happened half a lifetime ago?'

It was a valid defence. That was the trouble. Especially given that Kennedy was neither a warring civil servant nor a Sicilian with a vengeful gene that continued through the generations.

'I'd say you were clutching at straws but our old English master used to abhor clichés. Who are you going after next? Sophie Diaz, because he dumped her? Or Gary Sadiq, our Anglo-Indian because he used to taunt him about having a touch of the tar brush? Or Alice Douglas because she was a charity case and Ainsley never let her forget it?'

It seemed Sebastian Kennedy was keen on spreading their suspicions as wide as possible. Softly, Rafferty said, 'A charity case? What do you mean?'

'She was here on a bursary. Her parents certainly couldn't have afforded to send her here otherwise. So you see, Inspector, you've got quite a good mix of motives to choose from. May I wish you joy of them.' So saying, Sebastian Kennedy lay back and reached for another can.

It was a dismissal. Rafferty couldn't see how he could dismiss the dismissal with any dignity, so he merely said, 'No doubt I'll speak to you again,' to Kennedy and made for the door.

'Let's find Simon Fairweather,' he said to Llewellyn once they were outside with the door closed. 'We'll try the library.'

But the only people in the library were Victoria 'Brains' Watson and Alice Douglas. Rafferty asked if they'd seen Fairweather and they both said no.

'Perhaps he's in the pub again. Let's walk down to the village. It would be good to stretch our legs and it's a shame to waste the nice weather, cooped up inside.'

It was a pleasant walk, past ripening fields of corn and rape seed, the latter still seeming to Rafferty to be an improbably deep colour for the English countryside, which used to sport more mellow hues. A gentle breeze kept the day cool and ruffled his auburn hair into more than usual disorder. He felt like he was playing hookey and wished he were. But he had still to re-interview Simon Fairweather in light of this new evidence. And depending on whether he protested his innocence too much, he might yet well have a purple-faced Long-Pockets on his hands. But perhaps, if the Home Office man exuded guilt on being confronted with his victim status at Ainsley's hands, he could depute Llewellyn to break that particular piece of bad news to the superintendent? What else were sergeants for but the rough stuff? And he was so much more diplomatic. Just showed what an expensive education could do for a man.

Simon Fairweather wasn't in the pub, nor anywhere around the village, either, so they took a slow stroll back to the school. But although they wandered right round the school, its classrooms, playing fields and swimming pool, and asked everyone they met if they'd seen him, Fairweather wasn't anywhere to be found.

FIVE

'Perhaps he's done a bunk?' Rafferty suggested. Of course, Llewellyn immediately punched a hole in the idea.

'Hardly likely, I would have thought. Any case against him is extremely thin. He's an intelligent man; he must have worked that out for himself. And as you yourself pointed out, civil servants are a hardy breed. Not easily intimidated.'

'Must have changed then, from when he was a boy, seeing as he was a victim of Ainsley's bullying. Could be he's the exception that proves the rule. Oh well. I'm not going to go chasing him all round the countryside. No doubt you're right, as usual, and he'll turn up. He'll wait. But my throat won't. All this walking's given me a thirst. Let's go back to the pub while we consider what we've learned.'

'I really don't think we should be frequenting pubs with this regularity. Superintendent Bradley wouldn't like it.'

'What difference does it make if we do our thinking in a fusty office or a pub beer garden? All that fresh air and oxygen must be good for the brain.'

'I doubt the beer is.'

'There speaks the teetotaller. What do you know about it, anyway?'

'There have been various studies and—'

'Oh. Studies. Each one contradicting the one before. I never take any notice of studies. You'd do well to ignore them as well.'

Llewellyn had made his point. He said nothing more till they reached the pub.

'Orange juice or mineral water, Daff?'

Llewellyn thawed sufficiently to say, 'Do you know, I think I'll have a coke.'

'Why not? Let's push the boat out. I think I'll have a Jameson's.'

'In the middle of the day?'

'Don't start that again you killjoy. Anyway, as the song says, "it's five o'clock somewhere".' Rafferty ordered the drinks and took them outside to the beer garden. They sat in silence for a while, Rafferty savouring his whiskey and Llewellyn staring at his coke as if he regretted ordering it. Five minutes went by in this fashion, and then, Rafferty said, 'Drink up, Daff and I'll get you another one.'

'I don't think so, thank you all the same. One is more than enough. I've seen what this stuff does to copper coins.'

'So have I. You should have had the Water of Life, like me. Far healthier. Barley in it, not like that muck, which has God knows what ingredients.'

'If you say so. Actually, I think I'll have a coffee.' Llewellyn stood up. 'I'll go. Can I get you another?'

'Go on, then. You've twisted my arm. You're driving, after all. And I need something with a kick to it to help me withstand my madhouse of a home at the moment.'

'You've still got the religious gentleman staying with you?'

'Yeah. And he's still trying to turn me on to God. He seems to consider my lapsed Catholic condition as something of a challenge. Maybe if I give in and let him think I've succumbed to his God-botherer blandishments, he'll stop trying so hard.'

'Possibly. Or perhaps he'll start on Abra and then the fireworks will begin.'

'They already have. You wouldn't believe the flak I'm getting. It's not as if it's my fault that Ma's foisted four far-flung family on us, though you'd never think so to listen to Abra.'

'The female of the species was ever thus. Abra's never taken kindly to having someone tell her what she should believe.'

'Nor me. I had enough of that when I was a kid.' Rafferty sighed and stared morosely at his whiskey. 'And to think I've got over another week of this. Perhaps you ought to order some hemlock instead of the Jameson's?'

'Oh dear. Are things really that bad, Joseph?'

'Not far off.' Llewellyn's use of his forename made him

think he was perhaps complaining too much; he rarely used it when they were working, in spite of Rafferty asking him to stop 'sirring' him time after time. He sighed again and decided he might as well get sympathy from Llewellyn as there was none coming from any other quarter. 'Of course, cousin Nigel managed to slime his way out of putting up anybody.' Nigel Blythe, aka Jerry Kelly, had the gift of tongues, like all estate agents, and had apparently got out of putting up any of the Rafferty and Kelly families' Empire-spread relations without raising a sweat. 'I wouldn't mind, but he's got more room than anyone else with that whacking great swanky warehouse apartment of his. Ma let him get away with it as well. She never lets me get away with anything.'

'She's a strong-minded woman, your mother.'

'You can say that again. I hope she doesn't make these family reunions an annual event. I wouldn't put it past her. Trouble is, she's lonely. After having six kids, she's used to a houseful and feels it now she's on her own. She's always liked people to look after. When I go there she always stuffs me with food as if I'm one of those geese the French turn into pâté de fois gras.'

'Perhaps you could encourage your mother to get a lodger? Someone whose path through life she can guide and whose stomach she can feed up. Students are always hungry. It could be a perfect match.'

'Yeah. Someone young and gormless, who thinks Ma's a harmless old lady. Good idea. I'll put an ad on the notice board of the local college. Should get someone suitable. See how Ma likes getting dumped on.'

'It might be advisable to ask her first if she wants a lodger.'

'Why? Maybe I should just tell her she's going to have one, like she did me. Only I've got four of 'em. She'll be getting away lightly.'

Llewellyn must have thought it prudent to say no more, for he excused himself and went to get the drinks, leaving Rafferty to brood on his plight.

The next morning, Rafferty, having learned his lesson, got up at six and fetched Abra her tea himself.

'Is that to madam's satisfaction?' he asked.

'Mmm,' said Abra, taking a sip. 'Though it's a bit dawn

chorus, considering it's the weekend. I suppose you're going to be early into work and late back again? It's Saturday, so that means I'll have Cyrus and crew all day.'

'I have got a murder on, sweetheart. It's what I do. Anyway, the weather seems set fair. They'll probably go out somewhere.'

'Good. Just as long as they don't expect me to join them. Knowing churchy Cyrus he'll want to take a tour of all the area's praying holes, rather than the watering holes.'

'He is one of my family, Abra. It's only right to be hospitable. I'd be the same if it was your family.'

'I doubt it. And it's not what you said last night. You were as fed up with him as me.'

'Yeah, well. I'm an indecisive Libran, Abs. You surely don't expect me to be of the same opinion twice in a row, do you?'

Abra just went 'Hrmph', downed the rest of her tea and burrowed back under the duvet.

Rafferty took himself off to work. He stopped off at the stationer's on the way and bought a pack of plain postcards. He only wanted the one, but they didn't sell them singly. Back in his car, he found a pen in the glove compartment and began to write: *WANTED – Elmhurst. Two single lodgers. Reasonable terms. Inclusive of dinner, phone and utilities. Contact . . .*

He put his mobile number, rather than his ma's landline; he wanted to get his ma's lodgers sorted out before he told her a word about it. He pulled up at the local college and saw the secretary, giving her the postcard and paying her for a month. He rubbed his hands together. 'Now let's see how Ma likes it.'

Simon Fairweather had returned. Rafferty didn't know if he'd stayed out all night or if he'd returned after he and Llewellyn had gone home, but either way, it didn't matter. At least he was here now.

They took him into their office for privacy and asked him again how he had felt about Adam Ainsley. 'In view of the fact that he was a bully and you were one of his victims,' Rafferty added.

'What's this? Because Adam was nasty to me many moons ago you think I killed him? Maybe I should rethink my disinclination to complain to your superiors?'

'That's your prerogative, sir,' said Rafferty stiffly.

'Only joking, Inspector. Relax. You shouldn't be so sensitive.'

You'd be sensitive if you had a boss like mine, was Rafferty's thought. But it was true that Fairweather's face had puckered into that impish smile. Rafferty wished he could appreciate his sense of humour.

'Please, Inspector, don't waste your time. I took Adam's punishment like a man, as did most of his other victims. Looking back, I think he was more to be pitied than anything else. Most bullies are unhappy souls. How could they be otherwise? Few people enjoy being actively hated, unless they've got a Stalin complex.'

'That's very forgiving of you.'

'I've never been one to harbour grudges. I've never seen the point. Besides, working in the civil service as I do, such a tendency could leave you seriously exhausted with no energy for anything else. You'd be surprised at all the little vendettas that are going on at any one time amongst the mandarins.'

'I wouldn't be surprised at all, sir,' said Rafferty with feeling. 'The Home Office has impinged on my working life much as it has yours.'

'Just so.' Fairweather bowed his head and Rafferty let him go, feeling as if he'd been talked out of suspicion-mode by mandarin-speak, despite Fairweather's previous protestations that he didn't go in for bureaucratic doubletalk.

Cyrus Rafferty didn't go in for doubletalk, either. When Rafferty got home that evening, he could hear him holding forth in Christian brethren mode as soon as he opened the front door. He found him leaning on the dining-room table as if it was a pulpit. He suspected Abra had come in here, which wasn't a room they'd used much, since they moved in at the beginning of July, to get away from Cyrus and had been followed in.

'Ah. Joe. Ah was just telling Abra here something about ma early days as a lay preacher. Ah took ma first examples from two outstanding evangelical preachers from the 1700s – Jonathan Edwards and the Rev George Whitfield. Fine preachers, both of them. Men of steel, too, as preaching in those days wasn't a profession for the faint-hearted. As itinerants, even occasional ones, not only had to travel miles in all weathers, they also had to deal with drunken rowdies. And then, of course, there's the redoubtable Billy Graham from our own times. How many sinners that man must have saved from the eternal flame. My usual text is from Acts of the Apostles. You can find enough examples in there to touch the heart of the most determined backslider and—'

He was interrupted in his oratory by Wendy, his wife. 'Oh, there you are, Cy. You're not preaching at poor Abra again, are you, honey? Do give it a rest. You're a guest in their home, not an invited speaker.' Wendy turned to Rafferty. 'I'm sorry, Joe, Abra. Once he gets going it's hard to stop him.'

As if he didn't know. He'd had plenty of examples of Cyrus's oratory already.

'Ah'm preaching the word of the Lord, Wendy, as is ma duty. After these good folks' hospitality, Ah couldn't live with myself if Ah didn't reciprocate by snatching their souls from the snares of Lucifer.'

'Their souls are their own responsibility, Cyrus. They're adults, not children in your Sunday School class and can make their own decisions. Come on now and come out for a walk with me. You don't want poor Abra going to bed with a sick headache again, do you?'

'Ah was just a trahin' to do ma duty. And—' Cyrus's Southern twang was getting more pronounced, Rafferty noticed.

'Yes. We know, sugar. But you know what the doctor said about your throat. He told you to rest your voice, didn't he?'

'Well. Yes. Ah guess he did. But Lord, Wendy, it's hard when Ah see folks in need of ma ministry.'

'I guess they're just not so into preachers in England, sugar. I've not seen a single televangelist on TV.'

'No. And that's another thing—'

'Cyrus.' Wendy's voice was firm. She gave Rafferty and Abra an apologetic smile as she led Cyrus from the room. 'We'll be no more than an hour. What say we bring a take-away back with us?'

'Would you?' said Abra, brightening at the idea she would be relieved of kitchen duties for the evening. 'That would be great.'

'Sure, honey. You work all week. You shouldn't have to cook of a weekend. We'll see y'all later.'

When they heard the front door slam, Rafferty took Abra by the hand and led her back into the living room. 'Sit. I know what you need.'

'And it isn't being preached at.'

'No.' Rafferty poured a large Jameson's out and then another for himself. He passed Abra hers. 'Ah. Peace,' he murmured as he slumped on the settee. 'How little we appreciated it. Where are Angel and Louis?'

Angel and Louis Kelly were more cousins, on his mother's side this time. They were New Yorkers, a surprisingly quiet couple and, given Cyrus's domination of the conversation, Rafferty had hardly got to know anything about them. They'd quickly taken Cyrus's measure and had proclaimed themselves born-again converts – who presumably didn't require preaching at – and went out every morning loudly expressing their intention to find a 'cute little church' on their travels that would meet all their religious needs for the day.

'They said they'd be out till late. They were going to town to do the London Dungeon, Madame Tussauds and Buck House. Then I think they were going to take in the Tower of London. They said they'd stay in town for dinner and maybe take in a show if they could get tickets.'

'I admire their energy. Sounds like a recipe for exhaustion, to me. They were able to tell you all that? Without being interrupted? Did Cyrus take himself out for another walk?'

'Funnily enough, yes. Angel's sweet. God, the things she told me while Cyrus was out. I had her life history this morning. She and Louis were High School sweethearts and have been married for forty years coming up. It'll be their anniversary while they're over here. I thought we might take them out for a celebratory meal.'

'Good idea. Thanks, sweetheart. I know how much you hate having your home invaded by strangers.'

'They're strangers to you, too, for all they're your family. I'm sorry if I've given you a hard time over this, Joe. Have I been a perfect bitch?'

'You know everything you do is done perfectly, my sweet.'

'Ooh, you!' But she laughed and downed half her whiskey. 'Promise I'll try harder. But if you could just pray Cyrus gets laryngitis . . .'

Rafferty stayed long enough to eat the Chinese takeaway that Wendy and Cyrus brought back and then he returned to the office for an hour. It was as well that he did, for, unusually, Bradley showed his face. It wasn't like him to put in an appearance at a weekend and Rafferty guessed he'd turned up specially to berate him. It seemed Simon Fairweather's status as a suspect really had got him seriously rattled.

The investigation wasn't progressing well. It wasn't progressing at all, in Bradley's opinion, as he told Rafferty with all the force of a Cyrus led revival meeting.

But Rafferty couldn't find fault with his super's logic. Much as he'd like to. All of the suspects had managed to refute any suspicion of guilt by the simple expedient of saying that their previous relationship with Ainsley was such old history that it had cobwebs. Not only that, it was also true that any time over the previous seventeen years one of them intent on revenge could have found the high-profile Adam Ainsley with little difficulty. A simple study of his movements and habits, which the media were happy to supply, would presumably have provided the opportunity for murder if such was their inclination. They wouldn't have needed to wait for the next reunion and the slim possibility that Ainsley would attend when he never had before.

There must be something else. Something he didn't know about. 'I think we'll have to do a bit more digging, Dafyd. Maybe Ainsley had some juicy knowledge about one of them and tried a spot of blackmail. His parents don't live too fancy and being a school sports instructor can't bring in much money. Maybe he had an expensive gambling habit. It's all the rage amongst sportsmen; they'd bet on which of two raindrops would reach the bottom of the window first, some of them. Only being over-confident, Ainsley would likely favour the front-on approach to extracting money.'

'It's certainly a theory.'

'Just not one to your taste? Oh well, I'm sure to come up with another one. Theories are something I've never been short of. There's always the chance that his alcohol troubles had run up debts. Let's get over to that school where Ainsley worked as a sports master and see if we can't find out something scandalous. There might be someone there even though it's the holidays. But perhaps you'd better give them a ring first to save us a wasted journey.'

Stainforth College was ten miles the other side of Chelmsford. It was a large Victorian edifice with grounds as extensive as Griffin's. He'd got Llewellyn to phone ahead to check whether anyone would be there and had managed to speak to the Deputy Head, who had come in to organize the new term's timetables. She had proved amenable to speaking to him even after he had told her the reason he needed to find out more about Adam Ainsley.

Mrs Hall was a casually dressed forty-something. She'd unlocked the main door for them and given them directions to her office. They'd found her with no trouble and once they were seated in front of her desk that was piled high with papers and files, Rafferty soon brought her to the point of discussing Ainsley.

'I gather he studied for a career as a Sports Instructor after his professional rugby career finished, which is how he ended up here?'

'That's right, Inspector. He came to us straight from college. He was very keen and really threw himself into his new role.'

'Do I detect a but?'

Mrs Hall smiled. 'How sensitive of you.' Beside him, Llewellyn managed to maintain a straight face at Rafferty's unabashed receipt of such an unusual compliment. 'Yes, there is a but. I'm afraid Adam's enthusiasm for teaching students palled after the first year. I think he really began to miss being part of a team, rather than being the instructor. He missed the camaraderie and the triumphs. Of course he had a few of those as we're quite a sporty establishment, but it wasn't the same for him. The triumphs weren't so triumphant and the failures failed to bring forth the supportive team spirit. Of course, it was part of Adam's job to raise the spirits of the team, but he had difficulty raising his own. He'd been used to being a star and found the transition difficult. I was against the appointment, but the Head's a keen rugby man and he over-ruled me.'

'What was he like with the students?' Rafferty asked. 'We've been speaking to some of his old schoolmates and it seems Mr Ainsley was inclined to be heavy-handed.'

'He was a bully, you mean?'

Rafferty lowered his head in acquiescence.

'Several of the boys complained to their parents about his manner to them. He could be very sarcastic, particularly to the students who didn't come up to his sporting ideal. It was a verbal bullying only. We wouldn't have tolerated any other sort. In fact, we weren't prepared to tolerate the verbal sort either. Stainforth's ethos is one of encouragement and support.

Adam's services were dispensed with at the end of the summer term.'

'Really?' That was something that hadn't been mentioned by any of the Griffin reunees. Rafferty could only suppose Ainsley had kept quiet about his sacking. For a man whose entire working life had been one of success and achievement, it must have been a dent to his pride that he wouldn't want his old schoolmates to know about. It explained why he had been putting feelers out re another job.

It was something else to think about, something to weigh in the suicide versus murder debate. A lot of men killed themselves after losing their jobs; employment was said to be a stabilising factor in a man's life. It gave him standing and pride and income. And with the income came a certain lifestyle. Had Ainsley's lifestyle lowered drastically after the end of his professional career? Had he any savings from his high-earning days to tide him through unemployment? Or had he lived high on the hog and spent his income as he earned it? In view of this latest information, Rafferty began to wonder if he hadn't plumped on the side of murder way too soon.

They had yet to pay a visit to Ainsley's home and Rafferty decided they'd return to the station, collect the keys and see if the place yielded up any clues to his death. His bank statements would at least tell him something about his financial health even if they yielded up no clues about his emotional wellbeing.

Ainsley had lived in Elmhurst; he'd had a flat around the corner from the Norman castle. It was a quiet neighbourhood and while he searched through the late Adam Ainsley's possessions, Rafferty deputed Llewellyn to learn what he could from the neighbours.

It was a small, two-room flat, with a shower room and galley kitchen, not at all the style of home that Rafferty had imagined and it indicated that Ainsley's finances hadn't been of the healthiest. It was furnished in a modern style, with blonde wood and white walls against which were arrayed Ainsley's sporting cups and medals. Grouped around these were blown-up portraits of his sporting triumphs. Some of the medals were showing signs of tarnish as if the gloss of success had worn off them. Of course it must be three, four years since he'd played professionally.

Maybe depression at his current life had caused Ainsley to neglect the trophies. Or maybe he'd never been one for spit and polish. But this isn't getting the job done, Rafferty reminded himself.

He began in the bedroom. There was a desk in the corner with the usual computer and its assorted accessories. He'd leave that to Llewellyn to investigate if he could. Rafferty concentrated on the desk drawers. He found a heap of fan letters just thrown in a couple of box files with no indication that they had been answered. He found sporting contracts and letters from his agent. He even found the email from Griffin School inviting Ainsley to the reunion. It had been a fulsome epistle, with plenty of admiring superlatives about his sporting career. No wonder Ainsley had taken the trouble to print it out. Rafferty thought Paxton had laid it on a bit thick. It wasn't as if Ainsley had really hit the heights and made it into the England rugby team that won the World Cup. Or any England team, for that matter. No wonder Ainsley had decided to attend the reunion. He must have hoped for further compliments. It would be the balm his poor, sacked soul would crave.

Llewellyn returned as he was reading Paxton's email and Rafferty handed it to him after the Welshman reported that the neighbours had been no help as Ainsley had only been in the flat for a few months and hadn't socialized with them. Stifling a sigh, Rafferty made a start on the bank statements. He didn't have to go far through them to discover that Ainsley had lived up to his star income until relatively recently, but now, his account hovered dangerously near the red every month. Perhaps he had savings? Rafferty searched the desk some more, expecting to unearth evidence of ISAs, stocks and shares and other marks of a wealthy man, but there was nothing and he sat back.

'I've got more money than Ainsley seems to have had. What the hell did he do with it all? If the papers are to be believed, he earned fabulous sums. All right, he wouldn't have earned the sponsorship money of the top rugby men, but he'd have got some.'

'He had two ex-wives, remember. And perhaps, as you suggested before, he was a gambler? Have you found evidence of any bookmaker's accounts?'

'Not so far. Perhaps he preferred to do his betting, if any, in person and went to the races to bet on the Tote, rather than using a bookie. But get the team to trawl the local turf accountants and find out if Ainsley was a regular customer. Get them to check out the local racecourse as well. And friends. He must have friends, even if they were just the hangers on that every successful sportsman attracts. They'll be likely to know more of his habits than we've so far found here.'

Llewellyn nodded and pulled out his notebook. 'Maybe we also ought to check his old home? The neighbours said he used to live in Chelsea.'

'Good idea. He didn't confide in any of his old schoolmates; perhaps we'll find someone there to whom he let his hair down.'

Rafferty went through to make a start on the living room while Llewellyn got busy on the computer. But there were few places of concealment there; there wasn't even a bookcase wherein might have been hidden something incriminating to link Ainsley to blackmail.

Disgruntled, Rafferty tried the kitchen; maybe Ainsley kept any evidence in a biscuit tin? But there were no biscuit tins and no biscuits, which was a shame as he was starting to feel peckish. The one thing he did find was plenty of booze as evidence that Ainsley had started down the slippery slope that led to physical imperfection.

The bathroom was a last resort. But again he found nothing of interest. This room was blonde, like the rest of the flat. It was a larger bathroom than was usual with a flat of this size and was equipped with a small gym. There were dumb bells and a rowing machine and a treadmill. There was a thin coating of dust on all of them as if they hadn't been used recently. There were the usual assortment of unguents and a large selection of expensive aftershaves. He tried the bathroom cabinet, but beyond learning that Ainsley had suffered from piles, there was nothing else of interest. More in hope than expectation, he went back to the bedroom to see how Llewellyn was getting on with the computer.

'Anything of interest, Daff?'

'Not so far. He seems to have used his computer more for surfing the net than anything else. There's precious little in the way of personal correspondence; perhaps his agent dealt with it?'

'Someone else we should speak to.'

'Yes. I've made a note of his details.' Llewellyn paused. 'I wonder if Ainsley answered his own fan mail as I found a standard form letter in reply to his fan mail. He must have sent the same letter to each of them, printing them out as necessary.'

'Saves time, I suppose. No incriminating photos of one or more of the other Griffin reunees to support my blackmail theory?'

'No. I've checked the picture file and they're all of Mr Ainsley competing in sporting events. There's nothing here of his school years.'

'What about Facebook? Is he on there?'

Llewellyn nodded, 'I think so. He had it on Favourites and when I clicked it brought the site up, though I haven't been able to get beyond the login screen without his password.'

'Leave it to the boffins. It'll be something obvious, most likely.' He sighed. 'Looks like we've drawn a blank. Finish up checking the computer, then we'll head back.' Though back to what, Rafferty didn't know. He was running out of options. Unless he found something incriminating soon he'd have no reason to stop any of the reunees from returning home at the end of the reunion week. And wouldn't *that* please Bradley as he thought about his precious budget and the expense involved in motoring up and down the country in search of answers from the scattered reunees.

Disappointed that Ainsley's flat had revealed so little, Rafferty locked up behind him and handed the keys to Llewellyn for safekeeping. He could only hope that his agent was able to tell them more.

SIX

There was no one in the Senior Common Room when they returned to Griffin School, not even the lager-drinking Sebastian Kennedy. Rafferty concluded that the reunees were probably packing in anticipation of their return home tomorrow at the end of their week. He'd give anything to come up with the answer to the murder before they went, but he had nothing, nothing but intangible this and intangible that. None of it would be enough for the Crown Prosecution Service, who liked their proof of the conclusive sort.

He crossed the corridor to the office and he and Llewellyn started packing up, too, in anticipation of their own move back to the police station. There was no point in keeping on their temporary office with their suspects decamped. Once the packing was done, he went in search of the headmaster to return the key and tell him he could have the room back.

Paxton was in a canary yellow waistcoat this time, and with the prospective departure of both police and reunees, he seemed to have an end of term air about him, which the waistcoat only served to emphasize.

'I'm off on holiday as soon as I've shut this place up,' he told Rafferty. 'We own a villa in Portugal so we can go there whenever suits as we didn't let it out this year. There are no boarders on site as they've all managed either to return home or to snag a holiday with friends. I put my break off when the Board of Governors appointed me last year and asked me to step into the breech when the previous incumbent's health deteriorated and he retired early. So I organized this reunion. Now that that's over, I can return to my own plans. This time tomorrow, I'll be sunning myself on a Portuguese beach anticipating my next rum punch.'

'Lucky man.' This time tomorrow, Rafferty thought, he'd be anticipating nothing more than a bawling out from the super first thing Monday morning over his failure to solve the case before the reunion came to an end.

The thought of his holiday seemed to have a soothing effect on Paxton because the arm waving had almost ceased. His desk was clear, ready for an early start once the reunees had left in the morning, the sun was shining through the window and Jeremy was broadly smiling. This cheery atmosphere depressed Rafferty and he went in search of Mrs Benton to see if she would provide a cup of the beverage that helped the British through all their ills. Tea, hot and strong and three sugars sweet, was what he needed. He needed it even more when he thought of the morrow. Because Abra had decreed that, murder or no murder, it being Sunday, he would not slink off to the office to get away from Cyrus. She'd done her bit had been her refrain before they went to sleep last night. It was time he did his.

He wondered if Mrs Benton could be persuaded to put a drop of the hard stuff in his tea.

* * *

Dinner was over in the dining hall and there were only a few scattered diners left. Rafferty and Llewellyn had joined the last stragglers amongst the suspects in the hope that any conversational exchange, made more incautious through alcohol, would bring a slip of the tongue. But nothing that Rafferty recognized as evidence was revealed. Disgruntled, he finished the last of the wine that Sebastian had so generously donated to him from the bottles taken from the school's cellars. He'd never been much of a one for wine, preferring beer and spirits, but this red was bursting with a fruity flavour and certainly went down smoothly. He made a mental note of the name so he could buy a bottle or two for Abra, who was partial to the occasional glass.

Sophie Diaz got up from the dining table and said she was tired and was going to bed. Her slender, boyish body swayed slightly and she clutched the back of her chair and laughed. 'Ooh. I'm dizzy.'

'Had a few two many glasses of vino Sophie?' asked Sebastian Kennedy.

'You'd recognize the symptoms,' Sophie retorted as she walked off, with an unsteady gait.

Rafferty said it was time he and Llewellyn went home. He said good night to Sebastian Kennedy and they walked out into the fresh evening air and, after bidding each other goodbye, they got into their separate cars and drove home.

Dinner was long over and after saying hello to Abra and his four guests, Rafferty went out to the kitchen to make himself something to eat. He was surprised to find that Cyrus seemed to have lost his verbosity. He'd merely nodded a greeting and hadn't displayed any of his God-botherer rhetoric, for which Rafferty was thankful.

He put the kettle on. He'd had a big meal at lunchtime, so he only wanted a snack. He made a sandwich while he waited for the kettle to boil. Abra came into the kitchen and Rafferty asked her what sort of day she'd had.

'OK.' She laughed. 'More than OK, actually. You'll never guess, but Cyrus has lost his voice.'

'No? Really?' Rafferty grinned. 'And I didn't even have to pray for it as you suggested. But Glory be to God all the same. The Almighty must have got as sick of listening to it as we have.'

'Mmm. I could almost feel sorry for him. He doesn't know what to do with himself when he can't go in for his ever-lasting God-monologues.'

'Why don't you have an early night and a pampering bath?' Rafferty suggested as he made the tea. 'You've earned a bit of self-indulgence.'

'Good of you to suggest it on the only night that hasn't echoed to the glories of God.'

Rafferty took a bite of his sandwich and through the bread and ham, he said, 'I only thought it about time I sat up with the guests.' None of their houseguests were early to bed. Cyrus combined those two worst traits in a visitor, being both a late bird and an early one, so there was no peace either end of the day.

'Anyway, I'll take you up on your kind offer. Say good night to them for me.'

After kissing Abra and handing over her tea, Rafferty went into the living room. His guests were watching a film and it didn't take long for Cyrus, who had control of the TV remote, to make disgusted noises and switch over. But he could find nothing to his liking, so he switched off.

In a rasping whisper, which Rafferty had to strain to catch, Cyrus said, 'Ah think Ah've been overdoing it, Joe. Ah've lost ma voice.'

Trying to keep a straight face, Rafferty said he was sorry to hear it.

'It's happened to me before,' Cyrus rasped. 'But Ah know how to treat it. Ah've been gargling with some of your whiskey.'

Rafferty glanced at what had been a full bottle of Jamesons's. It was two-thirds empty. Cyrus must have had some gargling session. And he didn't suppose he'd spat it out after the gargling. Truth to tell, he looked a bit glassy-eyed.

'Ah'll do some more before ah go to bed. But don't worry. I'll replace the bottle tomorrow as I know how partial you are to your nightly glass. The Lord God will have me right as a shiny silver dollar by morning.'

'Will he?' Cyrus sounded confident that the Almighty would devote His overnight energies solely for his benefit. Rafferty wondered if he might have got answers on his various investigations a bit quicker down the years if he'd been a God-botherer like his guest. Maybe he'd surprise Father Kelly on Sunday and go to church. Praying seemed to be a powerful weapon in Cyrus's armoury; perhaps it could be in his. As a lapsed Catholic, he hadn't prayed for years, apart from the attendance at church for his wedding and just prior to it. Perhaps he'd been missing a trick?

Rafferty murmured what he remembered of the 'Our Father' when he went to bed, thankful that Abra was asleep and unable to tease.

Rafferty had prayed for a break in the case, but he hadn't expected his prayers to be answered so promptly. He hadn't even opened his eyelids the next morning when the phone rang beside the bed. It was Bill Beard, the duty officer at the station.

'Sorry to disturb your beauty sleep, my duck,' said Beard, 'but there's been a development in your murder case.'

'A development?' Rafferty questioned sleepily as he sat up and glanced at the clock with half-open eyes. He took no notice of Beard's endearment – the middle-aged constable had a habit of addressing everyone the same, even senior officers. He was something of an institution at the station, being the longest-serving officer there – and he was able to get away with things not permitted younger colleagues.

'A euphemism, my dear. I just thought I'd wake you gently as sudden shocks can be bad for a person of the older persuasion.'

Rafferty had turned forty the previous year. Sometimes he felt considerably older. 'Thanks for that, Beardy. So go on then, what's happened?'

'Another murder most likely.'

'Most likely? Don't you know?'

'No signs of injury. but there's reason to be suspicious, I think, when a young woman of previous good health dies in her sleep.'

'True. So who's died?'

'A Mrs Sophie Diaz. One of those reunees.'

'Yes. I know who she is. So what happened?'

'I've just told you, haven't I? She was found dead this morning by her room mate by the name of Alice Douglas, apparently pegged out in the night. I suppose you want me to wake Dr Dally also?'

'You bet,' said Rafferty. 'I prefer not to be the only one whose beauty sleep is disturbed.'

After he'd put the phone down, Rafferty was thoughtful. So they had another death. Why? He was shocked by this latest one. Who had reason to want to get rid of Sophie Diaz? Even more to the point *was* it murder or some previously unsuspected weakness in the heart? But he couldn't buy the latter. It was too much of a coincidence for her to die so soon after Adam Ainsley. This second death, for him, also removed the last possibility that Ainsley's death had been suicide.

He flung back the covers and got out of bed. He wasn't going to find the answers lolling here. Abra, still half-asleep, asked him who'd been on the phone.

'Bill Beard,' he told her. 'There's been another death at Griffin School.'

'Huh. See what your praying's achieved. I bet you didn't expect that.'

'No.' Rafferty hadn't realized that Abra had heard his prayers the previous night. He felt a bit shame-faced that she had witnessed it. Given his lapsed status, it was, he supposed, a bit hypocritical. 'I'll be a bit more careful what I pray for next time I plead with the Almighty.'

'Mmm. What time is it, anyway? Have you got time to make me tea?'

'It's seven o'clock. And yes. I'll make tea, unless Cyrus has beaten me to it. The woman's dead, so what's the rush? My speedy arrival's going to make no difference.'

Abra, not involved in the murder case, ignored his reference to the latest death and homed in on the reference to Cyrus, which *did* concern her.

'I woke and heard Cyrus go downstairs ten minutes ago. It's about time you tackled him and asked him to stay out of the kitchen first thing. It's not as if you've managed to teach him how to make a decent cup of tea.'

'I've tried, my sweet. I think it's just that he's past the age for learning new things.' Rafferty felt he couldn't blame Cyrus for that. Hadn't he one or two areas where he had failed to learn? Technology, for instance. God knew what he'd do if – when – Llewellyn passed his inspector's exams and applied for a post elsewhere. He didn't feel like revealing his ignorance to anyone else. He supposed he'd have to take a course for idiots. There must be one. His ma had been on a course for would-be silver surfers at the local Adult Education Institute and look at her now – able to ferret out family members on the other side of the globe. God knew what she'd be up to this time next year.

'And you needn't think this latest death absolves you from spending the day with Cyrus and Co,' Abra called after him as he made for the door. 'Dafyd's more than capable of taking charge for one day. I'll expect you back here at ten thirty sharp.'

'But Abra, how am I supposed to get away? You know how much work a second murder brings.'

'Yes. Work for forensics and fingerprints and the members of your team. You, I bet, give orders in a lordly manner and sit back to await results. And while you wait you'll spend your time coming up with a monkey-puzzle of theories. It's not as if you'll have any suspects on tap to question as you said they're all going home this morning and that you've got no evidence to hold any of them.'

Abra had unerringly put her finger on the crux of the matter. And she was right in that Dafyd was more than capable of taking charge. He'd probably do a better, more thorough, job than he would. No, Abra had him by the short and curlies and he had no excuse not to be back halfway through the morning, murder or no murder.

He tried one last throw of the dice. 'But what'll Bradley say?'

'Who cares? At this moment, I'm more concerned with what Cyrus will say if he gets his voice back this morning to find you've cried off this outing. He's been looking forward to it all week. He certainly gargled enough of your whiskey to cure any number of sore throats last night.'

With a muttered, 'See you later,' Rafferty made his escape.

When Rafferty got to Griffin School, he found the place in uproar. Most of the reunees had clustered around the headmaster's office to await the arrival of the police, all seemingly talking at once, such was the bedlam of noise that met him. There was panic after this death in the way that there hadn't been over Adam Ainsley's. Jeremy Paxton was hovering, clearly waiting for him.

'Inspector. You got my message, then?'

'Yes. The station rang me. Which room is Mrs Diaz in?'

'I'll show you.'

Paxton turned and led the way upstairs and along a corridor. He tapped on a door. It was opened by a red-eyed Alice Douglas. 'Inspector. Thank God you're here.'

Rafferty didn't know where else she expected him to be. 'May I come in?'

'Of course. I know I should probably be downstairs with the others, but I – I didn't like to leave her. It seemed wrong, somehow.'

'I understand. It's good that she had someone to sit with her, but I'll have to ask you to leave now.' If she'd wanted to interfere with the scene of death in any way she'd had plenty of time to do so. 'Perhaps you can wait in Mr Paxton's office? I'll need to ask you a few questions.'

Paxton nodded. 'Of course. Come along, Alice. I'll get Mrs Benton to make you something warming.'

Alice turned to Rafferty. 'What about my things? I'm supposed to be leaving today.'

'I'll get one of my female officers to pack your clothes and bring them along to Mr Paxton's office.'

They both nodded and walked away down the corridor, leaving Rafferty in possession of the room of the dead. He approached the bed. Sophie Diaz looked peaceful. She could have been asleep, but a quick touch to the carotid artery in her neck where a pulse should have been steadily beating proved she wasn't merely deeply asleep. He hadn't thought she had been. He looked down at her and asked, 'So what did you do, Sophie, to bring about your own death? Have you left me any clues?'

But a quick look around the room revealed nothing obvious. Llewellyn arrived five minutes later, with Sam Dally hard on his heels and, for the present, Rafferty abandoned his hunt. He should put some protective gear on before he got down to more serious searching, anyway.

Sam was able to add little to Rafferty's own findings.

'Reckon it's the same as killed Ainsley?'

'And how am I supposed to know?' Sam demanded. 'Can you see anything obvious? Because I can't.'

Rafferty had to admit that he couldn't.

'You've got your answer then. I'm a medical doctor not a witch doctor. I've no twigs to rattle or stones to throw.'

'All right, Sam. I only asked.'

'And I'm only telling you. Now.' Sam edged him away from the bed. 'If I could get on.'

Rafferty left him to it and went downstairs to the headmaster's study to question Alice Douglas. Paxton was with her, but he left at a gesture from Rafferty and he and Llewellyn sat down.

'What alerted you to the fact that Mrs Diaz was dead?' he asked.

'It was nothing specific. No loud scream in the night, if that's what you mean. It's just that I've learned that Sophie's woken early every morning and gone down to the kitchen to make toast, but this morning she didn't stir. It was so unusual that I called her name. Nothing. So then I shook her. Still nothing. Next, I really shook her. It was then that I knew she was dead.'

'Had she woken in the night complaining of feeling unwell?'

'No. Not as far as I know. But I'm a deep sleeper, Inspector. Though, having said that, I don't think she woke up. The bedclothes weren't disturbed at all. She just – fell asleep and didn't wake up.'

'Oh, I think it's rather more than that, Ms Douglas.'

'So do I,' she admitted, 'especially after what happened to Adam. It's very scary. It could have been me.'

'I don't think so. You should be perfectly safe. I imagine Sophie Diaz did something to bring her death on herself.' I just have to find out what it is, Rafferty thought.

By the time he got back to Sophie Diaz's bedside, the place was a confusion of activity. Adrian Appleby and his Scenes of Crime officers – or whatever the powers that be had decreed they were to be called this week – had arrived and were busy dusting and sweeping as many surfaces as the room contained. The photographer had also arrived and was busy taking wide shots from the door. Uniform were bustling about, keen to get a look-see. Not that Rafferty imagined all this activity would do any good. It seemed likely, whether Sam agreed or not, that Sophie Diaz had met her end from the same pernicious substance that had killed Ainsley; and that was likely not to have been administered here, but in the dining room, again just like Ainsley.

Alice Douglas had reluctantly admitted that she had sat at Sophie's table at dinner the previous evening. Rafferty already knew that Sebastian had and Alice had confirmed that the other occupants of the table were also the same as the day Ainsley died, so at least he didn't have another set of diners to add to the suspect list.

He still had no evidence to detain anyone. There was no reason why the reunees couldn't return home as planned, once they were questioned as to whether they had seen anything untoward the previous evening. He designated some of the uniforms that were milling about to get on with this task, while he and Llewellyn asked Sophie Diaz's tablemates to come upstairs.

He spoke to them all together in the Senior Common Room.

'Sophie Diaz has been confirmed dead,' he told them. 'And I suspect she may have died from the same cause as Adam Ainsley. That being the case, I have to ask you if any of you noticed anything suspicious at dinner.'

They all shook their heads and Sebastian said, 'To think I teased her about being tipsy when the hemlock must have already begun to take effect. Poor Sophie. I feel awful now.' He met Rafferty's gaze. 'So what now, Inspector? Are we to be allowed to go home?'

As Abra had already reminded him, he had no reason to detain any of them, as he explained. 'But before you leave Griffin I must ask some more questions. Did Mrs Diaz confide in any of you last night?'

The response was another lot of head shaking.

Rafferty turned to Alice. 'Ms Douglas. You shared a room with her. You must have had some late night conversations.'

Alice shrugged. 'Not many. Sophie and I were never close and, as Seb's just said, she'd drunk rather a lot of wine and pretty well crashed out. I read for a while, but she didn't stir. Terrible to think that the poison was doing its worst while she slept and I just lay there. If only I'd known, I might have been able to do something. Call an ambulance. I could have saved her.'

'I doubt that,' Rafferty assured her. 'Unless gastric lavage is started immediately after the poison is ingested, the victim invariably dies.' He had this from San Dally so he knew it was gospel. 'As a poison, on a list from one to six, hemlock is a six. The most deadly.'

'Who would want to do these dreadful things?' Alice burst out. 'It's like a nightmare from which one doesn't wake up.'

Rafferty nodded, thinking that it was rather more his nightmare than theirs, given that he had to find the answer to the question of who was the killer. And even if he managed that it could never be fast enough to satisfy Superintendent Bradley.

After questioning them closely for some minutes, Rafferty accepted that none of them were able to provide any more information. Or, if they were, they were most probably the killer and not about to share their knowledge with him. He said they could finish their packing and travel home. He had their home addresses so as soon as he thought up a few more questions to ask, he could get in touch.

He left them to a sombre silence that even the usual spokesman and organizer, Giles Harmsworth, didn't attempt to break.

The minutes were ticking away towards ten thirty, the time appointed for his return home, but it was only ten past when Rafferty told the team he'd see them later and made for his car. He couldn't concentrate and the interviews he'd had with the reunees were just a reiteration of what had gone before: they'd seen nothing; heard nothing, had no idea who had killed Sophie Diaz. But at least the suspect list hadn't increased as the same people as before were in the frame. He'd already fixed his time off with Llewellyn, so he made for home, wondering what the rest of the day held. At least – unless Abra was goaded beyond bearing – it should be free of murders.

Cyrus, unsurprisingly, had organized the day out for them all. The City, of all places not to be on a steaming hot day, their destination. To escape the kerfuffle as his houseful got ready for their outing, Rafferty headed upstairs to get changed out of his suit. At least he could wear something cool, he thought. He had another quick shower and dressed in t-shirt and shorts. He lingered for longer than strictly necessary in the bedroom and was hurried up by a loud shout from Cyrus, whose voice had returned with a vengeance. Rafferty had never thought he'd find himself cursing a bottle of whiskey.

'You ready, Joe? We're all set.'

'Coming,' Rafferty shouted back. With a heavy sigh, he opened the bedroom door and headed for whatever the fates had decreed for the day.

Cyrus, it seemed, had done his homework. As they made for

the train station, he patted the large shoulder bag he had decided it was necessary to lug with him, and said, 'Ah checked up on the internet, Joe, before Ah ever left the States and Ah know exactly where to go when we get to the City of London. Ah want to see St Paul's Cath-ee-dral and Westminster Abbey. And then Ah want to see St Giles-Without-Cripplegate – what a great name – the medieval church where Nathanial Eaton, the first schoolmaster of Harvard College, was christened in 1610. Then there's Robert Crawley, the social gospeller and Protestant polemicist. He was buried in the church in 1588 and John Foxe, author of the Book of Martyrs, who was buried there the previous year. Ah can't wait.'

Cyrus's enthusiasm was almost catching. But not quite. Rafferty had spent too much of his life in churches and around cadavers to voluntarily revisit either. He pushed his hair off his damp forehead, shut the front door behind them and plodded up the path after Cyrus, muttering under his breath as he went.

When they reached the station, Cyrus led them all straight to the platform. Rafferty volunteered to get the tickets but Cyrus told him he'd already got them.

'Ah bought them on Abra's laptop last week. Ma treat.'

It didn't take long to reach Liverpool Street, where they switched to the underground. They all filed out at St Paul's, again with Cyrus confidently in the vanguard.

'You seem to know your way about,' Rafferty commented. 'Have you visited London before?'

'No. But Ah've studied your London A – Z, which Ah bought on the internet and Ah've pored over the maps and Ah have all the streets up here.' He tapped his forehead. 'What say we start at St Paul's Cath-ee-dral?'

'OK. Whatever you say.' Cyrus seemed to know not only where he was going, but what he was doing, so Rafferty left him to it.

They reached St Paul's just in time for a service and Rafferty said, 'We can come back later, so we can see over the church.'

'Hell, no,' said Cyrus. 'Ah've done ma homework and Ah came here at this tahm deliberately to attend a service. Hush, now, Joe. Let's grab a seat. The service is about to begin. We'll see over the church after.'

Cyrus marched up to the front as if he owned the place, slotted his portly body into the pew and stared expectantly at the priest. The rest of them sat where they could find a place. Rafferty, two pews behind him, could hear Cyrus intoning the priest's part as well as the congregation's responses and he smiled to himself. At least Cyrus seemed to be enjoying himself. Wendy, Angel and Louis were gazing around taking it all in. Then the choir started up and even Rafferty found himself joining in, much to Abra's amusement.

The priest droned on a bit in his sermon. He seemed to be on Cyrus's wavelength, for he pontificated about the youth of today and their myriad faults and Cyrus nodded his agreement with every point. But eventually, it was over. Rafferty let the others wander round to check out tombs and statues and the rest, while he took his ease in his pew. Finally even Cyrus accepted that he'd thoroughly 'done' St Paul's and they all filed out.

'Right. Westminster Abbey is next on ma list. Follow me.'

Obediently, they all fell in behind and Cyrus, without referring to a map once, led them unerringly to the required church.

Abra and Rafferty lingered outside. They found a shady spot and took root. Abra took the opportunity to light up and Rafferty, who had given up smoking some time ago, appreciatively sniffed the smoke and yearned for a few drags. He sighed. It was hot and he was getting thirsty. He studied his watch. Surely even Cyrus must be getting hungry by now. He knew one or two good pubs in or around the City: There was the Prospect of Whitby at Wapping Wall or Dirty Dick's in EC2. Either would do for lunch.

Rafferty could almost taste the cool bitter and by the time Cyrus and the rest trailed out of the Abbey, an hour and a half later, his tongue was hanging out.

Before Cyrus could stride out towards another centre of religion, Rafferty said decisively, 'Lunch. I'm sure you're all getting hungry by now.'

The others, all but Cyrus, nodded agreement, but Wendy persuaded her husband to fall in with the majority.

It was time for Rafferty to take the lead. 'Follow me. I know a few good pubs around here.'

'Pubs? We don't need no pubs, Joseph,' Cyrus told him. 'Ah've got lunch raht here.' He patted the heavy shoulder bag and opened it to reveal packed lunches. 'Ah made the sandwiches maself. Ah went to the supamarket specially.'

So that was what Cyrus had lugged around all morning. He'd wondered what was in the bag. Now he knew. 'But surely you all want a drink?' Rafferty was getting desperate as he saw the prospect of a cool bitter slipping away. 'I know I do.'

'We can bah drinks on the way. It's too nahce a day to be cooped up inside. I thought we'd get the subway to St James's Park. Ah have it on good authority that you can see Buckingham Palace from there. Is that right, Joe?'

Rafferty confirmed that it was. But at least, as Cyrus surged in the direction of his latest tourist destination, Rafferty had some commiseration because Wendy nudged him and said, 'Don't worry, Joe. Ah've got a coupla beers in ma bag. They've got your name on them.'

At the prospect of an alcoholic drink, Rafferty brightened. And when they got to the park, he even helped to spread the tablecloth on the grass and hand out the plastic picnic plates. That done, he took a swig of the can that Wendy handed him and took the opportunity to ring Llewellyn.

'Anything?' he asked.

'No. Nothing new. The reunees have all packed up and gone, as has the headmaster. He's given me the spare keys and told me he'd collect them from the station on his return from holiday.'

'OK. See you later.' Rafferty snapped his mobile shut. It soon became clear that Cyrus was a dedicated tourist, for he urged them all on to eat and when they had finished, he packed everything back in his bag and got to his feet. 'Right, y'all. Let's go and do St Giles-Without-Cripplegate.'

Rafferty, with no pub in the offing, would have happily remained in the park for the afternoon, but there was no gainsaying Cyrus once he was set on something, so, once again, they all trooped behind him till they reached St Giles.

Rafferty hadn't been in this church before and when he was foolish enough to admit as much, Cyrus took it as his job to make sure he missed nothing. He dragged him round the church, from memorial to memorial, from tomb to tomb, till Rafferty felt he knew the church as well as he knew his own living room. Cyrus wanted to do the Palace next, but thankfully, Wendy, who seemed to be drooping, vetoed this latest idea and insisted that Cyrus call a halt, with the words, 'tomorrow's another day, honey. Ah'm pooped.'

Rafferty breathed a sigh of relief. He certainly didn't fancy trudging around Buck House. And tomorrow he'd be back at work.

It was still hot and the tube back to Liverpool Street was an airless Hell. Rafferty just shut his eyes and endured till they got on the train to Elmhurst.

As the others piled into a taxi at their destination, Rafferty said he'd walk the short distance into town and get a takeaway Chinese for their evening meal. He ordered a good variety of food, paid up and headed home. He rang Llewellyn again on the way. But, like Wendy, Rafferty was pooped and he hadn't sufficient energy left to take anything in, so he cut the call short.

Cyrus, for all that he was a similar age to Rafferty's ma, seemed to have bundles of stamina, for he had already transferred the photos from his camera to the computer and copied them to a CD by the time Rafferty got home. It seemed they were all to get a second taste of the day's doings. Rafferty, hot and tired, grabbed the Jameson bottle and a couple of glasses and prepared to sedate himself and his bride as Cyrus began the narration to the pictures on the TV.

SEVEN

Monday dawned with the steamy heat still hovering over Elmhurst. Rafferty peeled himself away from his sticky sheet and, hoping he had beaten the early rising Cyrus to the bathroom, went in search of a cool shower. Luckily, the bathroom was free, which probably meant that Cyrus was in the kitchen again, making tea. He'd tried to teach the American the finer points of tea making, but Cyrus seemed to have a blind spot where this particular beverage was concerned. Leastways, he still produced undrinkable cat's piss every morning, much to Abra's disgust.

Rafferty lingered in the shower, partly from a reluctance to leave its cool embrace and partly from a desire to let the Cyrus-made tea go cold and give him an excuse to make his own. But eventually he had to turn it off and step out of the stall. He felt sweaty again five minutes after leaving the shower, so he put on a double dose of his Pavanne's 'Cool Man' and went to get dressed.

Abra was awake and gasping for tea. So Rafferty threw on his clothes and went down to the kitchen. Thankfully, it was a Cyrus-free zone. Rafferty quickly made tea for six, gave his four guests their mugs, hoping that, this time, Cyrus would remember what a cup of tea *should* taste like, and went back to his bedroom. A sight to gladden the eye met him on his return, for Abra had thrown the sheet off and was wearing the flimsiest of baby doll nighties.

'You know,' he said, 'I could always come back in for a cuddle. I've got time and with Cyrus and the others here we haven't done much cuddling, for fear they'll hear.'

'It's too hot, so don't even think about it. Sticky skin against sticky skin and I haven't even had a shower yet. I just want to drink my tea and then get in the bathroom before Cyrus.'

'Spoilsport.' He hunted in his wardrobe for his lightest jacket, finished his tea and said, 'right. I'm off.' He kissed Abra. 'See you later, sweetheart.'

He went downstairs and stuck his head round the living room door. Cyrus was up and insisted on telling him, at length, about his and Wendy's plans for the day, which recitation resulted in Rafferty being late for work. He could only hope the heat had made Long-Pockets Bradley sluggish or he'd be waiting for him to give his report with steam coming out of his ears.

Bradley's Lexus wasn't in its usual spot in the car park, he noticed as he pulled up and he gave a relieved smile. It might give him a chance to further discuss the latest murder with Llewellyn after their too-brief and lethargic conversation late on the steamy Sunday.

Llewellyn, not discombobulated by the heat or any other weather a variable climate might throw at him, was at his desk, looking cool in a pale green linen jacket.

Rafferty's second tea of the day was on his desk and he drank it gratefully, parched from the heat of the car whose air-conditioning hardly had a chance to get started between home and his arrival at work. 'Right,' he said, his immediate wants met, 'let's be having your report again. I had a thumping headache yesterday evening and could hardly take it in.'

Llewellyn duly obliged, repeating the few things he'd learned during his day of sole responsibility for the case.

Rafferty quickly cut to the chase. 'It's not much, is it?' he complained. 'I can just hear the super pulling his usual holes with it and this heat's likely to make him fractious.'

'It's about as much as we got during the past week,' said Llewellyn, in a blithe reminder that they were in this together.

'Hmph. I suppose so. You certainly managed to make it sound more than it is. I suppose that's the benefits of a university education.' He got up and gave the air-conditioning unit a thump. 'Bloody thing.' He walked back to his desk and slumped in his seat. 'I suppose, once I've got Bradley off my back, we ought to think about doing something, though what, with the suspects flown on the four winds, I don't know. Did you get Ainsley's computer over to the boffins?'

'Yes.'

'What about the phone company? Have they let us have a list of his calls in the last month or two?'

'Yes. I've got the team checking them out. I've also taken the liberty of asking them for those of Sophie Diaz as well.'

'On the "just in case" principle? Good man.' His mobile went. 'Rafferty.'

'Oh. Hello, Mr Rafferty.' It was a young girl's voice. 'I'm Karen. I'm ringing about the room. Is it still available?'

He'd forgotten all about his advert and now he sat up expectantly. 'Oh yes. The room's still available. Both of them are, actually. I only put the card up a few days ago.'

'I know. I saw it this morning. I've been looking for lodgings for ages, so I pop in a couple of times a week in case Miss Cartwright had added anything to the board. How much is it a month?'

Rafferty told her.

'That's good. And it's inclusive of an evening meal, phone and utilities?'

Rafferty confirmed that it was.

'Could I come and see it?'

'Of course.' He told her the address and they arranged a mutually convenient date and Rafferty had no sooner said goodbye and shut his mobile than it went again. 'Rafferty.'

It was another enquirer about the rooms, a young man this time. Rafferty arranged to show him the rooms at the same time as Karen. He had a key to his ma's so could show them both round without having recourse to sleight of hand with a credit card. With a bit of luck Ma's American cousins would be out at the time he'd arranged for the viewing with the two youngsters. He grinned. Divine retribution wasn't in it. This was the Rafferty version.

'So you've done what you threatened?' Llewellyn's voice was disapproving and Rafferty frowned.

'You bet.'

'I hope you've told your mother.'

'Not yet. I will. Eventually. By the way, I wanted to ask if you can help me download a short-term tenancy agreement off the internet later.'

Llewellyn turned huffy. 'I want nothing to do with it. I don't think it's a nice trick to play on your mother. She's not a young woman. You should have asked her permission before arranging these viewings.'

'Get away. She's tougher than you and me put together. Besides, I want to teach her a lesson. She's way too fond of organizing my life.'

Just then the landline rang. It was the expected summons from Superintendent Bradley and Rafferty slunk off, expecting the usual critical reception of his efforts. But he was pleasantly surprised. Because, once he'd given his report, Bradley, instead of the expected bawling out after a second murder with no suspect in view, was quite complimentary.

'Heard from that headmaster at Griffin School. He rang up this morning from his holiday villa, specially to thank me for all your efforts this past week.' Of course he had to add his usual twopenn'orth. 'Though I'd have thought you might have come up with more than you gave me in your report.' Unfortunately, Bradley, too, was adept at sorting the wheat from the chaff. 'So what are you doing now?'

'I've got the boffins checking out Ainsley's computer and the team going through the phone calls made and received by him in the last few months.'

'That's *them*. I want to know what *you're* doing.'

The correct answer to this question was 'nothing much'. But that wasn't politically advisable, not with Bradley, who had always been far better at office politics than he was at police work. So instead, Rafferty waffled on for a while about their remaining lines of inquiry.

It was Bradley's turn to go 'Hmph,' and complain that they

didn't amount to much. 'This is a high-profile case, Rafferty, with plenty of high-ranking interested parties such as Simon Fairweather, the Home Office man. Did he have anything else to say when you last saw him?'

'No, though he didn't strike me as being ready to fire off letters of complaint in all directions.'

Bradley simply went 'Hmph,' again, then said, 'Well, you'd better get on with the pitifully few lines of inquiry that you *do* have. I shall want a report last thing this afternoon and I'll speak to you again in the morning.'

Rafferty didn't wait for a second invitation. Back in his own office, he said to Llewellyn, 'Organize a couple of the team to go to Chelsea to speak to Ainsley's old neighbours. As for you and me, I think we should go and see Alice Douglas. I've got a niggle where that young woman's concerned. She seemed a bit evasive to me. You've got her address to hand?'

Of course he had. Llewellyn was a man for the minutiae of a case.

'We'll go to see her this afternoon. Catch her just as she comes home from work. The post mortem on Sophie Diaz is scheduled for two o'clock so that gives us time to see the victims' old headmaster, Cedric Barmforth, and Ainsley's bank manager this morning. Might learn something about old hatreds and where Adam Ainsley's money's gone.'

Jeremy Paxton had told them that Cedric Barmforth had retired early owing to ill health, but when Rafferty and Llewellyn went to see him, he seemed bursting with vitality. Mr Barmforth was in his early sixties, with a great bush of grey hair. He was well over six feet and was firmly built. He certainly had a physical presence, and Rafferty could well imagine that he had kept his former pupils in line with ease and a disregard for pettifogging rules. Rafferty took to him immediately.

He told them he lived alone, having never married. Certainly his ramshackle bungalow was untidy, with half-read books scattered on the furniture and a Cromwellian army in the process of being painted, laid out on the dining table.

'Great man, Oliver Cromwell. Pity his son was so useless. "Falling down, Dick", they used to call him. But come out to the greenhouse. I'm having a bit of a tidy.'

They followed him outside to a garden whose grass needed

cutting and whose borders needed weeding, but for all that, it was a pretty garden, a bit wild, but full of plants and colour. He led them into a large greenhouse, which had borders populated with more weeds, but with trestles filled with plants and shrubs, which were being grown on.

'Potted these up last year. I'm a bit late getting them planted out.'

Rafferty wondered where he was going to put them, given that the borders already looked overfull, but perhaps, like his ma, he'd find somewhere to cram them.

'Your man said on the phone that you wanted to talk about young Ainsley. Terrible thing. Fine athlete, but a bit of a bully. Too much of a golden youth. Given too much, too soon. Only child. Parents too soft. Not a good combination, do you see?' All this was interspersed with vigorous attacks on the weed-strewn border, accompanied by plenty of huffing and puffing. Personally, Rafferty would have waited till the cooler weather returned. The borders looked as if they'd waited a while already so a bit longer wouldn't hurt.

Cedric Barmforth had just given Rafferty a potted history of Adam Ainsley's life and family background and saved him the usual painstaking questions and answers most witnesses forced him to go through.

'I gather he had something of a colourful love life?'

'You could say that. Matron had a stream of weeping girls in her room for tea and sympathy. Myself, I always thought Ainsley had a fine contempt for the fair sex. Flitted from one to another and never settled, breaking hearts left and right.'

'What about enemies? A sporty boy who was a hit with the girls must have created some resentment.'

'Lord, yes. But he was always a big lad, do you see? Few boys cared to take him on.'

'That indicates that some did.'

'Ha! Yes. One or two. Young Kennedy fancied his chances. Got a gang of boys together and beat the stuffing out of him. Gave him a good thrashing, of course. Wouldn't stand for private gangs.'

'Sebastian Kennedy, you mean?'

'That's the one. Rebellious youth. Always in my study. Clever, mind. Shame he didn't go to university. Lazy. Hardly worked. Passed his A Levels with ease. Did no studying. Took drugs. Thought I didn't know. Wasted life.'

'You've heard that Sophie Diaz, Sophie Chator, that was, has also been found dead?'

'Yes. Another lazy one. Married young. Invited me to the wedding. I went, too. Flashy show. Marquee on the lawn. Posh frocks. Morning suits. Looked the poor relation. Ha. Good spread. Give her that. Husband a banker. Filthy rich.'

'I understand Mrs Diaz was another one of Adam Ainsley's girlfriends?'

'Lasted longer than most. More weeping against matron's ample bosom. Often wished Griffin was still just a boys' school. Not my decision to let girls in. Board of Governors. Mistake. Claimed she was pregnant. Wanted to get Ainsley in trouble. Give him a fright. And it did. False alarm. More tears.'

His particular form of verbal shorthand conveyed more information than any amount of normal conversation and Rafferty was grateful for it. He hadn't known that Sophie Diaz had had a false alarm. He wondered if Ainsley had denied paternity and asked Mr Barmforth.

'Tried. Said she'd been with plenty of other boys. And she had. Little strumpet. There's always one. Bit of a hoo-ha before she found out her mistake. Took the wind out of Ainsley's sails for a bit. Stupid boy. Gave him some condoms and told him to use them. Catholic or no Catholic. Too many people in the world already.'

'Did any of his discarded girlfriends threaten revenge?'

'No, nothing like that. A tad Romeo and Juliet, and though Romeo didn't threaten suicide some of the girls did. Few angry fathers. Nothing serious. Tears and tantrums, but no lasting effects. Youngsters resilient.'

Maybe not all of them, was Rafferty's thought. He named the females amongst the seven reunees that had shared Ainsley's table and asked if any of them had been amongst those to threaten suicide.

'No. Not as I remember.'

Rafferty asked him about the other reunees, but Barmforth was able to give him little pertinent information. 'It's the bad ones that stick in the mind, do you see? Have more to do with them, of course. But only Sebastian Kennedy amongst your lot could be so described. Young Adam wasn't a lover of rules and regulations either, mind, but he didn't end up in my study as often. My Head Boy, Giles Harmsworth, used to deal with him mostly.'

By now the borders were weed-free. Barmforth was sweating profusely and he cast his shirt aside and, in his vest, he started to rake the weeds into a pile.

There was nothing else Rafferty could think to ask him, so they made their goodbyes.

'You know your way out? Must get on. Lot to do.'

They made their way through the untidy bungalow and back out into the sunshine. Rafferty was sweating. It had been like a sauna in the greenhouse. Just watching the energetic Barmforth had been enough to make him perspire. Not so Llewellyn, of course. Cool as a lime ice-lolly he looked in his pale green jacket. It made Rafferty want to spit. Once back in the car, he mopped his face with a wad of tissues from a box he kept in the glove compartment. The car was another steam bath and he began sweating again. He took a sniff of his armpit. His 'Cool Man' didn't seem able to cope with the current temperatures. He hoped he didn't offend the bank manager.

Mr Jarvis was a punctilious little man. He was bald and round and bore a striking resemblance to an egg. His office was in complete contrast to Cedric Barmforth's home. Fussy wasn't the word. After greeting them, he sat down and immediately straightened his already straight blotter, aligning his pen just so.

'Mr Adam Ainsley. You wanted to know about his finances? Not a prudent man with his money. He was sent the usual savings information, of course, but he never filled in the forms. A professional sportsman. They're not always very wise. A tad Lester Piggotish in their financial affairs.' Mr Jarvis smiled at his little joke.

'Are you saying he owed money to the taxman?'

'I don't know. But I shouldn't wonder. Certainly no payment to the Revenue and Customs came out of his account. Not since he moved it to this bank a year before he retired from playing professional rugby.'

'So he lived up to his income?'

'Lived beyond it, Inspector. Lived beyond it. Very foolish. He made no provision for the future. I tried to advise him, but he was a headstrong man. Seemed to think his stardom would guarantee him an income. It didn't, to judge from the state of his current account. I think he regretted his lack of prudence. Too late of course. Like a lot of my clients.'

Thinking of blackmail, whether as victim or otherwise, Rafferty asked, 'did he have any unusual or unexpected sums of money going into or coming out of his account?'

Jarvis gave him a sharp glance, straightened his pen and blotter again and then said, 'Funny you should ask, but yes. Several sums of money went into his account.'

'Who were they from?'

'I don't know. They were just paid in over the counter.'

'When was the last payment made?'

Jarvis checked his computer screen. 'A month ago. These sums were pretty regular.'

'Every month?'

'More or less.'

'How much?'

'A thousand pounds each time. Came to a tidy sum as it had been going on for the past twelve months.'

'How long do you keep your CCTV images for?'

'I thought of that, but I was too late, I'm afraid. The tapes from the day of the last payment have already been wiped and reused.'

So, apart from learning that Ainsley was a thousand pounds to the good every month from a mysterious source, they were no further forward. Who could have paid him the money and why? It was going to niggle at him until he found the answer.

He thanked Mr Jarvis, gave him one of his cards and led the way out down to the car and the post mortem.

Sam Dally was in good form. 'Someone take a photo. This once-only event needs to be recorded for posterity. Inspector Rafferty is on time for the post mortem.'

'Oh, ha ha,' went Rafferty. 'You're so droll. I just hope you're a better pathologist than you are a comedian.'

'Of course I am. I'm the *sine qua non* of pathologists. But enough of this badinage. I've got a lot on this afternoon, so I suggest we make a start.'

Sam fairly raced through the post mortem. Rafferty had never seen 'Dilly' Dally's knife slice so quickly. Rafferty concluded he must be on a promise. When it was over, he said, 'I'll want the toxicology report tagged as urgent.'

'Of course you will. So does every other detective.'

'Ah, but I'm the only one in the parish with a fresh murder case. That gets me priority.'

'If you say so.'

'So, what's on now, then, Sam? Got a date with your Mary for a bit of love in the afternoon?'

'At my age? I should be so lucky. My days of love in the afternoon are long gone. I'm hard pressed to fulfil the expected conjugals at night, never mind in the day as well.'

'You want to reply to some of those Viagra ad emails.'

'So do you with your child bride. How do you keep up with her?'

'I'm not that much older than Abra. Only twelve years.'

'Yes, but when she's forty-eight, you'll be sixty and reaching for your pipe and slippers. Anyway,' said Sam, breaking up this latest idle chitchat having had the last word, as usual. 'This lady was a healthy young woman. Her heart was in good nick as were her liver and lights. Altogether she should have lived to her three score years and ten and beyond.'

'So you don't know what killed her?'

'No.'

'And you a *sine qua non*. Slipping, or what?'

'I think you'll find it's "or what". But as you requested, my beautiful assistant will put a priority tag on for toxicology. Satisfied?'

'It'll do me.'

'We aim to please. So what have you got on? Some flitting around the country using up your superintendent's budget?'

'You bet. See you later, Sam.'

Alice Douglas lived in Norwich. It was a straight run once they got on the A11 and, even with the traffic, it took no more than an hour and a half to reach the city's ring road. 'Where now?' Rafferty asked. The heat had made the satnav go all cranky and Llewellyn consulted the notes he had taken from the A-Z of the city before giving him directions. The Welshman was as efficient in this as he was in everything else and, shortly after, Rafferty pulled up outside a neat terraced house in a suburban street.

The front garden was paved over to accommodate a car, but pots were dotted around the edges and sprouted red geraniums and poppies and tall, creamy lilies.

A young woman in her late teens answered the door and when Rafferty stated the nature of their business, she said, 'Mum's at work. I suppose this is about the murders at Griffin?'

Rafferty agreed that it was. 'What time do you expect your mother back?'

'Any time. She said she wouldn't be late.'

'Is it possible for us to come in and wait?'

The young woman looked doubtful. 'I don't know. Mum said not to let anyone in the house when I'm here alone.'

'We *are* police officers, Miss,' Llewellyn reminded her.

'Oh well, I suppose it will be all right.'

She led them to an untidy living room, in which, like Cedric Barmforth, books were a prominent feature. They overflowed from well-stuffed bookcases on to the floor and the top of the corner television cupboard.

'I'm Joanna.' Clearly feeling she had to fulfil the duties of a hostess, the teenager offered them tea, but seemed relieved when Rafferty declined. In spite of his parched throat, he was more keen on questioning the girl before her mother returned than he was in slurping tea.

'Are you enjoying the summer holidays, Joanna?' Rafferty asked in a polite pursuit of small talk, just to get the conversation started.

'Gosh, yes. I'm heading for uni in the autumn, so it's good to enjoy a few weeks of freedom before I have to settle down to more swotting.'

Llewellyn asked what she intended to study.

'History of Art. But sorry, won't you sit down?'

They did so and Rafferty decided to ask Joanna a few more questions about herself and her mother while he had the chance. 'Did you have some nice presents for your eighteenth birthday?'

'I'm not eighteen yet. My birthday's in April. Mum's throwing a party for me. She said I could invite all my school friends.'

'Ouch. That'll cost a bit,' said the ever-practical Rafferty. 'I bet your dad's wallet is wincing.'

Joanna's animation died. 'My father's not in our lives.'

'You must be a bright girl to be going to university early,' Llewellyn said.

Joanna brightened again, blushed and told him, 'I've been a year ahead of my peers since the second year of school.' She smiled. 'I'm hoping to get to spend some time with my dad next year. I managed to get Mum to promise she'd ask him to my birthday party, which surprised me as she never wants to talk about him.'

From the sound of it Rafferty guessed there was a less than amicable estrangement between Alice Douglas and Joanna's father. He was curious as to what had caused it and casually asked, 'Are your parents divorced, Joanna? Mine divorced when I was about your age,' he lied, hoping a bit of fellow feeling would encourage her into confidences. 'I remember how much it upset me.'

'No. They're not divorced. They never married.'

Her answer was abrupt. She didn't elaborate or look likely to, so Rafferty, having got what he was after, changed the subject to one she should find more to her taste. 'So, why did you decide on History of Art?'

'I love art, but I'm hopeless at painting, so this seemed the next best thing. I hope to get a job in one of the big London galleries when I graduate. Mum's paid for me to spend the last two summers in Italy –' no mention of Dad's contribution, Rafferty noted. Maybe the estrangement had been very bitter – 'so I've had the opportunity to learn the language, which will be a great asset in my career.'

They all seemed to run out of things to talk about then and Joanna excused herself and said she'd see if her mother was coming. It gave Rafferty and Llewellyn the opportunity to discuss what they'd learned from the girl.

'I was interested to discover that Joanne's birthday is in April,' said Llewellyn.

'And me. I've done the sums,' he boasted, albeit he didn't mention that he'd had to use his fingers for the arithmetic and that it had taken him a while before he'd twigged. 'I counted back the appropriate time. And judging from that, her mother would have fallen pregnant with Joanna during her last summer term at Griffin. So much for the abortion she claimed to have had. Wonder who the father was? Studious little Alice. Who'd have thought it? Reckon the daddy was another swot?'

'Possibly. They must have exercised discretion, as, apart

from the late Mrs Diaz, no one mentioned her having a boyfriend.'

'Mmm. Bet it was Giles Harmsworth. He was the only other swot in the group, though when he found the time for fornication, if you believe Sebastian Kennedy, he spent his leisure hours as a youth being the school sneak.'

Joanna came back then to tell them her mother was just parking the car and wouldn't be long.

'I wonder, Joanna,' said Rafferty, testing the water, 'if you can let me have your father's address.'

'I don't know it. I told you. I don't know who he is. Why do you want it?'

'Your mother became pregnant with you during her last summer term at Griffin School. You said she intended to ask your father to attend your eighteenth birthday party and I wondered if he might not be amongst the reunees. I'd like the opportunity to question him more deeply.'

'Really? Why?'

Rafferty, who'd launched into his request for her father's address without thinking through his reasons for wanting it, was relieved when Llewellyn spoke up.

'Your father's likely to have a double connection to the school: through his own attendance there and then through your mother. Once we know his identity, he might be able to give us more background than we thought to ask him for at the time.'

'As I said, I don't know his address. You'll have to ask Mum for it. If she has it.'

'Ask Mum for what?' Alice Douglas stood in the doorway and gazed quizzically from her daughter to the two policemen. 'Inspector Rafferty. You should have rung and let me know you were coming and I could have taken a few hours off.'

'I didn't want to put you to any trouble. Besides, your daughter's made us more than welcome.'

'Has she?'

The idea didn't seem to please her too well. But then, Rafferty supposed she hadn't expected them to just turn up on her doorstep and discover a teenage daughter in residence, one moreover who was the right age to be starting university. He waited until Joanna had gone off and then he said to Alice, 'You said you'd had an abortion, Ms Douglas. Why did you lie to us?'

She sat down in an armchair and said carefully, 'I suppose you could say it seemed a good idea at the time. It seemed an unnecessary complication to admit I'd had the baby. For one thing, I didn't think it was any of your business. And for another, it's not as if it's anything to do with Adam or Sophie's deaths.'

'But if Adam *isn't* your daughter's father, as you told me before, who is? Is it Giles Harmsworth?'

She didn't answer 'yes' and she didn't answer 'no'. Instead, she said, 'I still don't think the identity of the father's any of your business. Besides, I thought you had one, no, two, *murder* cases to solve, rather than paternity ones.'

But Rafferty thought that it was very much his business. He determined to find the answer to his question somehow when Alice Douglas stubbornly refused to tell them the man's identity. It just might take a while.

EIGHT

'Wonder why she kept it a secret that she had the child after all? Do you think it possible that Joanna *is* Adam Ainsley's child? It would explain why she lied to us.'

'It doesn't seem likely given that Ainsley had no interest in her at school beyond taunting her about being a charity case. It might pay us to get hold of a copy of Joanna's birth certificate, though, and see if Ms Douglas added the father's name.'

'Good idea. I wonder how many of our other suspects have deliberately misled us?' Rafferty said once they were in the car and making their way back to Elmhurst. He loosened his tie and undid the top two buttons of his shirt, but gained little relief from the heat. He'd already taken off his jacket and slung it on the back seat. 'Maybe we ought to check them out on their home turf, too. See what else we learn. It's certainly been illuminating in Alice Douglas's case.'

Llewellyn nodded. 'Who do you want to try first?'

'Let's try Giles Harmsworth. If Ainsley's not the father of Alice Douglas's daughter, then he strikes me as a possible. After that, I think Sophie Diaz's widower might be the most fruitful. It was her that Alice Douglas confided in about her unwanted pregnancy all those years ago. Maybe others confided their secrets there too, and more recently, and then regretted it. She might have shared any such secrets with her husband. Depending on where he lives, we could check it out this evening.'

Llewellyn flipped through his notebook. 'Mr Diaz lives in London. Notting Hill.'

'With the loveys, hey?' He wiped his brow. He'd had enough of London yesterday when Cyrus had trailed them round the tourist sites in the heat. 'I don't think I feel like venturing to Notting Hill as well as the City in this weather. The stop-start traffic. The fumes. The crowds. No, the morning will have to do for Mr Diaz. Perhaps a storm will have broken by then and cooled the air.'

* * *

Giles Harmsworth, when he met them for a coffee from his job in the City, was fidgety and ill at ease. Rafferty couldn't help but wonder why. He hadn't displayed any nervousness when they interviewed him at Griffin School, so why now?

'Tell me about Alice Douglas,' Rafferty invited once the coffee was served in the high-priced eatery in which Harmsworth had elected to meet them. Rafferty had briefly glanced at the menu and was stunned at the prices. Five pounds for a cup of coffee. He ought to do them for daylight robbery.

Giles frowned. 'Alice Douglas? What do you want to know?'

'Were you the father of her baby?'

'What baby?'

'You didn't know about it?'

'First I've heard of it.'

Either Giles Harmsworth was a very good actor or he was telling the truth.

'So when are we talking about?' he asked.

'That last summer term at Griffin. That's when Ms Douglas fell pregnant.'

'I'm sorry, Inspector, but I don't know anything about it.'

'So you don't know who was the father?'

'No. I only know it wasn't me.' He glanced at his watch. 'I really ought to get back. The bosses have got another purge on and I don't want to be one of the victims.'

Rafferty nodded and let him go. And that was his nervousness explained. It seemed Harmsworth was worried about losing his job. All in all, there seemed to be a few whose standard of living was either in danger of falling or had already done so for he'd heard rumours that Sophie Diaz hadn't presented as quite the up-to-the-minute fashionista as she had in previous years. The only one who seemed flush with cash was the trust fund boy, Sebastian Kennedy. But somehow, Rafferty couldn't see him lending his old school friend, Giles, a few quid should he get the sack. There must have been a few undercurrents at this Griffin school reunion between those who were doing well in life and the rest. He wondered whether, rather than being a blackmailer, Adam Ainsley had been a boaster and had boasted once too often about his successful sporting career and had prompted revenge from one of his jealous peers? It would certainly explain the choice of the muscle-paralyzing hemlock as the poison of preference. Ironic, if so, given his sacking and that his bank account was weighted only with the still unexplained grand a month. Really, the down-on-his-luck Ainsley had had little to boast about.

And as his own internet hunt had proved, the killer would not necessarily have to be knowledgeable about plants and poisons. Even his ma had managed to trawl the Internet for family for her reunion. It would be the simplest thing in the world for a killer of the computer generation to check out poisons on the World Wide Web. He wouldn't need to have scientific or plant biology qualifications to find an appropriate method of murder. Though, of course, the killer might have found it more difficult to identify the plant, so many plants looked similar, so maybe a bit of expertise would be called for there.

It was now six thirty and the traffic was building up. Rafferty had had second thoughts and had considered trying to fit Edward Diaz in today. But by the time they'd fought through the London traffic to get to Notting Hill it would be beyond time to turn back and head for home if Abra wasn't to have set up a lynching party to welcome him. It would have to wait till tomorrow.

Rafferty had sent two of the team to speak with Ainsley's old neighbours in Chelsea. They came back to the station shortly after Rafferty and Llewellyn with tales of nightclubs and sponsorship money and the good life.

But, as Gerry Hanks told him, all that had began to peter out about six months after his professional rugby career ended.

'One old girl I spoke to told me Mr Ainsley used to throw lavish parties at his house. He'd invite all the neighbours. These parties used to get quite rowdy, apparently. But there hadn't been any parties for the last two years of his tenancy.'

'He was only a tenant? He didn't own the Chelsea house?'

'No.'

'So he didn't even spend his money on property. What the hell did he do with it all?' Of course, he'd had two ex-wives batten on him and that would have taken a fair lump of his income, but even so, there should still be more. Surely no judge in a divorce case would leave a man without an income sufficient to live on.

'Spent it as soon as he earned it,' said Mary Carmody, 'according to this same lady, on wine, women and song. The usual story. It seems he used his money to buy the popularity that his personality didn't attract. Certainly he did so once his sporting career was over and he had no other means of attracting attention.'

'Hangers-on, you mean?'

'Yes. If he went out to dinner he would always end up picking up the tab. I'm afraid the only friends he attracted were the fair-weather sort.'

Rafferty nodded. 'Thanks Gerry. Thanks Mare. You've done well. What a turn-around from his schooldays,' Rafferty said to Llewellyn once Gerry Hanks and Mary Carmody had gone. 'Whatever happened to that popular boy his parents and Cedric Barmforth spoke about?'

'The usual too much too soon, I imagine,' opined Llewellyn. 'That and the modern cult of celebrity which makes stars out of nobodies or second-raters. As we know, Mr Ainsley never reached the top of the tree in his sporting career. Perhaps that niggled away at him and encouraged him to make more of less.'

'Oh well. I don't suppose we'll ever know now what drove him.'

Sophie Diaz had told them that no one else amongst her old schoolmates had confided anything to her. Rafferty wasn't sure he had believed her. After all, as the school 'bike', Sophie Diaz was an unlikely confidante of the quiet girl that Alice Douglas had been, so maybe it was possible that she was also the unlikely confidante of a few of the others. There was nothing like the aftermath of lovemaking for getting secrets out of a man – wasn't that something the old Soviet Union had turned to good use? What secrets could she have had whispered to her in her youth and what had she done with them? Had she discreetly forgotten them? Or harboured them against a rainy day? Perhaps, tomorrow, her widower would be able to tell them.

Edward Diaz had already been told of his wife's death by the Met, but Rafferty was keen to speak to him and not only to find out if his wife had used her mobile to apprise him of the latest happenings amongst her old school friends. He had always regarded it as a courtesy to speak with the bereaved as soon as practicable.

Besides, they were now armed with the results of the toxicology tests, Rafferty having begged and pleaded to have them moved up the queue, and could now let Mr Diaz know the cause of his wife's sudden death. It *had* been the same poison that had killed Ainsley, which wasn't any great surprise.

They stopped off at the local nick as another courtesy, to let them know he and Llewellyn were on their patch. 'How did he seem, Mr Diaz?' he asked the uniformed inspector he'd been directed to.

'Much as you'd expect him to seem,' said Inspector Trent. He stared at them curiously. 'So what brings Essex CID on to the Met's ground? I thought it was a natural death.'

'So did we. At first. For a while. But no. We had an earlier death at the school where she was staying. Poisoning. The toxicology results came in before we left Elmhurst this morning and Mrs Diaz was poisoned also. Hemlock. Same stuff as killed Socrates,' said Rafferty, keen to display his recently-garnered knowledge.

'Socrates? That footballer, do you mean?'

Rafferty sighed. He could see that his newly gained erudition was wasted on Trent. 'That's right.'

'Didn't know he was dead. Can't have been very old. Sad.'

'Isn't it?'

Edward Diaz was waiting at home for them as Llewellyn had rung him earlier to let him know to expect them. He lived in some style, in a three-storey, plus basement, house, the likely cost of which made Rafferty's eyes water. But he was a banker, he recalled and had the high earnings that Rafferty had been given to understand Sophie had thought was her due, though it was strange that the Griffin rumour mill had implied that she hadn't been up to the minute in the fashion stakes for her school reunion. Abra had taught him that was unusual: women were always keen to impress other women with their clothes and their style.

Edward Diaz was – given his surname – surprisingly fair, with light brown hair and sandy lashes. He was also older than Rafferty had expected, being fifty-five at least, and was fleshy, with the look of a man who indulged all his appetites. But this morning, he seemed a husk of a man. There were violet shadows under his eyes and a listless air about him that Rafferty put down to sleepless nights since the loss of his wife. He seemed almost pathetically glad to see them and immediately began talking about his wife as if he was anxious to keep her name alive.

'Who could want to kill her?' he asked, plaintively, once they had sat down in the large and opulent drawing room with its enormous TV and tiny stereo and explained how his wife had died. 'She had no enemies. She loved shopping and cooking and entertaining our friends. There was no harm in her. Everyone liked her. Who could want to kill her?' he asked again.

'I don't know, sir,' said Rafferty. 'But we'll do our best to find out. To that end, I'd like you to tell me everything you can about your wife. We've already learned she was a woman that others confided in and—'

'Was she? I didn't know that. Of course I heard her swapping girlie gossip on the phone, but that's all. I didn't realize she was some kind of agony aunt.'

Edward Diaz's comment didn't sound hopeful from Rafferty's point of view, but he pressed on optimistically. 'Yes. I wondered if she rang you while she was away at Griffin School?'

'Yes, yes, she did. We spoke every day.'

'And did she speak to you about the other reunees? Did she tell you anything she learned about them or from them?'

Diaz frowned. 'Like what?'

'Anything – the sort of thing that they probably wouldn't want to go any further.' He saw that Diaz was still floundering and he helped him out. 'Things like sexual peccadilloes, unwanted pregnancies, money problems. That sort of thing.'

Diaz's frown deepened, but it looked as if he was having trouble garnering his thoughts as a minute went by with no response.

'Mr Diaz?' Rafferty encouraged. 'The other reunees. Did your wife speak of them?'

'Sorry. My mind wandered off on to thoughts of Sophie. Yes. She said she was enjoying catching up on her fellow old boys and girls. She said a chap called Giles Harmsworth was as pompous and self-important as ever and was even trying to assume the lead of the police inquiry. That amused her.'

Rafferty, sensitive about his secondary modern background amongst the educationally privileged scions of Griffin School, wondered what she'd found so amusing about it and what she'd said about *him*.

'She said that a chap called Seb was still the lazy good-for-nothing he'd been at school.'

That wasn't the sort of thing Rafferty was interested in hearing. He knew all that already. 'Did she tell you anything more intimate?' he asked.

'Intimate? Like what?' To Rafferty's frustration, he immediately returned to his own miseries. 'Sophie was in a twin room with another woman so there was little privacy for sharing even the normal marital intimacies. I missed that,' he said sadly. 'My last memories of her are of brief phone calls rather than lengthy cuddles. Now all I have is memories. I don't know how I'm going to get through the days without her.'

'Perhaps you'll feel better when you get back to work, sir,' Rafferty suggested. 'Less time to brood.'

'Work? What work? I was made redundant after Christmas. I was a banker,' he told Rafferty, who nodded. 'I was one of those culled at the height of the recession.'

'I'm sorry,' was Rafferty's inadequate response. Here was yet another secret, something that Sophie Diaz had chosen not to confide to the other Griffin reunees. Or him. It certainly explained her turning up at the reunion in last year's fashions. It seemed that, for Sophie Diaz, the rainy days had arrived. 'Still you must have friends.'

'Not many. Life in my world was more about competing with colleagues than making bosom buddies of them. The pursuit of money doesn't make one many friends, Inspector.'

'Like the pursuit of criminals,' Rafferty murmured. 'But to get back to the other reunees,' he tried again. 'Did your wife really not discuss anything more serious than pomposity or idleness?'

Diaz frowned. 'She said – something. What was it?'

They waited.

'She said that she had seen something.'

'Seen something?' Rafferty repeated, imagination going into overdrive. 'Seen what, exactly, sir?'

'Sophie didn't elaborate. I got the impression that whatever it was, she thought there might be profit in it. God knows we – I – could do with the money as all my savings are gone. Not that I was ever a great saver. Live for the day was a motto Sophie and I shared. I got the impression that Sophie had put out feelers for a job for me with her old friends and wouldn't say anything more until she was certain of it.'

Or maybe, was Rafferty's thought, she was trying to put the touch on the killer, having witnessed him or her slipping the hemlock in Ainsley's lunch. 'And you say your wife said nothing further?' How frustrating was that? Rafferty had come here hoping for secrets from beyond the grave. Or at least beyond the mortuary slab, but all he'd found was a man pathetic in his grief who could tell them little.

'No. That was all she said as far as I can remember.' He wore a shame-faced expression as he admitted, 'I'm afraid my mind's turned to mush these last seven months. Lack of use, I suppose. And even if it was an employment possibility that Sophie had come across I really didn't see her pulling off a job for me, not from amongst her thirty-something old school friends. I'm a good few years older than Sophie and even with all my contacts I've been unable to get another post. I rather doubt I ever will.'

'Have you no prospects?'

'Beyond people who said they'd put a word in for me? No. And nothing's come of them so far. I'm considering re-training as a teacher as I think my days of being a big-earning banker are behind me.'

'What did your wife think of that?'

Diaz pulled a face. 'Sophie liked the money. Sometimes I think she loved that more than she did me. But no, I mustn't think like that. It's just that Sophie was used to the good things in life. She liked the latest designer fashions and the best restaurants. We've had to cut back a lot. Sophie even had to get rid of her beloved sports car. We were able to get her a cheap run-around with the money, but it wasn't very reliable. She had to take the train to the Griffin reunion as my own car was in the garage getting repaired. She was a bit upset about that. She was a bit upset that she had to wear last season's fashions when she got there as well. She always liked to cut a dash.' He brushed his hand across suddenly damp eyes. 'I was worried she'd leave me,' he told them, brokenly. 'I was never good-looking or witty. All I had was my income. My family don't have money. I was the first one to make any decent cash. Sophie was a very attractive woman. She could have had anyone. I was always amazed that she settled for me.'

These grief-stricken confidences made Rafferty uncomfortable. But they also told him something about the dead woman.

A woman who was 'used to the good things in life', and 'the latest designer fashions'. He'd never have guessed she wasn't wearing up to the minute stuff without the input of the other female reunees. Sophie Diaz had always looked very smart every time he'd seen her – chic, he supposed Llewellyn would call it. Women's clothes all looked the same to him. He wouldn't have recognized a designer dress if it had leapt up and emptied his wallet.

They'd searched the possessions that Sophie Diaz had brought to the reunion with her, but had found nothing of interest. Now, Rafferty said, 'I wonder, sir, if we could look through your wife's things?'

'Sophie's things? There's only her clothes and her jewellery and we've sold the best bits of that. Why would you want to look through them?'

'I'm hoping there might be something more, sir. Did your wife keep a diary?' They'd found none amongst her belongings at Griffin.

'A diary? No. Nothing like that.' He gave a taut smile. 'Unless she kept a secret one in which she complained about me.' He tried to laugh, but the laugh only ended in more tears, through which he said, 'Look if you like. I can't imagine you'll find anything. Sophie wasn't a woman for confiding her thoughts to paper. She has a laptop, but she hardly used it; she preferred the phone. You'll find it in our bedroom if you want to check it out. She preferred to confide in her women friends on the phone and in person. Many are the confidences I've interrupted as I've walked past when she's been on the phone, though none that would concern your murder case,' he was hasty to add.

'Her women friends,' said Rafferty thoughtfully. 'Maybe they'll be able to tell me more about your wife's life? Could you let us have their details?'

'There's an address book in the hall. I'll get it.' He lumbered his bulk off the sofa, across the drawing room and into the hall. He moved very slowly, like an old man whose legs were stricken with rheumatism. He was back more quickly than Rafferty had expected, as if it had occurred to him that for whatever reason his wife had been killed, she might indeed have confided something relevant to her girlfriends and he wanted to speed up their checking of it out.

He was holding a bulging pink book, which he, with evident

reluctance, handed to Rafferty. 'You should find the names and addresses of all Sophie's girlfriends in there. She was particularly close to Amanda Shaw.'

'Thank you, sir.'

Diaz held his hand out. 'Let me just take a note of a few numbers. Sophie's friends might be able to tell me something.'

Rafferty handed the address book back and waited while Diaz found a pen and paper to scribble down the phone numbers, then he handed the book back with a look of regret.

'Don't worry, sir,' Rafferty reassured. 'We'll let you have it back shortly. We'll look upstairs now, if that's all right?'

Diaz indicated his permission with a wave of his hand, before he sank back into his chair and his introspection, clutching the paper with the scribbled numbers and staring at them as if he sought to find the reason for his wife's murder scrawled in his shaky hand.

The Diaz marital bedroom was lavish, with wall-to-wall wardrobes and a carpet so thick Rafferty longed to take off his shoes and socks and feel his feet embraced by its softness. Getting poetical again, Rafferty, he warned himself. Don't go there. Not now, anyway.

There was a large en-suite with a sunken bath and double shower, but there was nothing in there that interested Rafferty. He pulled out the drawer in the bedside table on the side that, from the pile of girlie magazines and romantic comedies, was clearly Sophie's, but there was little but an assortment of sleeping tablets and anti-depressants, certainly no diary which would 'tell all'.

Llewellyn was checking the wardrobe; it stretched the length of the room, which must have been twenty-five feet and not far off as wide. Rafferty thought – if they weren't to be there all day – that he'd better help him, so he started checking through pockets at the other end. But countless expensive-looking outfits later, the pockets had yielded nothing. There were not even any soiled tissues or forgotten lipsticks. Clearly Sophie Diaz was a woman who valued her clothes and looked after them. Rafferty glanced briefly at some of the labels and was impressed; even *he'd* heard of some of them. The wardrobe seemed to contain nothing but Sophie Diaz's clothes, shoes and handbags and Rafferty presumed that her husband's clothes had been banished to a spare room. Next, he checked out the handbags, of which there were a large number. Abra had a bit of a thing about handbags and he guessed that she'd love these. They came in every size and a rainbow of colours. But, like the clothes, these also yielded nothing.

Dispirited, Rafferty plumped his behind down on the king-size. 'I've got a theory,' he told Llewellyn's back.

Llewellyn turned. 'Oh yes?' he said in tones of discouragement.

Rafferty smiled, aware that his educated Welsh sergeant had probably had a surfeit of his inspector's theories since they'd been working together. He knew he tended to the outlandish and outrageous. He wasn't sure whether it was just the Irish in him or whether he did it because he knew it riled Llewellyn.

'Don't say it like that,' Rafferty protested mildly. 'This is one of my better ones, promise. I was wondering, seeing as Sophie Diaz was a woman who seemed to love money so much, whether she might not, now her husband's as poor as an unfrocked vicar, have found another way of making the old spondoolicks.'

'Like what?'

'Blackmail.'

'Blackmail,' Llewellyn repeated. 'Again. You thought the unexplained thousand pounds a month going into Mr Ainsley's bank account might have been the proceeds of blackmail.'

'Yes, I know. Perhaps both of them were going in for it? I don't know. I'm only going on the evidence, Dafyd, and unexplained money and secrets shout blackmail to me, loud and clear. You heard her husband say that she'd seen something she thought there might be money in at this reunion. Rather than a job for Diaz, I was wondering if she saw Adam Ainsley's murderer in action.'

Rather to his surprise, Llewellyn didn't immediately squash the idea, so he added, 'and got herself murdered when she tried to put the squeeze on the killer.'

'A bit stupid of her.'

'No one said she had a brain to rival Einstein's. You've seen her wardrobe. Shopping seems to have been her greatest love, not mind expansion. She might think it worth it, down to last year's fashions as she was, to try to get her hands on some of the folding stuff that her old man had stopped providing.'

'It's a possibility, certainly,' Llewellyn opined slowly.

'Gee, thanks. Don't go too overboard.' A bit miffed at this ponderous response, Rafferty demanded, 'Well, what's your theory? Or don't you have one?'

'Personally, I've always liked to wait until I have some solid evidence before I start constructing theories. But, as you say, there would seem to be something there to support this theory. I wonder whether she tried to take any kind of precautions before she approached the killer. *If* she approached the killer.'

'Doesn't seem likely, does it? Seeing as she got herself murdered.'

'I can't believe anyone, even a woman obsessed with clothes, could be so foolhardy as to embark on blackmail without taking care to safeguard themselves.'

Rafferty, glad as he was to have another possible theory to play with, had to agree. 'Perhaps she thought there was safety in numbers and that the killer wouldn't go after her, surrounded as she was by all the other reunees.'

'I would have thought that the murder of Mr Ainsley himself would have folded away that particular comfort blanket. Besides, the reunion was only for a week. Could she really have thought the killer wouldn't target her once she got home?'

Rafferty tutted, as the Welshman dissected his theory and found it wanting. 'So what's your theory?' he challenged. 'You do have one, I take it?'

'Not as yet, no.' It was Llewellyn's turn to look peeved. 'Maybe we'll find some proof, one way or the other, when we speak to Mrs Diaz's girlfriends?'

Rafferty grinned as he was reminded that even though Llewellyn had just demolished his latest theory, life had its compensations. 'Take a look in her address book, Daff. See how well spaced out they are around the country. With a bit of luck they live all over and it will cost plenty to get there and back. This case might be giving me the pip, but it'll be nice to think that Bradley's going to break his dentures on a few himself before we're done.'

With a pained expression, Llewellyn opened Sophie Diaz's address book and, after leafing through it, confirmed Rafferty's hopes.

'You want the pleasure of telling Bradley that his budget's about to go through the roof? Oh, I don't know, though, what's the point of having the rank if you don't get the rewards that go with it? I'll do it. I like to watch him turn purple.'

Alice Douglas hadn't put the name of the father on her daughter's birth certificate, as Llewellyn discovered the next day, though whether that was her choice or whether the father – whoever he was – had refused to allow his name to be put on the document was anyone's guess. At any rate, Ms Douglas was still refusing to reveal the identity of the father. Her refusal irritated Rafferty. What was she hiding? It might be worth having another word with the daughter. Even if she didn't know her father's name, she might still, unbeknownst to herself, be able to provide them with a clue to his ID.

So while Llewellyn was hunting down Sophie's girlfriends with Mary Carmody to discover if there was anything worth following up, he would drive over to Norwich and see if he couldn't catch the daughter on her own.

Joanna Douglas, Alice's daughter, *was* home alone, which was a bit of luck. Rafferty got himself invited in without any trouble this time and accepted the cup of tea that was offered, confident that he could spin the drinking of it out to twenty, thirty minutes. In his experience, there was nothing like tea and sympathy for encouraging confidences.

After they had spoken for a little while about the degree course that Joanna would start in the autumn, Rafferty got on to what he really wanted to talk about. 'You said, last time I spoke to you, that you hoped to see your father at your birthday party in April. When did your mother promise to ask him?'

'Just before she went for that silly old reunion. I don't know why she went. She never has before though she gets an invitation every year.'

'Perhaps that was the only way she could contact your father? Working backwards from your birthday, your mother would have fallen pregnant with you during the July of her last term at Griffin, so it seems logical to suppose that one of her fellow students was your father. If she had lost his address and phone number, his attendance there would tell her that she would be able to speak to him then. I know a list of attendees is circulated among the old boys and girls, so your mother would know he would be there.'

'You know, I never thought of that. But you're right. She did speak of asking my father to my birthday party just after she'd received this year's invite from the school. The post hadn't come by the time she went to work and I remember she was late home that day. She had several large glasses of wine as soon as she came in and only then opened her post. She said she'd had a hard day. I think she only agreed to ask my father to my eighteenth party because she was tipsy. She became quite cross about it when I reminded her the next morning. But, as I said, she'd promised. She couldn't *un*promise.' Joanna stared at him excitedly. 'So do you think my father must be an Old Griffinian?'

'I don't know, but it sounds possible. She didn't say anything else about him at the time?'

'No. Not a thing. At least that gives me something to go on; I don't want to wait till April to meet him. It would be so much nicer to have become acquainted before then.'

Rafferty was disappointed that his attempt at further digging had got him nowhere. That Joanna's father was probably an old Griffinian was hardly news. But he wasn't done yet. He had an idea how he could find out who the father was. Or, rather, who he wasn't. It just required the girl's cooperation. He was thankful that Llewellyn hadn't come with him as he would be sure to disapprove of what Rafferty hoped to have the opportunity to do next.

NINE

'Are you sure my mother didn't say anything more about my father last time you spoke to her?' Joanna asked as he sipped his tea. 'I so want to know him. How can I wait all the months till April? It's light years away.' Breathlessly, she demanded, 'Are you sure mum didn't tell you who my father is? You're not keeping it from me, are you?'

'No, Joanna. Your mother didn't tell us. I'm sorry.'

Joanna's eyes filled with tears and Rafferty, under the attempt to comfort her, saw the answer to his dilemma and took it. It was unethical, of course, but cousin Nigel, the smooth-talking estate agent, wasn't the only one in the family who could ignore the ethics of a situation when it suited. He embraced the crying girl, patted her back and went, 'there, there.' Then, with some difficulty, he managed to hook the buttons on his jacket's sleeve around Joanne's long hair and in his apparent efforts to disengage them, he tugged several strands of hair, with their roots, from her head. He clutched them in his fist and hid his hand behind his back until he could put them in an evidence bag. 'Sorry, Miss,' he said. 'I hope I didn't hurt you?'

'No.' she said as she took the surprisingly clean tissue that Rafferty offered and wiped her eyes. 'I don't know why mum has to keep him such a secret. It's not as if I won't find out. Just wait till I'm eighteen. I'll be able to apply for a copy of my birth certificate then and she won't be able to keep it a secret any longer. I want to know something about him before my party, even if it's only his name.'

Aware that Joanna, destined to find a blank space where her father's name should be, was heading for another disappointment, he asked, 'Have you considered that your mother might have kept your father's identity a secret to save you from hurt?'

'No. Though maybe she's done it to save herself from embarrassment. Who knows? I might be the result of a tacky one-night stand, with a man whose name she didn't even remember. Maybe, in spite of her drunken promise to ask him to my party, she hasn't because she can't. Because she knows nothing about him.'

Rafferty, the not-so-innocent partner in a few tacky one-night stands of his own in his younger days, sprang to Alice Douglas's defence. 'I doubt that's true, or why would she, drunk or sober, feel able to make that promise? It's not as if your mother was promiscuous in her younger days, no one we've spoken to has said that. They've all said she was a studious girl and that they couldn't remember her dating anyone.'

'All the more reason then, I would have thought, for me to be the result of a one-night stand.'

Rafferty could no more argue with her logic than he was ever able to argue with Llewellyn's, so he just said, 'However you were conceived, your mother's brought you up, looked after you all these years. Surely that counts for something?'

Joanna didn't answer, but simply rose up from the settee in one swift movement and ran out of the room. He could hear her feet thumping on the stairs, leaving him in possession of the living room. Allowing himself a few indulgent seconds to feel pity for the girl, he carefully placed the hairs in an evidence bag and put it in his pocket. This was an opportunity to snoop that was too good to pass up.

But twenty minutes later, he had to admit defeat. He had found nothing of interest, nothing that might tell him the identity of Joanna's father. Doubtless Alice Douglas would keep such sensitive stuff in her bedroom, carefully locked away from her daughter's eyes. And even he didn't feel able to sneak up the stairs to find Alice's bedroom. He might just happen on Joanna's instead and then he'd have some explaining to do.

His attempt at playing a Dutch uncle clearly as much of a miserable failure as his hope of immediately discovering the identity of Joanna's father, Rafferty consoled himself that at least, with Joanna's hair and attached roots in an evidence bag, he was in with a chance of finding out who he *wasn't*. And even if it was later rather than sooner and the answer unofficial and inadmissible, the results might be far more revealing than that. Superintendent Bradley wouldn't like it, of course, but then he'd make sure he never found out. Rafferty, keen to get ahead in the case somehow, was sure that if he could find out the identity of Joanna's father for his own purposes, he would be able to get her mother to admit the truth without too much difficulty. A confident air and a knowing smile could work wonders.

Rafferty had arranged a time to meet the two student lodgers when he knew his ma wouldn't be in. She had her regular bingo and she went every week as if someone had wound her up and set her down in the right direction.

Luckily, her visiting cousins were out and the rooms they were using reasonably tidy. Unlikely as it seemed for students, Karen and Martin were on time and he hurriedly showed them round, urging them on in case the cousins returned before they'd finished. Young Karen's face seemed vaguely familiar, but he couldn't place her and when he asked her if they were acquainted, she opened her eyes wide and said, 'Oh no, Mr Rafferty. I don't think so.'

They loved Ma's two spare rooms and said they'd take them. He'd got copies of short-term tenancies on the internet after a lot of trouble and he'd cursed Llewellyn and Abra as he struggled. They'd both refused to have anything to do with his little plot. But he'd managed and eventually was able to print the agreements off.

He quickly filled in the youngsters' details. Money and rent books changed hands – he'd already asked for and received references. They were all set. He gave them keys and told them they could move in the day after Ma's American cousins were due to go home.

Rafferty, aware that the get-his-own-back joke on his ma had come full circle, rang her mobile once the two students had gone and he was back in his car, to let her know what he'd arranged, but all he got was voice mail. He'd try her later; he had plenty of time and he didn't want to leave a message.

To Rafferty's disappointment, Gary Sadiq was still in England, staying with relatives in Birmingham. He'd rather fancied a free trip to India – apart from anything else, the necessity of making the expensive journey would upset Superintendent Bradley, not to mention giving him a couple of days' break from Cyrus and his religious fervour. But it wasn't to be, so they battled their way up to Birmingham through the morning's rush hour and a stop-start journey under a still-blazing sun to discover precisely nothing. Though, of course, the semi in Birmingham wasn't Sadiq's home. Maybe, if he could persuade Bradley to fund the trip he might yet find out something to his advantage on the sub-continent. But Gary Sadiq, when they saw him, was very circumspect and answered Rafferty's questions as if his words were rationed. In any event, they got nothing useful out of him.

So far, none of the other reunees they'd spoken to had revealed as much as a morsel of new evidence to raise them up the suspects' list, so it was a reluctant Rafferty, on their return from Birmingham, that slouched his way along the corridor to report his failure to Bradley. He then slunk home to Abra and Cyrus, who was in even fuller voice than Bradley had been.

'Joe. Hi. How's your case going?' He didn't wait for Rafferty to answer, but continued blithely on. 'Ah was saying to Wendy, although Ah've bin praying for you. Of course Ah have, Ah thought a bit of *in*tense praying would be mighty helpful. So this evening, Ah'm going to retire early to ma room and spend some hours on ma knees. Me and God are on good terms, and Ah'm confident Ah'll get a positive response. Ah'll start now, if you don't mind. It seems rude to deprive you of ma company when Ah'm a guest in your home, but Ah know how much good it will do.'

Bemused, but grateful to have an evening free of Cyrusisms, Rafferty thanked his guest solemnly, kissed Abra and helped himself to a large Jameson's.

It was a few days later. Rafferty had rushed off Joanna Douglas's hair to the forensic laboratory requesting it be prioritised and he was pleased when Llewellyn told him they had some results in. Then Llewellyn frowned and looked at him from narrowed brown eyes. 'That's funny, they're from Joanna Douglas's hair. When did you obtain strands of her hair? You never mentioned you were doing so?'

'Didn't I? Must have slipped my mind.' He learned forward expectantly. 'And?'

'Adam Ainsley, not Giles Harmsworth, was the father of Ms Douglas's daughter.'

'Bingo! No wonder she fought shy of telling us the father's identity. We need to have another word with her.' Rafferty glanced at his watch. 'She'll still be at work. Why don't we beard her at the British Library? After first telling us she'd had an abortion, then denying Joanna was Ainsley's child and then outright refusing to supply us with the identity of who was the father, I don't think she's entitled to our consideration.'

Llewellyn was looking pensive. 'You know, you haven't said how you got that lock of Joanna Douglas's hair.'

'Haven't I?'

'She's a minor, so I hope you asked her mother's permission.'

'I got the hair, didn't I?'

'As long as it wasn't obtained in such a way as to render it inadmissible.'

'As if. You know me, Dafyd.'

'Yes. I do, don't I? That's the problem.'

'You want to trust more and suspect less, Dafyd. All that tense suspicion can make a person constipated.' He paused, then added airily, 'though it might be a good idea not to mention it to Alice Douglas. No point in complicating matters. I shouldn't be surprised if she hasn't forgotten giving her permission. You know how absentminded these academics can be.'

Llewellyn stared at him, sighed and shook his head, but he said nothing further, much to Rafferty's relief. He'd never been able to persuade the by-the-book Welshman that, sometimes, it was necessary to use a bit of unofficial sleight-of-hand to get answers.

Thankfully, the weather had broken and the day was cool with a threat of rain. Perhaps as well as successfully praying for a break in the case, Cyrus had also prayed for a break in the weather. Rafferty, after getting confirmation that Adam Ainsley was indeed the father of Alice's daughter, wasn't about to look the second gift horse in the mouth, so was duly grateful. He just hoped Cyrus wasn't too unbearably triumphant when he told him that his prayers had been answered.

The run to London was far more comfortable than it had been when they'd made the journey to Notting Hill to see Edward Diaz.

Leaving Llewellyn to find a place to park, Rafferty entered the British Library and went in search of Alice Douglas. He tracked her down to one of the offices.

She was surprised to see him and even more surprised when she discovered the purpose of his visit.

'How did you find out that Adam was Joanna's father? His name's not on her birth certificate.'

Her question put Rafferty in something of a quandary, given that he had obtained a sample of her daughter's hair illicitly – Bradley would go spare if he heard – so he temporised. 'Let's just say that, given your reticence about identifying the father, I put two and two together.' Airily, he added, 'I can, of course, obtain DNA evidence if you wish.'

She grimaced. 'What's the point? It would only delay things for a short while. Yes. All right, Adam was Joanna's father. Or rather, his was the seed that helped to create her. He certainly had no interest in being a father to her or in supporting me, as I soon discovered. He made quite clear that he didn't want to be burdened with a "brat", as he called our child. He was going places and he didn't want either me or his little bastard tagging along behind him.'

'You must have hated him for it.'

'I did for a time. But life moves on, Inspector. And I moved on with it. The stardust dropped from my eyes pretty quickly and I realized that he had only ever taken up with me because his pride was wounded when he found out that Sophie had cut a swathe through most of the class.'

'Surely he knew that all along? Wouldn't the other lads boast of it?'

'Perhaps, if it had been another boy. But Adam was the school's sporting hero as well as having the reputation as something of a bully; the combination encouraged Sophie's conquests to keep their bedpost notches to themselves.'

'One of them must have let it slip.'

'Yes. But I don't know which one. Adam never said. He refused to talk about it at all.' She cast a sudden, sharp look at Rafferty. 'And if you think I killed him because of something that happened when I was a foolish girl, you're mistaken.'

Poor off for suspects that had a really strong motive for wanting Ainsley dead, Rafferty was reluctant to let Alice Douglas go quite so easily. She was the only passable suspect he had. Unwanted pregnancies caused high feelings and blighted lives. Perhaps that was the case here. Unfortunately, Ms Douglas was quick to disabuse him of that theory.

'My pregnancy didn't ruin my hopes of a career, Inspector, as you can see. Nor did it breed resentment if that is what you were hoping.'

'I just like to check, Miss. It's called being thorough. A man has been murdered. He might not have been a very nice man, but he was entitled to enjoy his life.'

'Unlike the child I was expecting? The one he gave me money to abort?' When Rafferty didn't answer, she questioned his silence. 'I suppose, like Adam, you'd have wanted me to get rid of the child?'

Rafferty thought for a moment of his dead first wife, Angie, and the probably fake pregnancy that had forced him to the altar, then he said, 'No. I'm a Catholic, too, Ms Douglas. Disposing of a life as if it was so much rubbish is not something I could ever feel comfortable with.'

'Then you'll understand why I decided to keep my baby. Luckily, I had an inheritance from my grandmother and was able to employ a nanny to look after Joanna while I was at university.'

'Wouldn't your parents help?'

'No.'

The answer was abrupt and Rafferty was intrigued by it. 'Why not?'

With a marked degree of reluctance, after a few moments, she admitted, 'They were ashamed of me. They were always very strict churchgoers and thought I had let the family down. They refused to help. I learned to manage without them. You'd think they'd have given me some credit for not having the abortion that Sophie advised. They'd have been even more appalled if I'd done that.'

'Even with your grandmother's inheritance, it can't have been easy.'

'No. It wasn't. But now I have a lovely daughter who's about to go to university herself. She's bright and should do well. I'm very proud of her. Her existence is a great comfort to me. And I have Adam to thank for that. I had no reason to want to kill him, Inspector. None at all.'

'Not for your own sake, perhaps, but maybe you did for that of your daughter.'

She turned wary eyes on him. 'What do you mean?'

'I went to see Joanna the other day. She told me that you'd agreed to invite her father to her birthday party.'

Alice's lips tightened and she said faintly, 'She told you that?'

Rafferty nodded.

Alice sighed and stared down at her desk. 'You can't know how bitterly I regretted those few glasses of wine and that stupid promise.'

'But a promise is a promise.'

'Yes.

'So, did he say he'd go to the party?'

Alice raised her head and smiled at him. 'Yes. He might not have shown any interest in the baby in my womb, but a daughter all grown up and about to go to uni intrigued him. He said he'd be there.'

'Your daughter would have been pleased. Shame he's dead.'

'Yes.'

He bid her good day then and went in search of Llewellyn.

Llewellyn must have had trouble parking the car because he only entered the building just as Rafferty was leaving it. He told the Welshman what Alice Douglas had said.

'And do you believe her that Mr Ainsley agreed to attend his daughter's party?'

Rafferty shrugged. 'Why not? Ainsley was no longer a callow youth, but a grown man. He has no other children that we know of, so why wouldn't seeing his only child intrigue him?'

Showing an unlikely reluctance to let go of Rafferty's theory, Llewellyn said, 'To kill a man because he had rejected her child was about the best motive we had.'

'I know.' At least he didn't say the *only* motive, thought Rafferty.

'Though, I suppose, as you said before, she'd had seventeen years to pay him back if that had been her inclination. And it's not as if Ainsley wasn't high profile and easily found if she wanted to find him. She didn't need to wait for him to attend a reunion in order to kill him.'

'No.' Rafferty sighed. 'It would seem our best motive is smashed into smithereens.'

'Maybe something had happened more recently to bring a resurgence of any hatred she might have felt then?'

'Yes, but what?

For once, the intellectual Welshman had no answer.

Between one thing and another, Rafferty forgot all about ringing his ma again and advising her of the situation *via-a-vis* her new lodgers. He was only reminded of it when she got him on the phone several days later. He was in his office, wrestling with what remained of his assorted theories and trying to decide whether he should plump for one of them and pursue it for all he was worth when he was forced to acknowledge that wrestling with theories was easy as opposed to jousting words with his ma.

'Thanks for organizing my new lodgers, son. And thanks for telling me about it. It was good of you.'

Rafferty's mouth fell open in astonishment. How had she found out? Who could possibly have told her? The only ones who knew were Abra and Llewellyn. Had one of them . . .?

'Have you got nothing to say for yourself?'

Rafferty felt like a naughty schoolboy dragged in front of the headmaster. 'Sorry, Ma. I did try to ring you, but you didn't answer your mobile and I didn't want to leave a message.'

'And then you forgot. Never mind, I had other ways of finding out.'

That didn't surprise him. His ma had a more extensive network of spies than the Kremlin. 'I suppose it was Llewellyn?'

'You suppose wrong. Though I must say I'm surprised that Dafyd knew what you were up to and didn't stop you.'

'There's no need to have a go at him, Ma. He disapproved and tried to dissuade me.'

'Yes, well. That's as may be. I suppose your Abra knew as well?'

His guilty silence was all the answer she needed. He quickly changed the subject. 'So who told you?'

'Young Karen is an old school friend of Gemma. She knew you immediately when she rang you.'

'She never said.' Rafferty frowned. He had thought when he'd met her that there was something familiar about the girl, but he hadn't been able to put his finger on it. It didn't help that Gemma changed her friends like he changed his shirt. There was a regular parade of them through his sister, Maggie's front room.

'No. She thought it a bit odd that you should be taking in lodgers. It was clear you didn't recognize her, so she played along.' It was a well-known family joke that Rafferty was averse to having overnight guests. 'She told Gemma and Gemma told me. And when Karen told us the address where the rooms to rent were to be found, we soon worked out what you were up to.'

'So you knew all along?'

'Well, of course I did. You'll have to grow a lot older and plenty more canny before you manage to put something over on your mother, Joseph.'

'Are they very disappointed?'

'Who?'

'Well, Karen and Martin, of course. Who else?'

'And why would they be disappointed? Sure and they like the rooms and I like them. They were worried that I'd ruin your little plot and tell them I didn't want lodgers and for all my protestations to the contrary once I'd got used to the idea, they didn't believe me. So I've been keeping in contact with them. We've been getting on like a house on fire. It'll be a treat to have youngsters in the house again. It's done me a favour, you have, though you didn't know it. Oh and by the way. Where's my rent?'

A few minutes later he put the phone down and turned to see Llewellyn positively grinning at him. Rafferty realized it was the first time he'd seen the Welshman's teeth. They were as well ordered as the rest of him and gleamed with a positive relish.

'Seems like your mother surprised *you*, Joseph.'

'Yeah.' Rafferty ran his hand through his unruly auburn hair. He still hadn't found time to go to the barber's. 'You can say that again. She knew about my plan all along. Right from the start. You'd think she'd have said something.'

'She probably thinks the same of you.'

Rafferty nodded. Slowly a grin formed. 'Trust ma. I've never got the better of her yet. One day, though. One day.'

There was something niggling at Rafferty's brain, but he couldn't pin it down. What could it be? But for all that he kept pressing his mind, he came up with nothing. Of course, it didn't help that he couldn't look forward to peaceful evenings. Cyrus showed no sign of running out of either steam or bible quotations and he was still assailing Rafferty's eardrums every evening and giving him tea poisoning every morning.

He'd got so desperate that he'd even gone over to his ma, with his tail between his legs after his lodger stunt, to see if he couldn't talk her into an exchange of lodgers, but she wouldn't play ball. 'Sure and why should I discommode them all when they'll be packing to go home soon enough?'

'Because I ask it of you.'

His ma smiled that smile that, for all her love of the church, hinted at devilment – no soft touch, she, and said, 'Is it pricking your conscience what Cyrus has been doing, son? After all, you did promise Father Kelly before your wedding that you'd start going to church a bit more regularly. But he says he hasn't seen hide or hair of you.'

Frustrated, he burst out, 'Why did you have to go and land me with a religious maniac?', after she had ignored his own concerns and got a poke of her own in for good measure. 'You must have known what Cyrus is like and know very well that I don't go in for all that stuff.'

'Why do you think? Father Kelly and I both felt you needed a bit of religious encouragement to get you back to the Church.'

'You mean you *sicked* Cyrus on me deliberately? If you think

Cyrus's presence in my home has turned me back on to religion, you've got another think coming.'

'Sure and I thought it worth a try. So did Father Kelly. In fact, he was keener on the idea than I was, so if you want an argument you should go and find our holy priest. He positively encouraged me once he'd fully considered the state of your soul. You can explain your broken promise to him while you're at it.'

'God, Ma, you don't just take the biscuit. You take the whole bloody packet.'

'Don't swear, Joseph. You know it's a sin.'

'Sin be damned. Cyrus is enough to make God Himself into a sinner. The man never stops. It's a wonder Abra hasn't left me again.' Abra had left him and gone back to her own flat not long before their wedding and he'd despaired of getting her back. This reminder served to put his ma rather on the back foot.

'There's no need to exaggerate, Joseph. And Abra's still with you, isn't she?'

'She is for now. But that may be because she hasn't any longer got her own flat to swan off to. She'd probably invite herself over to Dafyd's place only his pernickety ways get on her nerves.'

'It's not much to ask to have you put up a couple of cousins. Cyrus has got a good heart.'

'He's got an even better mouth. It never stops.'

'You could learn something from him, son. You should listen to him instead of complaining and shutting your ears. He's a good, Christian soul and could teach you a lot.'

'Yes, a lot of things I've already been force-fed once in my life. I'm a grown man now, Ma, and able to make my own decision about religion.'

'Yes, the wrong one. You'll be sorry when the Day of Judgement comes.'

'God's all forgiving, Ma. He'll overlook my frailties.'

'Maybe He will and maybe He won't. But His forgiveness is less likely, I'm thinking, when you've already been given the gift of the truth and persist in rejecting it.'

He gave up then, let his ma win the argument and went home.

* * *

Rafferty woke the next morning to find that the hot weather had returned in the night. It was only seven o'clock, but already the heat was intense. He grabbed a quick shower, grabbed an even quicker tea for himself and Abra, and made for the car.

Thinking the cooler climes likely to persist, he hadn't listened to the weather forecast, and had parked the car in the drive, well away from any shading trees. Furnace-heat wasn't in it. He opened the door and all the windows and waited five minutes for things to cool down a bit before he climbed in and drove to the station.

Llewellyn looked as if he'd found a shady spot for his car; perhaps, the prudent Welshman had taken the precaution of listening to the forecast. Not a drop of sweat sullied his brow, which immediately put Rafferty in a bad mood. 'Tell me nothing else has come in.'

Llewellyn duly obliged. 'Nothing else has come in.'

Rafferty sighed. 'Has Bradley shown his face yet?'

'Yes, the superintendent looked in a little while ago. He asked after you.'

'I'll bet. What did you tell him?'

'I said you were out pursuing investigations.'

'Did he believe you?'

'He didn't intimate an opinion.'

'OK. If he didn't "intimate an opinion", what colour was he when he left?'

'Strawberry going on overripe tomato.'

'And I suppose he said I was to go up as soon as I came in?'

'I didn't like to say, seeing as you're so tetchy, but, yes, as a matter of fact, he did.'

'Stuff him. He can wait till I've finished my tea at least.' Rafferty slouched back in his executive chair and tried to cool off, mind and body. But this cooling off took a good ten minutes and it seemed the superintendent wasn't prepared to wait because all of a sudden, the door was thrust open and Bradley's bulk filled the open space.

'So you *are* in,' he accused. 'I said you were to come up immediately and what do I find but you taking your ease and swilling tea. Have you any interest in solving this case, Rafferty?'

Rafferty felt surly and didn't trouble to reply. But it seemed

Bradley's question had been a rhetorical one that didn't require an answer.

'Well, seeing as the mountain chose not to come to Mohammed so we could speak in private, I'll speak to you here. What's happening, Rafferty? The investigation seems to have come to a premature halt. Have you got anything to follow up on today, but?'

Still feeling surly and out of sorts, Rafferty just managed to update him re Sophie Diaz and her possible blackmail attempt on the killer and the identity of the father of Alice Douglas's daughter.

'And what about their women friends? Have you questioned them?

'That's next on the agenda.'

Bradley consulted his watch in an ostentatious manner. 'It's nigh on time you got yourself out and talked to them then. And workmates? What about them?'

'They're next on the agenda as well. At least, for Alice Douglas. Sophie Diaz was a lady of leisure.'

Fortunately, the super was a big man and the heat seemed to have sapped his energy, for he did nothing but shake his head in a disappointed manner and bark, 'See to it, then,' before he slammed his way out.

'It's all right for him,' Rafferty complained. 'He hasn't got to drive all over the country in this heat.'

'I thought you liked making inroads into his budget. Besides, it's scarcely "all over the country", sir. Alice Douglas only lives in Norwich, so I presume we're likely to find her friends there, too. At least we can question the neighbours until we're able to ascertain who her friends are. And Sophie Diaz lived in Notting Hill and although her friends are more scattered, there are several in the area, including her best friend, Amanda Shaw, who was out when I tried before. Mary Carmody and I whittled down to three the list of Mrs Diaz's friends to whom you might like to speak yourself. We could easily fit them all in this morning if we make a move and go back to Norwich this afternoon.'

'Only if you put your foot down.'

This, of course, was anathema to the cautious Welshman, who believed slow and steady was the best driving course to take.

'Come on, then.' Reluctantly, Rafferty stood up and grabbed his jacket. 'Let's go. We'll take Notting Hill and surrounds first. You've checked Sophie Diaz's book for her friends' addresses?'

Llewellyn nodded. 'The London ones are all within reasonable proximity of Notting Hill, though it might pay us to park the car and take the tube.'

The thought of a hot, sweaty underground stuffed with jabbering foreign tourists and their bruising backpacks did nothing to improve Rafferty's humour.

TEN

Adam Ainsley's agent had his office in London, in Fulham, and Rafferty had thought he might as well kill another bird with the same stone and save himself an extra, sweaty journey, so he had got Llewellyn to arrange a meeting with him for forty-five minutes before they were due to meet Sophie Diaz's girlfriends.

The agent, Michael Gottlieb, was a lean man, who seemed to exude energy. He pumped Rafferty's and Llewellyn's hands enthusiastically in both of his and invited them to sit down. Gottlieb's walls were covered with posed photographs of his clients. Rafferty recognised most of them; it seemed Gottlieb specialized in sporting stars. He recognized Ainsley's portrait shot off to one side on the wall behind the desk. He was posed in a rugby jersey, with a ball clutched to his chest and his head forward as if he was just about to score a try.

'Tell me about Adam,' Rafferty invited. 'As his agent, you must have known him better than most.'

Gottlieb nodded. 'You could say that. Agents are the first to get it in the neck when things aren't going well.'

'And they weren't going well for Mr Ainsley?'

'No. He was what is known in agents' circles as a difficult client. Whatever you'd do for him, he always wanted more. More money, more appearances, more this, more that. I tried to get him set up on the speaking circuit, but he was hopeless. Never did his homework and didn't do jokes. The bookings soon petered out. He blamed me, he blamed his speaking agency; everyone but himself.'

'You sound as if you didn't like him.'

'You suppose right. In fact, I was about to send him our letter advising him to find a new agent. Life's too short to put up with the Adam Ainsleys of this world.'

Rafferty was silent for a few moments. Then he said, 'You mentioned money. Do I take it that Mr Ainsley wasn't earning as much as he thought he should?'

'Yes. His income had dropped drastically from his playing days. He wasn't suited to the cult of celebrity. Oh, he liked the limelight, all right, but he had little to say once the spotlight was on him. It was a case of 'I'm Adam Ainsley, the rugby star' and that was it. He could never even pretend an interest in the person he was speaking to.'

Rafferty asked Gottlieb about the unexplained thousand pounds a month that was being paid into Ainsley's bank account, but the agent knew nothing of it.

'Perhaps he'd applied to one of the sporting charities for a pension?'

Rafferty shook his head. 'No. It's not a BACs transfer or a cheque. It's in cash and the money is just paid in over the counter, according to the bank manager.'

'Mmm, you're right. That's not the way a sporting charity, or any other charity, would behave. Perhaps it's one of his wealthier admirers.'

'Is that likely?'

'Oh yes. Some people can be quite fanatical about their sport, quite obsessive about their favourite players. Sometimes you have them donating cash gifts to an ex-player down on his luck.'

Rafferty wished they did the same for coppers. 'And you think that's what might have happened in this case?'

'It's only an idea. Adam could be arrogant with fans, not always willing to sign autographs and so on. He thought it should be enough that his fans see him without expecting him to put himself to any trouble, so a generous fan is less likely in his case.'

'I see. And you can't think of anyone else who might pay a grand a month into his bank account?'

Gottlieb shook his head. 'No. Sorry, Inspector.'

Rafferty had had high hopes of Ainsley's agent, but it had proved a false hope. He stood up and handed Gottlieb one of his cards. 'In case you should think of something. Thanks for your help.'

Next on the agenda were Sophie Diaz's girlfriends. Rafferty had high hopes of these, too, but, after his failure to gain any useful information from Ainsley's agent, his hopes faded a bit.

Rather than see each one individually, Rafferty had asked that they meet them all together and they had elected to meet in a Notting Hill pub. Rafferty was nothing loath.

Sophie Diaz's girlfriends turned out to be a disparate bunch, to Rafferty's surprise. He had expected 'ladies who lunch', but Kate Carrow, Sue Daniels and Amanda Shaw were all suited and stilettoed suitable for high-flying careers, which, as it turned out, was what they had. Kate Carrow was a barrister, Sue Daniels worked for an investment bank and Amanda Shaw was a General Practitioner.

'How did you meet?' Rafferty asked, once the introductions and career checks were over. 'Were you all at Griffin School?'

'God, no,' Kate told him. 'I was a grammar school girl, one of the few that successive governments have left alone. Sue was the same, though Amanda was at Griffin with Sophie.'

'You didn't attend the reunion?' Rafferty asked, curious why not.

'No. I try to avoid such functions. As a GP, I find people have a tendency to buttonhole me about their ailments.' Amanda smiled and said, 'My mechanic told me he has the same problem, but with cars. In social situations, he's apparently always having people trying to describe the funny noises coming from their engines, expecting him to diagnose it for free. I get the funny pains. Both are equally tedious, I'm sure. But you wanted to know how we met Sophie. You already know about me. As for Sue and Kate, they're both on the boards of the same charity of which Sophie was also a member. I hadn't seen Sophie since school, but as a doctor, I tend to get involved with several local charities, which is how we met up again. We each found we liked the grown-up version of the other and we both knew Kate and Sue. We all got on and gradually we got around to having the occasional lunch or dinner. Apart from Sophie, we are all busy people, so they didn't happen too often, but they were often enough to keep us apprised of each other's doings.'

'And what was Sophie doing? Did she mention whether she was doing anything likely to get her killed?'

Amanda, who seemed to be the women's spokesperson, said, 'She rang me while she was at the Griffin reunion. Updated me on everyone I could remember and said she had something she wanted to talk to me about.'

'Really?' Rafferty sat forward. 'And what was it?'

Amanda shrugged. 'I don't know. She wouldn't go into it over the phone. She said she needed to meet me for a girly lunch. I couldn't make it that week, so we arranged it for this Friday.'

And Sophie Diaz had died before she could confide in her friend. Rafferty chewed his lip in frustration, then asked Amanda, 'Did she ever speak of Adam Ainsley? The boy she had an affair with during that last summer term at Griffin?'

She shook her head and said, 'She would always clam up when I tried to get her to speak about first loves. Even after all these years, that Adam Ainsley had dumped her was still a painful subject for her. She had always said that he was the love of her life, but beyond that, she would say nothing at all. I learned to leave it alone after a while.'

Stymied on that front, he tried from another angle. 'What was Mrs Diaz like?'

'Sophie was a people person,' Kate told him.

'What do you mean by that, exactly?'

'Just that she liked people and was interested in what made them tick.' She grinned. 'In other words, she was incredibly nosy.'

'God, yes,' Sue Daniels interrupted. 'If she sniffed out a bit of gossip, she wasn't happy until she had got to the bottom of it.'

'And did she sniff out any hot gossip while she attended the reunion?' he asked Amanda.

'No. Nothing worth killing her for, anyway. Or nothing that she told me about.'

'Did she do anything with all this gossip?'

'Oh, no,' they all agreed. 'She wasn't spiteful or malicious. She just liked to know things. And the who and the what and the why.'

Rafferty was thoughtful after he and Llewellyn had said goodbye to Sophie's friends. 'Sounds more and more like she knew someone's secret. More and more like she knew Ainsley's killer.'

For once, Llewellyn didn't disagree with his theory. But he did say, 'I wonder why, if so, she never spoke privately to us and confided this dangerous knowledge.'

'You heard her friends. Sophie Diaz not only liked to know the who and the what. She also liked to know the *why*. It seems likely that her curiosity overcame her good sense and she asked the killer why they had done it before she could confide in us. Foolish. Very foolish.'

By now it was after one and the sun blazed down ever more unbearably from an azure sky. Rafferty, between the failure of his 'Cool Man' and his sweaty hair that clung to his neck and forehead, felt as messy as a melted ice cream. 'Lunch!' he said in tones that brooked no argument. Even though the sticky heat had taken away his appetite, he knew he had to keep his strength up, if only to have the stamina for Superintendent Bradley and Cyrus.

'Yes, but where? Any pub with a garden will be bursting at the seams.'

Rafferty was amused to discover that if he'd trained his teetotal sergeant up in nothing else, at least he'd managed to get him to see pubs as natural lunch venues. But today pubs weren't on the cards; as Llewellyn had said, they'd be overflowing with perspiring customers. But he had learned a trick from Cyrus and had decided to follow his example. 'I thought we'd buy a couple of cans, some sandwiches and retire to Kensington Gardens. Find a shady tree to sit under and watch the world go by.'

'A *picnic*?' Llewellyn's face was a study. 'In the middle of a murder investigation?'

'And what better time to have one? A bit of fresh air will blow the cobwebs away.'

Llewellyn still looked affronted. 'You want me to sit on the grass? In this suit?'

'Well stand up, then. It's all the same to me.' Llewellyn's Beau Brummell instincts notwithstanding, the idea of a picnic was becoming more appealing by the second. Rafferty spotted a handy wine merchant's with a sandwich bar two doors down and set off in pursuit of refreshment. Llewellyn trailed reluctantly after him.

Refreshments purchased, Rafferty headed up Notting Hill Gate towards Bayswater and the park and his appointment with some shade.

Lolling under a sturdy oak tree, Rafferty finished the last of his ham rolls and pulled the tag on his second can of bitter. He gave a contented sigh. Bradley, Cyrus, the murders, all seemed a million miles away. All around them tourists were sitting, taking their ease and enjoying the occasional tiny breeze. Some energetic Australians were playing football and Rafferty found himself watching them desultorily until the ball headed in his direction and he had to duck. 'Colonials,' he muttered before pouring the rest of his beer down his throat. 'Time we weren't here,' he said.

Llewellyn – who had deigned to sit on the grass after all – got up and made a big show of dusting himself down.

Rafferty ignored him and headed for the nearest exit.

From Sophie Diaz's friends they had learned that Sophie had been quite a nosy woman who liked to know things. They didn't intimate that she liked to make use of whatever knowledge she came by, just that she liked to have it. Even so, such a habit was a nasty one and could be dangerous, as it seemed likely to have been in this case, especially if, short of funds for the first time in her life, she had decided to turn knowledge to profit.

Rafferty, with some of the steam taken out of his temper and his body by their shady sojourn under the oak tree, relented and let Llewellyn take the wheel for the drive to Norwich, which slowed things down somewhat. But Rafferty was happy to stay out of the office for the rest of the day and out of Bradley's hair, so he just sat back and let Llewellyn concentrate on the road ahead.

Even with Llewellyn at the wheel, they made reasonable time and were parked up and knocking on the first neighbour's door by three twenty.

A woman of about thirty, carrying a grizzling child, answered the door.

Rafferty explained their business and she invited them in.

She led them to the kitchen and asked them to sit down at the pine table. Rafferty tried to question her, his questions punctuated by more and ever louder grizzles, which turned to full-blown wails.

'He's tired. He doesn't like this heat. Let me put him down for an hour. I won't be a minute.' She disappeared. The grizzles retreated till they were barely audible.

'Thank God for that,' he said. 'Do you think she'll make us some tea? I'm parched.'

The woman, whose name was Mrs O'Neill, came back, said, 'He won't settle,' and immediately put the kettle on. Rafferty brightened.

She turned back to them while she was waiting for the kettle to boil. 'You said you wanted to ask me questions about Alice next door?'

'That's right. You know there was a murder – two murders now – while she was attending a reunion at her old school?'

'Yes. She mentioned it. It shocked me.'

'Did she happen to mention anything that happened during the reunion?'

'Like what?'

Rafferty didn't know. He was going through a straw-clutching exercise. 'Anything. Anything at all. Was there anything about her daughter?'

'Joanna?' She shook her head. 'No. I don't think so. I can't think of anything, though Joanna did talk about the birthday party she's having next spring and that she expected her father to be there. Poor girl didn't know him. It's very sad.'

Rafferty hadn't liked to break the news to Joanna that she wouldn't be meeting her father in April or any other time. He had decided to leave that to Alice Douglas. Maybe, seeing as she wasn't after all to meet her father, Alice might relent early and let the girl know his identity now. She was entitled to know where she came from. Rafferty believed that was a basic right that was denied to too many people in these permissive days.

Foiled from gathering any worthwhile information, Rafferty sat back and gazed hopefully at the now boiling kettle. After the stifling journey from London, he was as dry as a desert gulch and would welcome some hot, sweet tea.

Mrs O'Neill picked up the kettle, but she didn't reach for the mugs that were hanging on hooks under the top cupboard, but for a Pyrex basin that was sitting on the side. She half-filled this with boiling water, took a milk-filled baby's bottle from the fridge and plonked it in the basin. The grizzler's lunch. 'A bit old-fashioned,' she commented, seeing Rafferty watching her. 'But I don't like using the microwave to heat my baby's milk. Just in case.'

Rafferty just stopped himself exclaiming in disappointment. He was about to ask for tea outright, when Llewellyn forestalled him, said, 'thank you for your help, Mrs O'Neill,' and stood up, leaving Rafferty with no option but to do likewise.

'She'd have made us tea,' Rafferty grumped when they were outside. 'If you'd only have waited. I was just about to ask.'

'I know. Why do you think I called a halt to the interview when I did? You shouldn't importune gratis drinks from the public. It's unprofessional.'

'Unprofessional my arse! I only wanted a cup of tea, not the favour of her boudoir.'

'Even so.'

Rafferty scowled. Sometimes he wondered just which of them was the senior officer. Llewellyn could take things on himself at times. It was a trait he would be wise to squash, although he had a sneaking feeling that he had left such squashing too late. After thirteen completed murder investigations together, he suspected they were both now set in their ways.

But Llewellyn had his good points, as he was reminded, when the Welshman said, 'I noticed a workman's café on the corner. Perhaps we could stop there?'

'Why not?' Better still, such a café was likely to serve a decent mug of tea: big and strong and sweet as a nut. 'Lead me to this oasis, McDaff.'

It was while Rafferty was sipping his tea that something occurred to him. He was mulling over the day's events when he sat up straight and said, 'Dafyd.' He waited till he had got the Welshman's attention and then said, "I've got it! It was something Alice Douglas's daughter said. The neighbour reminded me. She said that she hoped to meet her father at her eighteenth birthday party. Maybe I was wrong to dismiss it. What if Alice invited Adam to their daughter's birthday party, sure he'd be interested in a grown up daughter when he hadn't been in a foetus? Why wouldn't she think that? I thought the same. But what if he'd rejected his child all over again? It could have brought a resurgence of the hate that Alice had felt for him when she was young and had just found out she was pregnant and that as a father he was not only unwilling but deadly.'

'You could be on to something, sir.'

Rafferty grinned. 'I could, couldn't I?'

'Or, rather, you could, if it wasn't for the means of death. The use of hemlock indicates premeditation, not the sudden upsurge of a hate originally felt nearly two decades ago.'

Rafferty, hot in pursuit of his latest theory, ignored him. 'Joanna told me that she intended to obtain her birth certificate when she came of age. I imagine, in one of her teenage strops, she told her mother the same thing. We both know she would have found no information about her father there. Do you reckon she would have continued to try to find out her father's identity? Maybe she'd succeed? Joanna struck me as the tenacious sort. Maybe she would have turned her attention then to Griffin School and her mother's old schoolmates. Admittedly Paxton wouldn't have given her any information about them, but he might well have agreed to pass a letter on to each of them. Alice would know her own daughter, would know she wouldn't give up. Must have worried that one of her old school mates would remember something that would give the girl a lead. Maybe she and Adam weren't quite as discreet in their little romance as she'd thought.' He was on a roll now and said, 'what if Sophie Diaz not only saw her slip the hemlock into Ainsley's lunch, but also knew about Alice's affair with him?'

Rafferty finished the rest of his tea in a hurry and said, 'Come on. We'll speak to the rest of Alice's neighbours while we wait.'

'While we wait for what?' Llewellyn asked as he finished his own tea.

'While we wait for Alice to return home from work, of course.'

'And do you think she's likely to admit that Mr Ainsley refused her eighteenth birthday party invitation? She's already told you the opposite once.'

'I don't know, do I? But it can't hurt to ask. Even if it's just to see her reaction.'

They drove back to Alice Douglas's street and interviewed her other neighbours to no avail. By the time they'd spoken to the last one, it was gone five, so they elected to wait in the car for Alice to come home.

'My daughter wouldn't find out the name of her father because none of my classmates know it.' Alice Douglas stared hard at him, as if daring him to refute her statement.

'Are you sure about that?' Rafferty asked. 'I wonder if Sophie Diaz guessed. Adam had just dumped her. Maybe she spied on him, looking for a way to get even? Maybe she even tackled you about it.'

He could see that he had hit a nerve and he pushed it – hard. 'Is that why she had to die, too? Was she someone else who knew your secret? Someone else who knew your shame that you'd allowed yourself to be used by Adam? Did she see you put the hemlock in Adam's lunch and tell you that she'd seen you do it?'

Alice Douglas had gone deathly pale, but she spoke up spiritedly enough. 'You're talking nonsense, Inspector. Sophie didn't see me doing anything murderous because I didn't kill Adam. And, for the record, Sophie didn't know that Adam was the father of my baby. Nobody knew.'

'Except Adam himself?'

His accusation of murder had made her incautious. Now she said, 'What makes you think he'd admit to paternity to our daughter even if someone put her on the right track? The thought of what he might lose if Joanna pursued him would be enough to have him running scared. He'd have admitted nothing and left Joanna to chase him through the courts if she had the money, which a few discreet checks would soon tell him she didn't have.'

'Maybe not. But what a lot of unwelcome pressure that would put on you. You told me last time we spoke that Adam had agreed to attend your daughter's eighteenth birthday party, but, from what you say now, it seems you lied to me. Again.'

She didn't answer. Rafferty knew, from the way her face had closed up tight, that he would get no more out of her. He'd have charged her there and then, but for the fact that everything was still only circumstantial. He wanted more.

By the time they'd had more tea at the local working men's café and driven back to Elmhurst, it was gone seven. At least the nine-to-five Bradley should have long since gone home.

And so it proved, as they turned into the Bacon Lane car park, Rafferty saw that Bradley's Lexus wasn't in its bay. He felt quite light-hearted as he got out of the car and climbed the stairs to their second floor office.

'Let's see if you can't beat your own record in getting these interviews typed up,' Rafferty said. 'Then we can go home. It seems to have been a long day. While you do that, I'll get the tea.'

Rafferty sauntered along to the canteen and ordered up two brews, which he brought back to the office, even managing to retain most of the hot liquid rather than slopping it over the beige carpet in the corridor.

'Here we are, Daff. Mother's helper rather than Mother's ruin.' He put Llewellyn's mug down beside the industrious Welshman and sat down behind his desk to sip his own tea. He returned to his latest theory.

'Alice Douglas has already lied to us twice: once about having an abortion and again, when she denied that Ainsley was the father. Lying would seem to be something of a habit for her. It strikes me as only too likely that she'd have lied to us a third time, especially given her response when we questioned her about what was Adam's reaction when he discovered for the first time that he was a daddy.

'Maybe what actually happened, was that he'd told her she could take her birthday invitation and shove it. This second rejection, something she must have already suspected would happen even before she attended the reunion, would answer the premeditation question,' he added quickly before Llewellyn could interrupt with more theory-quashing, 'could well give Alice Douglas a motive for killing him. A planned killing for an expected second rebuff of her much-loved child.'

Rafferty, satisfied he'd successfully resolved his clever Welsh sergeant's previous objections to his theory, sat back and sipped his tea thoughtfully, well pleased with himself. 'It'll be something to tell Bradley in the morning. He wanted a breakthrough. This could be it.'

ELEVEN

Rafferty, well chuffed, not only with his latest theory, but also the fact that Llewellyn had been unable to come up with any more arguments against it, was even able to welcome Cyrus's religious benediction when he got home. In fact he was overcome with benevolence and hail-fellow-well-metitis and he found himself saying:

'And God bless you, too, Cy. What say you, me, and Louis take a stroll to the corner and the nearest pub? It's about time we had a boys' night out and gave the girls a break. They can download a slushy DVD and enjoy it without us yobboes criticising from the stalls. They serve bar meals in the evening.' He hadn't actually been in this particular pub before as they'd only moved house a month or so ago, but he'd seen the sign about all-day meals outside and had kept it in mind.

Cyrus broke into jowly beams at this invitation. 'Why, Joe, that's a mighty fine idea.'

Whether it was the thought of a cold pint on a hot day or a whole new audience for his proselytizing, that brought the beaming smile, Rafferty didn't know. Nor did he care. If it was the beer, at least Cyrus would have something else other than words to occupy his gob and if it was the latter, Rafferty's ears would get a well-deserved rest. It promised to be a perfect evening.

After Rafferty had had a quick shower to remove the day's accumulated grime, they strolled the couple of hundred yards to the pub, the Horse and Groom. It was another sticky evening and they were all three in shirtsleeves, but apart from the heat, it was a pleasant stroll, through tree-lined streets with a prepon derance of flower pots and hanging baskets. They'd moved a bit up-market now he and Abra had been able to pool their financial resources after the sale of their respective flats and Rafferty smiled to see the streets were free of the youths who had assembled outside his old flat. It was a much nicer area, with teenage sons who didn't get involved in gangs and teenage daughters who didn't fall pregnant as career alternatives. Still, whatever its advantages, he missed the close location to the centre of town that his old flat had had and its ease of access to the shops and other facilities. Now, unless he fancied a longish walk, he had to get the car out every time he needed to visit the centre.

There weren't many customers in the pub and Rafferty hoped that wasn't an indication that the landlord didn't pay his beer the attention it deserved. But then he spotted the Adnams sign on a beer pump and immediately brightened as he recognized a connoisseur. It was good to know that the only pub within easy walking distance sold his favourite beer. He turned to Cyrus and asked him what he'd like to drink.

'I'll trust to your judgement, Joe and have what you're having.'

Louis said the same.

'OK. That's three pints of Adnam's Bitter, please Miss,' Rafferty said to the barmaid. 'Let's sit down,' he said when the barmaid had pulled three pints.

He took a long pull of his bitter, let out an even longer breath and sat back.

Louis wandered off to play the one-armed bandit. Cyrus watched him for a little while as if checking that he was settled there for a bit, then he said, 'Ah'm glad to have this opportunity to talk to you, Joe.'

'Oh?' Rafferty thought Cyrus had done way too much talking to him already.

'Yes. Ah've been meaning to speak to you, but the raht tahm never seemed to present itself.'

'It's here now. Say what's on your mind.' Rafferty thought he had half an idea already – Cyrus couldn't be said to be backward in coming forward – and so it proved.

Cyrus placed his bitter neatly on its beer mat and sat back against the upholstered bench. 'Ah thought you and Abra didn't want me – us – in your home. And Ah'm sorry about that. Ah've heard that the British are reserved.'

Cyrus was being tactful. Unwelcoming, he meant and Rafferty knew he had a point. Guiltily, he asked, 'what made you think that?'

'The way Abra goes to bed most nights with a sick headache. The way you work till all hours or if you get home early, disappear upstairs to your room. Are we in the way, Joe? Would you like us to leave?' Before Rafferty could say anything or come up with a bunch of words that hung together as an explanation, Cyrus went on. 'Ah can see that your mother probably foisted us on you.' He smiled. 'Ah've known Kitty for many more years than you have, Joe – we keep in touch with regular letters – so Ah know how determined she can be. And she was dead set on this family reunion. Dead set on saving us money.

'Most of us are seniors, without big bucks, so she said she'd arrange to put us up for nothing. It was mighty good of her. Mighty good of you and Abra. But we'll understand if you'd prefer to be on your own.'

Cyrus was speaking from the heart and Rafferty thought he deserved nothing less in return. 'You're right. Ma did foist you on us. But you must remember that Abra and I are just back from our honeymoon. We're trying for a baby.' It was only a little white lie as they probably *would* be trying for a baby in the not too distant future. 'That's why we keep disappearing.'

'A baby! My, that's neat.' Cyrus's beam reappeared. It threatened to split his dentures. 'Another generation of Raffertys? So that's why. And I thought we were unwelcome.'

'Not at all, Cyrus. Tell you what, we'll put the trying for a baby on the back burner for the rest of your stay. How does that suit you?'

'You don't have to do that, Joe. Not now Ah know. You can make as many babies as you like.'

'One's enough. For now, anyway.'

'Ah'm glad we've had this little chat. Wendy'll be relieved when Ah tell her.'

Still feeling guilty that he hadn't been more gracious about their unwanted lodgers, Rafferty changed the subject.'How do you like the beer?'

'It's different.' Cyrus tried another sip. 'But it's growing on me.'

'Adnams Brewery is an old-fashioned firm. Their beers are still handcrafted, not like the gassy stuff the big chains produce. They do a number of different seasonal beers you can try while you're here.'

Rafferty was amazed, but relieved, when Cyrus kept off the subject of religion for the rest of the evening – perhaps Wendy's promise to 'have a word with him' had finally borne fruit? – and he just chatted about the sports teams he supported, which gave Rafferty the opportunity to speak about the recent football World Cup and how their two teams had fared. The United States and England had been paired for their first match and the States had got a lucky equalizer when the England goalkeeper had fluffed a catch. But although Cyrus listened patiently, it soon became clear that he didn't really follow football – or soccer, as he referred to it. It wasn't that big a sport in America. Cyrus followed baseball and was a keen fan of the Atlanta Braves and the team's pitchers Tommy Hanson and Dontrelle Willis.

'Dontrelle's a black guy –' Rafferty caught a whiff of Southern prejudice – 'but he's not bad, though Hanson's my favourite.'

Rafferty, who knew nothing about baseball and cared less, said, 'Drink up, Cyrus and I'll get us another.'

'It's ma turn. Put your cash back in your pocket.' Cyrus picked up the glasses. 'What was that beer called again?'

Rafferty told him and watched as Cyrus walked up to the bar and attracted the barmaid's eye. For all his preaching, Rafferty guessed that Cyrus was something of a barfly; he certainly seemed to feel at home in the pub and with its rituals. Rafferty noticed he must have even told the barmaid to 'have one yourself', because a radiant smile appeared on her rather sullen face.

Maybe he'd try getting Cyrus on a pub-crawl next. A few drinks out of the house seemed to make him more human, more of a normal bloke or 'regular guy' as he supposed Cyrus would phrase it.

By the next day, Rafferty's confidence in his latest theory had suffered the usual overnight trauma and doubts – after all they still had no evidence against Alice Douglas other than the circumstantial – and he decreed that he and Llewellyn would have another chat to Adam Ainsley's ex-wives. 'I reckon there's more they could tell us if properly prompted. A lot more.'

Llewellyn nodded. 'You're probably right.'

'Though, this time, I think we'll go together as I'm not too confident in your technique with embittered exes.'

'I learned more from my ex-Mrs Ainsley than you did from yours,' Llewellyn pointed out.

'Maybe. Maybe not. Though, if you did, that might be down to Mary Carmody's mother hen approach. But there was something the first ex said that stuck in my mind. She said that Ainsley "wasn't the marrying kind". I want to find out – given that he was enthusiastic enough about the state of matrimony to get hitched twice – what she meant by that.'

'It could be just that he wasn't faithful.'

'True. But maybe there was something else as well.'

'Like what?'

'I don't know, do I? Just . . . something. Trust me. I'm a policeman. There's something else there. I'm sure of it. I just didn't pick up on it at the time.'

The first ex-Mrs Ainsley was surprised to see them again, but she welcomed them into her home and made them tea.

Once she'd sat down and served the tea, Rafferty explained the reason for their second visit. 'You said last time I spoke to you that your ex-husband "wasn't the marrying kind". What did you mean by that?'

Stella Ainsley didn't reply immediately. Instead she sipped her tea and gave Rafferty an assessing glance. Then, as if coming to a decision, she set her tea down on the glass coffee table and sat back, her slender figure holding the posture of the ex-model that he guessed she might have been; a trophy wife for the sporting star.

'I've no proof of what I'm about to say. I just feel it here.' She placed a hand on her stomach. 'It's a gut thing.'

Rafferty nodded. He knew all about gut feelings; he'd had plenty of them in his career and most of them had turned out to be right. 'Go on, please.'

She told them that she had, for much of their marriage, suspected that her husband was gay. 'As I said, I've no proof but a wife's natural instincts. He was never that keen on sex and used sporting tiredness or minor injuries as excuses. I think he was in denial,' she said, 'which was one reason why he went in for all the sports, all the women. I got the impression that he thought he could alter his inclinations if he tried hard enough.'

'It must have been difficult for you,' Rafferty said as he thought to himself, 'Gay?' and wondered what other areas of investigation this might point up.

'Yes. Though, for much of our marriage, I was in denial as well. And when he left me for another *woman*, I was more astonished than upset. It was rather a relief to put an end to the charade, actually. For all his courage on the rugby field he didn't have the balls to come out, any more than I had the courage to challenge him and even after his second marriage, I often read about him in the gossip columns squiring other women. In the end I thought it was all rather sad.'

They left the first ex-Mrs Ainsley and headed for the home of the second, Annabel. She was another model-girl type, with slender hips and a flat chest that cried out for surgical enhancement. He should certainly have wondered a bit about Ainsley's seeming preference for the boyish figure, the first ex-Mrs Ainsley's ample bosom notwithstanding. Rafferty thought it more than likely that she had had her cup size increased after her divorce as a confidence booster. What the second Mrs Ainsley had to tell them was even more revelatory than her boyish figure.

After they were settled in another good-sized house with more superior furnishings – Rafferty couldn't help wondering how much his two divorces had cost the dead man – and more tea, he got straight to the point.

'Why did you and Adam split up?'

She didn't even pause to give him an assessing glance, but just told him bluntly, 'I told you before that I found him in bed with a neighbour. What I didn't say was that that neighbour was a young lad.'

Rafferty nodded. Here was confirmation of what Stella Ainsley had told them. It seemed her natural instincts had been spot on. 'Why didn't you tell us this before? Surely you could see that it might be relevant to your ex-husband's murder?'

'I suppose so. But how would *you* like to admit that your wife preferred other women?'

Rafferty, while flattered that she had clearly put him down as the macho sort, had to admit that she had a point. God, what *would* he do if he'd found Abra in bed with another woman? He'd go spare. He'd be mortified, humiliated, shamed. It would be bad enough having to suffer the family's concern, but once it did the rounds of the cop shop . . . He felt his insides shrivel at the mere thought, so he said, 'I can understand why you preferred not to mention it. But, now you have, why do you think he did it? In your bed, I mean. Do you think he wanted you to find him? Do you think he had decided to use it as a shock method of bringing your marriage to an end?'

'No. I don't think that. I don't think he'd have ever done that for fear of what I'd do and say and who I'd say it to. I was supposed to be away for the weekend, so he must have felt perfectly safe. But on the way to my parents' house, I felt ill and drove home. That's when I caught them. Adam was terrified I'd go to the papers.'

'You said this boy was a neighbour. Can you give us his name?'

'I can, as it happens. His name was David Paxton. As I said, he and his family used to be our neighbours.'

'Paxton?' Llewellyn chimed in. 'Any relation to Jeremy Paxton, the headmaster of Griffin School?'

'Yes. David was his nephew. Or rather his half nephew, the son of Jeremy's half brother – or maybe that should be a quarter-nephew? If there is such a thing. Anyway, I don't think they knew one another well. Jeremy wasn't a regular visitor. He didn't get on that well with his half brother. Neither did young David. I got the impression that he often felt like a changeling in his own family. I know his mother was worried about him.'

Rafferty had picked up on the past tense and now he asked, '*Was* Jeremy's half nephew?'

'David's dead. He killed himself. Just after Christmas last year. After Adam dumped him. Poor boy, he didn't realize that Adam wasn't worth killing himself over. Adam only ever really loved Adam.'

Rafferty needed to think. It looked like they now had evidence to suspect Jeremy Paxton. Though surely the suicide of a half or quarter, nephew, barely a blood relative at all, was a bit tenuous? And another thing – how could Jeremy Paxton have introduced the poison into Ainsley's food? Even if he'd wanted to, was another question altogether. He had sat several tables away, at the High Table and wouldn't have had easy access to Ainsley's food.

Although it seemed that his new evidence was sliding away even more quickly than it had been gathered in, he still needed to speak to Paxton. Only trouble was he was in Portugal. And he didn't know where. But for now, he could interview the dead boy's parents. They must be able to tell him something. He got the address from Annabel Ainsley and Llewellyn noted it down. Once that was done, Rafferty couldn't get out of the second ex-Mrs Ainsley's home quickly enough, keen as a hound after the scent of a fox to get on this latest trail.

Once in the car, Llewellyn glanced at him and said, 'It is intriguing, isn't it? Given his own well-kept and potentially career-damaging secret, I really can't imagine Adam Ainsley attempting to blackmail someone else about their guilty secret.'

'No. I think you're right. That would be a bit too close to home for comfort. He would have thought, there but for the grace of God . . .'

Llewellyn nodded.

For once they were in agreement. Rafferty grinned to himself at the realization. Though he'd still like to know where that grand a month came from.

On the way to the Paxtons' home, Rafferty borrowed Llewellyn's notebook, found the telephone number of Ainsley's agent and rang it.

Gottlieb's secretary quickly put him through and after re-introducing himself and reminding him of the reason he was calling, Rafferty asked, 'Did you know Ainsley was gay?'

Gottlieb said yes. 'Give him his due, he told me when we first signed the contract. It wasn't a problem. He was never a painted queen. He dressed conservatively and did his best to project a macho image. He was tall and broad shouldered, which helped. I've often wondered if his inability to give more of himself when he did appearances wasn't partly down to the fact that he was gay. He was always scared someone would out him and choose one of his public appearances at which to do it. You remember there was a spate of outings of celebrities some years ago?'

'Why didn't he come out and save himself the worry?'

'Because he hadn't come out to himself. He hated that side of his nature and did his best to sublimate it in the image that all his photos proclaimed: that of a manly professional, who'd made his name in the most physical of sports.'

It was much the same as what Ainsley's first wife had told them. All in all, Ainsley's homosexuality seemed to have been a very well kept secret. Had someone outside the charmed circle of his agent and his ex-wives found out about it? But that wouldn't explain the thousand pounds that had found its way into Ainsley's bank account every month. The money would be going *out* of the account, not into it if Ainsley was a victim of blackmail. And if he was why was he also a murder victim? Blackmailers didn't often kill their victims. Why lose a nice little earner? It was a puzzle and he didn't like puzzles. Not ones that he seemed unable to solve, anyway. It was some consolation that his clever sergeant seemed unable to solve it, either.

Mr and Mrs Paxton were a middle-class couple in their forties and lived in some splendour in an Edwardian mansion in Chichester. Although they were perfectly polite, Rafferty sensed a reserve in the couple, as if they would prefer not to talk about their dead son and he set his secret weapon, the ever so diplomatic Llewellyn on them. Dafyd Llewellyn, unlike Rafferty, tended to think before he spoke. He chose his words with care and wouldn't offend anyone's sensibilities. But then, with his Methodist minister father's insistence on his young son accompanying him to break news of death, he'd had plenty of practice. And even though he fought shy of such situations, the Welshman had a delicate way of handling potentially awkward encounters.

Rafferty watched in admiration as the Welshman sidled up to the subject of their son's suicide and the reason for it.

'The loss of a child is one of the worst forms of bereavement. I can't imagine how you must have felt. Still feel.'

Mrs Paxton thawed at this show of sensitivity. 'Yes. What made it worse, was that David was an only child. I could only have the one,' she told them. 'I was too upset to delve too deeply into the reasons for my son's suicide for some time. I didn't even read the note David left. It was still too raw, too painful. I suppose, also, that I was scared he'd blame me. I just handed it to the first policeman who showed up and left it at that. It was only later, when the worst of my grief had passed, that I started wanting to know more. To know *why*. David had everything to live for. Or so I thought. My son was bright, attractive, popular. He excelled at sports and loved his rugby. What possible reason could he have for killing himself?'

Rafferty, beyond curious, wanting some quick answers, forgot his resolve to leave the questioning to Llewellyn and interrupted to ask, 'You mentioned his rugby. Was that how he met Adam Ainsley?'

Mrs Paxton looked sharply at him, then she admitted, 'Yes. Yes, it was. If only he hadn't, my son would still be alive.' She cast a single, tight-lipped glance in her husband's direction, then looked down at her tautly clenched hands.

Rafferty forbore from suggesting that their gay son, in denial and vulnerable, could have suffered just as much from an association with another mature and predatory gay male. Professional sport had its share of such men – and women – as any other walk of life.

'David hero-worshipped him. He'd followed the local rugby team from the time he was a young boy. He went to every home game. He joined the supporters' group and played for the youth team.' Mrs Paxton's lips tightened some more and her next words, when they came, were bitter. 'He was easy prey. My son had always been a too sensitive boy. That was why my husband suggested he take up rugby again after he left school.'

'I thought it would toughen him up,' Mr Paxton said and although he was a no-nonsense Northerner, the defensive note in his voice was evident. Rafferty guessed the question had been gone over more than once between the couple. He could imagine that Paxton would have little time for his son's sensitivity. Between his doomed first gay love affair and someone of his father's character, David Paxton must have felt he had no one to turn to. No wonder Mrs Paxton seemed to blame her husband for the boy's death.

'Did he confide in you at all?' Llewellyn picked up the questioning again. 'I know teenagers often find it impossible to talk to their parents about sex. It's such a difficult age. Such a difficult subject.'

Mr Paxton answered when his wife hesitated. 'No. He didn't confide in us. I don't think he confided in anyone.'

Mrs Paxton interrupted. 'He was a boy for bottling up his feelings. If only he'd felt able to tell us he was gay . . . I would have understood, accepted it. He was my son, after all.'

Mrs Paxton's fingers gripped ever more tightly together and Rafferty wondered, would she, though? Would he? David had been an only child, the only chance of them having grandchildren. Would they have been so accepting with that in view? Perhaps their son had sensed the opposite, which would explain why he had told them nothing about being gay, nothing about his abortive first venture into homosexual love with Ainsley.

Mrs Paxton seemed to have read his mind because she said, 'He as good as killed my son. He seduced him. Made him fall in love with him. Then he dropped him. Just like that. David put it all in his suicide note.'

'Really? I don't remember reading anything about it.' But if what his mother said was true, the boy, after his earlier hero-worship, must have been even more vulnerable when Adam Ainsley had befriended him, seduced him, even more devastated when he had chucked him.

'You wouldn't. The Coroner suppressed the contents of my son's letter. Though whether he did it for my sake or his own is debatable. He was another rugby fan,' she added flatly. 'Another of Ainsley's admirers. If it wasn't for the thought of the journalists we'd have camping on the doorstep, I'd give the news to the media myself.'

'Not much point now,' said her husband. 'Not with Ainsley dead. And I wouldn't want David's name bandied all over the press. Nor mine neither. Do you think I could bear the pity?'

His wife shot him a sharp glance, looked as if she was about to say something, then deflated as if she recognized the pointlessness of it, the pointlessness of everything now her only child was gone.

'Why did Ainsley drop him?' Rafferty asked her. 'Do you know?'

'Because he was still denying his own homosexuality – that's what Annabel, his wife, told me. Poor Annabel. Did you know she found my son in bed with her husband? In her own bed?'

'She told us.'

'He dated woman after woman trying to chase away his real desires. My husband told me he saw him out on the town several times with other women, though he never told me at the time. A male solidarity thing, I suppose. Anyway, Ainsley could never succeed in subduing his real preferences. His wife told me all about it and about how she'd found my son and Ainsley in bed together. This was some months after David's death and the inquest.' Mrs Paxton knitted her hands together. Her husband, beside her on the sofa, began to put his arm around her, but she edged away. 'I've tried to be charitable. Adam Ainsley, the great sportsman, the great rugby hero, had never admitted his homosexuality. He'd never come out. He was as much in denial as David. If he'd the courage of his convictions, he wouldn't have dropped David so abruptly, so cruelly, to my son's devastation. And death.'

Rafferty got behind the wheel of the car, but he didn't turn the ignition. 'Given this latest information, we really need to speak to Jeremy Paxton. Shame the bugger's on holiday in Portugal.'

'What are you thinking?' Llewellyn asked. 'Are you thinking that it's likely that Mr Paxton would want revenge for his half nephew's suicide? I have to say, I don't agree. After all, his relationship with the boy was fractional. And from what Mrs Paxton said, he can have hardly known David.'

'I know.' Llewellyn was expressing the thoughts that had already occurred to him, debunking his latest theory before he'd even mentioned it. 'But it's got to be investigated, even if it comes to nothing. Maybe his neighbours would know exactly where in Portugal he went?'

But in the event, they didn't have to talk to Jeremy Paxton's neighbours. Because when they drove round to their street, they saw Paxton's car on his driveway and the man himself, sponge in hand, in the process of washing it.

'Mr Paxton. I thought you were on holiday?'

'I was, Inspector. But my wife convinced me that I should come home. She felt it wasn't right for us to be sunning ourselves on a Portuguese beach when two people have died at my school. It's the sort of thing the newspapers would jump on, quoting term fees and making us sound heartless. All bad publicity for the school, and the governors wouldn't be happy. So . . . how is the investigation going?'

'We have various avenues that we're pursuing,' Rafferty told him without going into any of them. Paxton didn't pick him up on it. 'I'm glad to see you because I wanted to talk to you.'

'Oh yes?'

'Yes. I understand that Adam Ainsley could be held morally responsible for the suicide of your young half nephew, David. I wondered how you felt about that?'

'How I felt about it?' Paxton looked thoughtful. 'I know of his suicide, of course. It's tragic. But I scarcely knew the boy.'

He sounded somewhat wistful. Rafferty had learned that

Jeremy Paxton was the father of three daughters; perhaps he would have liked to consider young David a proxy son but hadn't received any encouragement from his half brother.

'I gather from my half brother that David was sports mad. Anyway, he was nearly always out when I visited, which wasn't often. Perhaps a couple of times a year. My half brother and I are not close.'

'I see. So you didn't want revenge for David's untimely death?'

'Revenge? I'm a Christian, Inspector. I turn the other cheek.' He smiled. 'Or I try to.'

'There are many Christians who don't.'

'I'm not one of them. Besides, there was no reason for me to want to kill Adam. As I said, I hardly knew my half nephew and there was no way I could have poisoned Ainsley.'

That was true enough. Which left them with Alice Douglas. Rafferty bid Jeremy Paxton good day and returned to the office. There, he sat and watched Llewellyn while he typed up the reports of their latest interviews, updated Bradley and then went home.

TWELVE

The previous night, after their late return from the restaurant meal Abra had organized to celebrate Angel and Louis's fortieth anniversary, Rafferty had told her about his and Cyrus's conversation in the pub. It was another humid night and they'd thrown the covers off along with their clothes.

Rafferty lay, admiring the curve of Abra's thigh, as she admitted she felt as embarrassed as he did that Cyrus and the others had picked up on their less than wholehearted welcome.

'Let's try, then, during the remainder of their stay, to make sure they have a good time,' she said. 'I suppose I have been a bit mean. And he's a nice enough bloke. He just talks too much.'

'I can take Cyrus out again, give you a break. I thought a pub-crawl with my brothers? Maybe I'll even invite Nigel.' Nigel Blythe, or 'Jerry Kelly', the moniker his proud parents had bestowed on him and which had met with a distinct lack of approval from their upwardly mobile, estate agent son, was a cousin on his mother's side. It was about time he shared some of the familial burden of this reunion. He'd got away scot-free so far.

'Why not? Just don't get Cyrus too sozzled. I doubt Wendy would like it.'

'I wouldn't worry. The way he's been going at my whiskey, he can handle his drink better than I can.'

'Even so. And as for you, you said you told Cyrus you were hoping to be a daddy. We don't want your sperm getting so pie-eyed that they lose their sense of direction.'

'That's the excuse I made to Cyrus for our less than sociable behaviour. I didn't mean that we had to go in for having a kid for real.'

Abra put her head on one side, threw her plait back over her shoulder and said thoughtfully, 'Maybe we should. Let's face it, you're no spring chicken, Joe. You don't want to be on a Zimmer frame by the time any kid of ours hits eighteen.'

'Succinct, as always, my sweet.'

'Someone's got to call a spade a bloody shovel. So what do you say? Should we get the ball rolling in the sprog department?'

Rafferty was thoughtful for a few moments, then he nodded. 'Perhaps we'd better. After all, when you think about it, I'm not the only one in this marriage that's ageing at a rate of knots. Your eggs are getting on for three decades old.'

'Delicately put.'

'I thought so. But if we are going in for having a kid, for God's sake don't tell Ma. She'll give us the third degree for sure if she knows. If you don't get pregnant immediately she'll think I'm doing something wrong.'

Abra laughed. 'She might be right. You know how uptight you are about sex.'

'I'm not uptight,' Rafferty defended himself. 'I just prefer to do it within marriage. Blame religion. With all his exhortations against fornication on a Sunday when I was a kid, Father Kelly's brainwashed me. I have fewer inhibitions about getting down and dirty now we're married.'

'Mmm. I noticed. But I don't see why we shouldn't tell your ma. Between us we should sort you out if you show yourself lacking in the baby-making department. And if you don't get me up the duff immediately, we can always consult Father Kelly,' she teased. 'He's got a direct line to God, after all.'

'So has Cyrus, and I don't intend to consult him, either. No. Please, Abra. Let's keep it just between ourselves for now. Well, between you, me and Cyrus.' He just hoped Cyrus could keep a secret. He must impress on him that the impregnating of Abra was at a delicate stage and not to be bandied abroad. Particularly not to Ma.

Rafferty glanced across at Abra as she lay beside him. He put a possessive hand on her flat belly and said, 'right, Mrs Rafferty, what say we get down to making Ma and Father Kelly a Catholic baby they can dote on?'

'You romantic old thing, you. I thought you'd never ask.'

The next morning, Rafferty was juggling the statements of the most likely possibilities amongst the suspects. 'We ought to get ourselves along to the rugby club. Talk to the manager and players and hangers-on. Never know, we might learn something to our advantage.'

Llewellyn nodded, said, 'I'll slot it in.'

Five minutes later, Rafferty murmured, 'Alice Douglas. She's still odds-on favourite for me. What about you?'

'I should think so,' said Llewellyn. 'Her life can't have been easy as a single mother without support. At the very least, she must have held a grudge against Mr Ainsley. Like most men in these situations, he got away lightly.'

'Mmm.' Rafferty thought of his own prospective fatherhood and felt quite smug. It would put him one up on Llewellyn, who, in spite of marrying before him, had yet to produce a child. He wondered if his intellectual blue stocking cousin, Maureen, wanted kids at all or whether she preferred to concentrate on her career. He must ask Ma. She'd be sure to know. There again, perhaps that wasn't a good idea. Get Ma started on the subject of kids and God knew where it might end up, although he had a pretty good idea.

'So we've got Alice Douglas, who could have killed Adam for her daughter's sake; we've got Jeremy Paxton doing the deed for the sake of his dead half nephew; we've got Gary Sadiq, who could have done ditto for his pride's sake after Adam gave him the silent treatment and made racist comments about him. Then we've got Sebastian Kennedy and Simon

Fairweather – their pride must also have taken a few dents after Ainsley bullied them at school.' Rafferty, with a younger brother who had suffered in a similar way, knew how long the victim could brood about it. How much they wanted closure of the sort that would give them back their pride. 'What about Victoria Watson and Giles Harmsworth? Has the team come up with anything more on them yet?'

'Not so far.'

'Tell them to keep trying. Shame Ainsley's two ex-wives weren't at the reunion lunch that day. We might have been able to make a good case against one of them.'

'Perhaps we should stick to the possibles, rather than the *im*possibles.'

'Just doing a bit of wistful musing, that's all.'

'Or theorising from the basis of no evidence at all. I thought you already had all the theories you could handle.'

'You take all the fun out of police work, Dafyd, did I ever tell you that?'

'Once or twice.'

'Right.' He paused for thought. Llewellyn's comment had touched a raw spot, and tentatively, he added, 'Maybe we've been concentrating our forces a little too narrowly. I think we should have another bash at Victoria Watson, Sebastian Kennedy, Simon Fairweather, Gary Sadiq and Giles Harmsworth. You'd better check whether Sadiq is still in the country or if he's returned home to India.'

'We've interviewed them all twice and failed to discover good enough reasons why they would want Mr Ainsley dead.'

'I know that. Doesn't mean there isn't one. Perhaps it's just a bit less obvious than Alice Douglas's bastard daughter or Paxton's dead half nephew. Get on that phone and set up the interviews, Daff. Let's not give Bradley the opportunity to think we're slacking. Besides, it'll be good to spend a bit more of his precious budget.'

The first of the interviews that Llewellyn had set up was for the following morning, at the rugby club, but they learned little more there than they had elsewhere, only that Ainsley had been a selfish player, with no close friends, and with a tendency to hog the ball rather than pass it, which they could have surmised from their other evidence.

Next came their interview with Sebastian Kennedy, the idle trust-fund reunee. Kennedy lived in a bachelor pad in Hampstead, one of a group of twelve apartments. The apartment was even swankier than that of the upwardly mobile cousin Nigel, with marble floors and leather-covered walls, which displayed pictures of more naked ladies than Rafferty had ever seen in his life. He didn't know where to look.

Kennedy must have noticed his dilemma because he laughed. 'No need to get a Catholic conscience about looking at my pretty ladies, Inspector. I don't. The female form is to be enjoyed, whatever those spoilsport priests thought back when we were both young. Can I get you a drink? You look like a whiskey man to me.'

'I won't, thank you, sir.' It was barely ten o'clock in the morning and a bit early even for an Irishman, though it seemed Kennedy didn't agree, as he poured himself a large one.

'I can't offer you coffee. My machine's on the blink. Besides, I never learned how to use it and my man is out.'

His *man*! Rafferty was astonished to learn that anyone still had a *man*. It was like something out of P G Wodehouse. It sounded odd coming from the lips of Sebastian Kennedy, the school rebel, who had also, as the computer had revealed, been a member of the communist party in his youth. Marches and sit-ins and protests seemed to have occupied most of his time after he'd left school, when he wasn't swanning off to the continent to spend his inherited wealth. 'That's all right, sir. I'm not thirsty.'

'I am.' So saying, he downed his first whiskey and poured himself a second, even larger, one. 'And what's with the "sir"? I thought we were drinking buddies. Call me Seb, why don't you? Everyone does. Or Sebastian at least.'

'Right. Sebastian. My sergeant here will have explained why we've come when he rang.'

'He said you're covering your backs.' Rafferty darted a sharp glance at Llewellyn and Kennedy laughed again. All in all, he seemed to be finding their visit a laugh a minute. 'Oh not in so many words, but I got the drift. You've been through the most likely possibilities – whoever they are – and now you're starting on the less likely because you haven't been able to make a case against the former. Does that about sum it up?'

It did. A bit too well for Rafferty's liking. He gave a strained smile and said, 'If we could sit down?'

'Of course.' Kennedy waved an expansive arm. 'Feel free. My home is your home and all that.'

They sat and Rafferty gave Llewellyn the nod to begin the questioning.

'We've made one or two discoveries since we last spoke to you, Mr Kennedy,' said Llewellyn, who didn't believe in getting too chummy with potential suspects. Not for the more formal Llewellyn the casual use of Sebastian. 'One of them was that Mr Ainsley was homosexual.' Nor did he go in for the modern 'gay' euphemism, preferring the more formal version.

'Queer? Really? It seems I had a narrow escape then.'

'You mean Mr Ainsley never made advances to you?'

'Advances?' Kennedy laughed. 'How very maiden aunt of you, Sergeant. No, he never made "advances" to me. I'd have known where to kick him if he had.'

'Even though you admit that he bullied you?'

'I was a scrawny kid. An easy victim. The sort Ainsley liked. But he never tried it on with me. Perhaps he just didn't fancy me? Besides, he was too busy working his way through the girls at school to have time for me. He must have been horrified that his macho school sporting hero self was queer. No wonder he tried to work it off by shagging as many girls as he could. What a result.'

Kennedy sounded triumphant rather than surprised to learn of Ainsley's real sexual orientation. And though Ainsley hadn't, apparently, forced him into sex, or rather, that was what he *claimed*, Rafferty reminded himself that he had still been a victim of Ainsley's bullying. He wondered how far that had gone and how frequently it had happened. It could still be a motive for wanting to kill Ainsley. Meeting him after so many years, it seemed likely that it would have come into the forefront of his mind where he'd brooded on it. Maybe he had thought it was time he got his own back? But if that was so, Kennedy didn't seem worried or remotely repentant. He was positively chirpy during the rest of the interview and showed no sign of the Catholic conscience that would have bedevilled Rafferty if he'd been guilty of the mortal sin of murder. But then, he'd shown no evidence of finding unmarried sex a guilt-trip, either. But Rafferty thought he could tag the carefree Sebastian as amoral. If he'd been poor he'd have probably turned to crime. It was only his wealth that protected him from a seamier lifestyle. Some people had it every which way.

The drive to Cambridge to see Victoria 'Brains' Watson was smooth, with no traffic hiccups and they arrived just before lunch. Ms Watson saw them in her college rooms. She didn't invite them to eat with her at High Table. Which was a shame, as Rafferty was starving and he'd heard how well college professors did for themselves at table, particularly the older, richer colleges like Corpus Christi. He supposed he'd have to settle for sandwiches from the nearest baker's.

Victoria Watson's rooms were utilitarian in the extreme, with none of the lavish ostentation for which Rafferty had heard Oxbridge professors were renowned. He and Llewellyn perched on a wooden settle by the window and Victoria Watson sat on an equally uncomfortable looking upright chair opposite them. She seemed to have no interest in clothes, either, because she wore another of the shapeless jumpers that he remembered from her reunion visit to Griffin School. Her hair was a short, no-nonsense style with a few more hints of grey than there had been since their last meeting. Once again, she wore no make-up. She reminded Rafferty of his blue-stocking cousin, Maureen, though at least, if *her* hair was greying, Maureen took the trouble to apply a concealing dye.

'I still have no idea who killed Adam,' she told them once the courtesies were gone through. 'Though, given the way he had always carried on, I would have thought a jealous husband might have fitted the bill. Poison rules that out, of course.'

'Unless he was carrying on with the wife or girlfriend of one of his table-mates.' Or one of their husbands, was Rafferty's irreverent thought. He didn't share it with Victoria Watson, who seemed to be unaware of Adam Ainsley's proclivities.

'I've no idea. I don't listen to gossip. I find all this casual modern-day infidelity very tedious and pay it no heed. I was never what you'd call a people person, so I didn't notice if there were any subtle nuances during the day he died. I've always preferred the certainties of science to the illogicality of man. And before you ask, I don't know who murdered Sophie Diaz, either.'

Altogether, for a woman with the school nickname 'Brains', she didn't seem to know much, was Rafferty's thought.

Although, given the sparsely furnished room and the baggy jumpers, he could well believe that Victoria Watson's interest was solely invested in her love of science, rather than people or things.

'Tell me, Ms Watson – did you like Adam Ainsley?'

'Like him?' She wrinkled her forehead as if such an emotion was a strange concept. She shrugged. 'I never had that much to do with him. Even at school, we were in different streams and had different interests. His were always in sport and mine in science. I had no reason to hate him, if that's what you mean.'

As their investigations so far had told them. But perhaps, like Alice Douglas and Sophie Diaz, the young Victoria had experienced the usual uncontrollable adolescent urges? Perhaps she had had a crush on a pop star? Or the school sporting hero? If she had been solely concentrated on her schoolwork before that, she could have been knocked sideways by the intensity of first love. How would she have felt if she'd been rebuffed or worse, used and discarded? Was it possible that she, again, like Alice, had fallen pregnant? Or, like Sophie, had thought she had? The teenage, science-mad Victoria was unlikely to have been on the contraceptive pill, so a pregnancy was a possibility. And somehow, he thought that Victoria would have dealt with an unwanted pregnancy in a pragmatic way and without confiding in anyone, unlike Alice Douglas who had succumbed to the usual love affair between mother and foetus and gone in for the messy, difficult business of single parenthood. He decided to ask her outright and see how she responded.

'Have you ever had children, Ms Watson? Or contemplated the possibility of them?'

'Children? What an odd question. What has it to do with Adam's death? Or Sophie's, for that matter?'

Nothing, as far as he knew, was the answer. But he wondered why she was prevaricating by turning the questions back on him. 'You'd be surprised at the avenues that have to be explored during a murder investigation. We never know where we might get to in the way of evidence. But if you could answer the question.'

'Very well. No, I've never had children. I haven't contemplated them much, either. I seem to lack maternal feelings, though I admit, once or twice, lately, I've wondered how any children of mine might have turned out. But such thoughts haven't had me rushing to an Italian gynaecologist for help in family planning. There was never any room for children in my life.'

'Not even when you were a teenager?'

'God, no. I'm not like Alice, Inspector. I could never have contemplated being a single mother. I doubt I'd have achieved my professorship here if I had.'

'You knew she had a child?'

'I only found out at the reunion. Adam told me. Though why Alice should tell him is beyond me.' Rafferty smiled to himself. Here was another indicator that Alice Douglas had talked to Ainsley about their daughter. 'Sophie had mentioned that Alice had fallen pregnant at the end of that last year, but she'd thought she'd had an abortion. She hadn't seen her since.'

'And you didn't think to mention it to us?'

Victoria looked puzzled. 'Mention it to you? Why would I? Again, what has Alice's pregnancy to do with these murders?'

Perhaps a lot. Perhaps nothing. Rafferty wished he knew. He also wished he knew for certain how Ainsley had taken Alice's news that he had a grown up daughter. He must have got the shock of his life when Alice told him that, rather than having their child aborted as he'd expected and paid for, she was shortly to celebrate her majority.

On the drive back to Elmhurst from Cambridge, Rafferty decreed that they would stop for a proper lunch, rather than just buying sandwiches. 'Though we're not stopping here in the city. Cambridge is such a tourist trap, it's going to have tourist-type prices that Bradley will be sure to kick off about. Even I'm not foolish enough to goad a bull elephant too far.'

'I always found the prices reasonable when I was a poor student here,' Llewellyn said.

'That was a long time ago,' Rafferty told him. 'Times change. Anyway, I'm not lining the pockets of some profit-hungry landlord here in the city. I'd rather do it a few miles down the road, where the profit might be a bit leaner.' As he hated the food at roadside so-called services, he pulled off the main drag and made for one of the villages sprinkled like confetti around the city and found a pretty, but unpretentious pub within a few minutes' drive. The food on the menu sounded simple but wholesome and Rafferty plumped for rump steak with all the trimmings.

Llewellyn, who went for the cheaper, salad, option, said, 'I thought you were paying heed to Superintendent Bradley's strictures on spending?'

Rafferty sniffed. 'I am. But I don't see any point in going too far. Where's the fun in that?'

The food was plentiful when it came and they both tucked in with a will. Rafferty had staved off the worst of his hunger when something struck him. 'Mrs Paxton,' he said. 'Did you notice that she kept referring to David as 'my' son, rather than 'our' son?'

'Did she?' Llewellyn frowned in recollection. 'Yes, she did, didn't she?

'I got the distinct impression that she blamed her husband for the boy's death, at least in part, even if only subconsciously. Thinking about it now, she certainly seemed to. If their son was the sensitive type she said he was, he and his father must have been chalk and cheese. She must have wondered if David would have confided in his father about his troubles if he'd been a different man. It would be only human to do so.'

He stabbed a particularly succulent morsel of steak and forked it into his mouth. It was wonderfully tender and the pepper sauce was particularly flavoursome, way better than their local steak house's offerings.

'Could be,' said Llewellyn as he finished his meal, pushed his plate aside and reached for his mineral water. 'Tragic situation.'

'Mmm. Do you want that last bread roll?'

Llewellyn shook his head.

The Welshman had made appointments for the next day with the other three reunees: Gary Sadiq, Giles Harmsworth and Simon Fairweather; Rafferty mentioned these appointments and with regard to the latter, said, 'I've always wanted to see where the Home Office mandarins work. I've heard they do even better for themselves than Cambridge professors.'

'I've heard the same. In fact, some time ago, I remember watching a documentary about the Home Office as part of a series on the great offices of state.'

'Shucks. I missed it. Good was it?'

'Revelatory.'

Llewellyn said no more, but just sipped his water.

'Well come on, then,' said Rafferty. 'Aren't you going to tell me all the gory details?'

'I didn't think you were interested.'

'I'm interested. I'm interested. So, what amazing revelations did the programme make?'

Llewellyn took his time. He wiped his mouth with his napkin and smiled. 'Amongst other things that the mandarins are every bit as tricksy as we've always thought them to be.'

Rafferty pulled a face. 'Tell me something I don't know,' he said. 'They have to deal with politicians every day, who are an even more tricksy bunch. So, is that it? The full Monty?'

'As the mandarins would say. I couldn't possibly comment. Have you finished?' he asked as Rafferty downed the remains of his pint of Adnams. 'Shall we go?'

Whatever Llewellyn had discovered from watching his documentary, there was nothing revelatory awaiting them on their return to the station. Apart from Superintendent Bradley who they met on the stairs and who revealed that he wasn't happy with the progress of the case.

Tell me something new, was Rafferty's thought, before he forced a polite, subordinate's smile to his face and asked with what aspects, in particular, his beloved leader wasn't happy.

'All of it, Rafferty. You're jigging up and down the country, eating up the miles and doing the very devil of damage to my budget and what are you achieving?'

Nothing much would have been the honest response. But Rafferty had learned in the course of his career under Bradley that honesty was definitely not the best policy when it came to the super. The truth needed to be painted over, gilded, decorated with scented roses, anything but delivered plain and unvarnished. So now he said, 'We've several worthwhile leads. I've already told you about Alice Douglas having an illegitimate daughter by Adam Ainsley and—'

'Yes, yes. As you say, you've already told me about it. What else have you found out?'

'That Adam Ainsley was gay and—'

'Gay. Gay. Don't use such euphemisms with me, Rafferty.' Bradley was another blunt Northerner, in the mould of Stephen Paxton and, like Abra, was inclined to call a spade a bloody shovel, though, of course, since the advent of the politically correct brigade into positions of high office, Bradley had tempered his language and could, when he had to, use euphemisms and long-winded circumlocutions with the best of them.

'As I said, Ainsley was gay. Homosexual. And could be said to be morally responsible for a young lad's death.' He went on to explain about the connection to David and Jeremy Paxton.

'A bit tenuous, isn't it, but?' The super repeated what he himself had earlier thought. 'The dead boy wasn't even a proper nephew, which, I agree, might have given Paxton a motive.' Bradley drew himself up and his red face developed a scarlet tinge. 'And that's it? The sum total of your discoveries?'

Unwillingly, Rafferty admitted that it was.

'And you're off out on your excursions again tomorrow?'

Rafferty made the second admission. It earned him a scowl. To hear Bradley talk, you'd think their trips out were to Disneyland.

'Eating costly meals on expenses, I suppose?'

'Even lowly sergeants and inspectors have to eat, sir. We try to be as economical as we can.' Which was an out and out lie. Wait till he sees the bill from the pub for rump steak, was his next thought.

After another few minutes' interrogation, Bradley took himself and his congested visage off back to his first floor lair, grumbling as he went. And Rafferty headed off to their office to see if there was anything interesting awaiting their return.

But all they found were several notes left earlier by Bradley, each one more Abra-succinct than the previous one.

THIRTEEN

Rafferty's brothers, Mickey and Patrick Sean, were more than willing to accompany Cyrus, Louis and himself on a pub-crawl. To his surprise, so was Nigel.

'I've been working hard,' his cousin told Rafferty when he rang him, 'selling houses and making money. It can get tiring.' Poor diddums, thought Rafferty. He doubted his cousin knew what a hard day's work was. 'I could do with a good night out.'

'I thought you were out most nights of the week.'

'I am, dear boy,' Nigel said in his usual patronising manner. 'But those nights are with assorted lady friends or clients. Doesn't do in either case to drink more than a couple. With the clients it's necessary to keep one's wits about one and with the ladies it's necessary to keep one's pecker up rather than suffering from brewer's droop. I've a reputation to maintain with both parties.'

'If you say so. Anyway, we're meeting at the Horse and Groom, the pub near me, at eight this evening. You can meet Cyrus and Louis at last. I'll see you there.'

'The Horse and Groom at eight. Got it.'

Rafferty put the phone down and got back to work. Some of the latest witness statements from the other ninety-odd reunees who didn't feature on their suspect list made interesting reading. All of human nature was there: the gossip, the spite, the remembered grievances, the petty tale telling. It was all manna from heaven to a policeman. Or it might have been earlier in the case when he was looking for lines of inquiry. But now, the trouble was, spite and gossip was all it was, not evidence. None of it gave him a fresh lead. Or at least not a conclusive one.

'Listen to this,' he said to Llewellyn. 'This statement's from a man called Robin Nash. "Adam was over-fond of the younger boys. He was well known for it, though neither the teachers nor the lovesick girls seemed to suspect a thing. His favourite spot for these meetings was the sports pavilion, which conveniently housed a rubber mat for the high jump, so he could do his canoodling in cushioned comfort". Shame he didn't confide that little snippet the first time we talked to him.

'Here's another one. From a woman this time. "Adam might have been popular with the other sports-mad boys at school, but to the non-sporty boys and the plain or dumpy girls, he could be nasty. He specialized in making up cruel nicknames. I won't tell you what he called me. It still hurts".'

'Mmm. We've already discovered that Mr Ainsley could be an unpleasant chap, though it's interesting that he wasn't so bashful about "coming out" with boys younger than himself. It seems to have been a particularly well-kept secret. I've certainly never read any speculation about his sexuality in the newspapers.'

'Nor me. I suppose his victims were only too keen to keep any assault quiet. They'll all be adults by now, with careers, wives, children. Imagine the embarrassment if it got out that you had been a victim of rape, if, like most of the pupils, you have a high-powered job.'

'Nobody actually says that Mr Ainsley went that far.'

'They don't say that he didn't, either. And if they've kept quiet about it for all these years, I can't see them confiding in a police officer during a murder investigation. Imagine what they'd go through when it came to court. Though perhaps we ought to find out the identities of a few of his likely victims. It's all just speculation and rumour so far. Who knows? Alice Douglas might not be the only one amongst our suspects with whom Ainsley had a secret affair that ended badly.'

These other witness statements were still trickling in as people returned from holidays and business trips. Most were innocuous, the typical statement given by those who didn't want any involvement with the police, which contained plenty of 'I don't knows' and 'I can't remembers', certainly far more cautious and circumspect than the original statements when news of the murder had shocked them into unwise indiscretions.

'We'll pass the more juicy statements on to Superintendent Bradley. Let him pick the flies out of them.' Rafferty put the paperwork on one side and said, 'Has the team re-interviewed everyone who was present at the school reunion now?'

'Yes. That's the last of them, though there are one or two that Gerry Hanks thought might be worth questioning again.'

'Probably scrappy scrabbling after nothing very much.' Which meant that there were no belated juicy morsels heading their way; at least none from the reunees themselves. Rafferty didn't know whether to be pleased or sorry. But, at the moment, he was floundering through unwanted pregnancies, discarded lovers, probable male rape, suicide, bullying and a first murder victim who seemed to change his sexual allegiance even more often than he changed his lady friends, and a second who was way too keen on ferreting out information on other people than was healthy. There was just too much of everything. One thing he did know – he needed a break from the endless statements and his own, nearly as endless, theories.

'Let's get out of here,' he said to Llewellyn. 'My brain feels like it's drowning in blasted paperwork.' He was surprised when Llewellyn, too, said he felt like he was swimming through a heavy tide. It was unlike the Welshman to complain. Llewellyn had the protestant work ethic to the nth degree and often put Rafferty to shame.

'We'll drive out to Griffin,' Rafferty decided, 'and have a wander round. We'll get the keys off the caretaker.'

The sultry weather had passed away and the day was inviting, with pale blue skies and breeze-scudded white clouds. It was weather to blow the cobwebs away and Rafferty breathed in deeply when he got out to the car park, hoping that all the oxygen to the brain would pump something loose that would lead to the end of the case. He handed the keys to Llewellyn and said, 'You can drive.'

Griffin School had the forlorn air of all empty buildings. The school summer holidays were not yet over and the only person on the premises was Tom Harrison. Rafferty found him in his flat, having elevenses. He still wore his cap, even though he was indoors. He grumbled a bit when Rafferty asked for the keys to the school.

'They're my responsibility, you know. I'm sure Mr Paxton and the board of governors won't like outsiders wandering around, certainly not unaccompanied. I'll come with you.' He finished the remains of his tea and stood up. He adjusted his cap over his thick and curly dark hair that only now, although Harrison must be in his fifties, was starting to show signs of grey. The movement showed off a fine set of rippling muscles under the baggy grey tee shirt that Rafferty hadn't noticed before. The man must keep himself fit, he'd say that for him.

Rafferty would rather make the rounds of the school without Harrison in tow, and now he said, 'Don't let me drag you away from your elevenses, Mr Harrison. I'm sure your wife wouldn't like it.'

'Wife? What wife? I live here on my own. Anyway, I've finished my break. I don't take liberties, even though I'm virtually my own boss.'

Rafferty gave in gracefully. It wasn't as if he had any idea why he had wanted to come here. What could he expect to find, but empty classrooms and silence? He wouldn't even find Adam Ainsley's spirit here as he had died in Dedman Wood.

But he was here now and he might as well look round, even if just to vex the grumbling Harrison. Once the caretaker had unlocked the main doors and let them in, he locked them behind them again and led them to the part of the school that housed the school's Griffin emblem. It occupied pride of place on one of the white walls near the headmaster's study and gleamed gold from the shafts of sunlight streaming through the oriel window.

'I've been meaning to ask about that,' Rafferty said to Llewellyn. 'What is a griffin, anyway?'

Llewellyn's lips twitched and made an infinitesimal curve upwards as he launched himself on one of his lectures. 'It's a legendary creature, with, as you can see, the body of a lion and the head and wings of an eagle. The griffin was believed to be especially powerful and majestic as it was made up of the king of the beasts and the king of the birds. It was considered a guardian of riches, and education is considered a precious treasure. The griffin is also the enemy of ignorance.'

'Good job it's not likely to come alive then,' Rafferty joked. 'Or it might attack me.'

'Lot of nonsense,' said Harrison, his rugged features set in a mould of contempt. 'Legendary beasts, indeed. They should be learning about the real world, not made up stuff.'

'Shakespeare's "made up stuff", Mr Harrison,' said Llewellyn. 'And no one suggests they shouldn't study his plays.'

'Plays are different. I'm not talking about plays, but beasts that never existed. Why bother to invent them? Aren't there enough animals in the world, without having to make more up?'

'I'm with you, Mr Harrison,' said Rafferty, whose Roman Catholic secondary modern school had had no such legendary emblems. Such a beast as the griffin would probably be regarded as idolatrous, particularly one given such prominence. Christ suffering on the cross was the only symbol given pride of place at St Joseph's; that and pictures of Jesus exposing his blood-red heart. Cheerful stuff.

Harrison walked along the corridor and opened up one of the classrooms. It was the IT department. Each desk had a modern, slim-line computer, scanner and printer. Rafferty had a sniff around and, for Harrison's benefit, tried to look preoccupied with great thoughts, but he wasn't sure he succeeded.

'You finished in here, then?' Harrison asked after Rafferty had walked up and down between the desks, fingering computers as he went.

'Yes,' said Rafferty. 'Let's go up to the Senior Common Room. It's the sixth form's particular place and it might yet tell me something.'

'It's an empty room,' Harrison grumbled. 'What can it possibly tell you? I've got plenty of other things awaiting my attention, you know. I hope you're not going to want to poke your noses in every blasted room in the place.'

'No,' Rafferty reassured him. 'It's only a general feel of the place that I want. I don't need to go into every room for that.'

'Waste of time if you ask me. Haven't you already been all over the school once?'

He had. He had asked Paxton to show him round at the start of the case. Rafferty was beginning to think Harrison was right. He didn't know what he had hoped to find, but, so far, he hadn't found it. Nevertheless, he followed behind him through the Senior Common Room and another half dozen classrooms, before he and Harrison both seemed to have had enough. They were on their way out when they bumped into Paxton himself.

'Hello,' he said. 'What are you doing here?'

'I might ask you the same thing,' said Harrison, clearly not cowed by Paxton's headmasterly authority. 'The old headmaster, Mr B, never came near the school in the holidays. Apart from a teacher baby-sitting the holiday refugees, it's always been my domain during such times. I hope you're not going to start checking up on me.'

'Not at all. Let's just say it's a case of new men and new brooms, Mr Harrison,' said Paxton, resplendent in his holiday wear of a turquoise velvet smoking jacket. 'I came here looking for a bit of peace. With three young daughters of my own at home, it's bedlam. They're all dancing round the living room to the latest pop sensation and I can't get any work done. Don't worry, I'll lock up after myself.'

'See that you do, then. Or I can't be held responsible.'

Jeremy Paxton seemed more amused than offended by Tom Harrison's complaints and strictures; perhaps a truculent groundsman/caretaker was a school tradition, along with the eccentric headmaster. Nevertheless, from a certain glint in the headmaster's eye Rafferty found himself wondering how soon it would be before Paxton's new broom had swept the surly caretaker right out of the school. In these competitive days, you didn't get to become headmaster of such a prestigious pillar of education without knowing how to hire and fire. Or at least make recommendations. And it had to be said that Tom Harrison wasn't much of an advert for the school. If he was always this surly and insolent to visitors, it was a wonder he'd lasted as long as he had. Even Rafferty could see that the caretaker didn't project the right image. And nowadays, image was all. A case of never mind the quality, feel the width. But, apart from his efficient way with lawns and playing fields, Harrison, it had to be said, had neither width nor quality.

The 'boys' in the boys' night out, consisting of Rafferty, his two brothers, Mickey and Patrick Sean, Cyrus, Louis and cousin Nigel, all met up, as planned, in the Horse and Groom, Rafferty's new local. After introducing the two Americans to the family, Rafferty introduced them to the concept of having a kitty and they both coughed up without a murmur. There was some discussion about who was going to hold the money, there being no non-drinking and ever-scrupulous Llewellyn in the party, but eventually, after much humming and hawing, Cyrus was elected to the office of cash holder, it being thought that, as a man of God, he could be trusted not to dip into the kitty for extra drinks for himself. As he took the money, Cyrus confided to Rafferty, he had hopes of converting the barmaid he had met during their previous sojourn in the pub, who had taken a shine to him.

He's a Yank, thought Rafferty. She probably thinks he's rich. Still, it had to be said that Cyrus, when he wasn't preaching to the unconverted, had a certain earnest charm about him. He heard the barmaid tell him she loved his accent and, right on cue, Cyrus came back with 'And Ah love yours, too, honey. You'll have a drink with me?'

Of course, the barmaid said yes. Rafferty, as it dawned on him that he should have kept hold of the kitty himself, hoped Cyrus wasn't going to make a habit during the evening of buying new acquaintances drinks out of their kitty or they would end the night sober.

Cyrus came back with the drinks and they all sat down. 'Not going to push your advantage with the barmaid?' Rafferty asked him.

'Shucks, no. This is a family evening. Ah was just gauging her general openness to the Lord. Besides, Wendy told me Ah'm being too pressing about religion. She said it doesn't go down well in this little old country of yours. She told me Ah've yammered into your ears till they've started to bleed.'

Good old Wendy. Rafferty didn't contradict him. Maybe things were looking up on the Cyrus front. Now all he had to do was curtail his ma's eternal religious offensive as well as that of Father Kelly and he'd be home and dry. Atheism, here I come, he thought. He wished.

On the other side of Rafferty, Nigel drawled in his ear, 'So how are you coping with all this family thing? Want to run away screaming yet?'

Rafferty took a sip of his Jameson's, then said quietly, so as not to be heard by Cyrus or Louis, 'I might not have been keen on acting as a lodging house, I admit that, but at least I've made the effort, which is more than you've done.'

'The way I heard it you weren't given much choice, so don't come that old self-righteous crap with me. Besides, families, I find, can be too claustrophobic up close. It's an illness. I can't help it.'

'Bollocks,' said Rafferty. 'Let's face it, Nig, you're just selfish to the core.'

Nigel wasn't even offended. 'Very true. I find it's the only way to be to get on in this world. Maybe you'd have got higher in the police if you'd learned to put number one first, last and in between. And you might get on better with your superintendent if you kissed his arse occasionally, like I have to do with my wealthy clients.'

'He'd probably fart in my face if I tried. No, I think I'll stick to tweaking his ego and his budget.' He turned to Cyrus and Louis. 'Fancy a game of darts?'

Cyrus, up for experiencing everything English, enthusiastically agreed. 'The local bar in ma neighbourhood has a darts board. Ah'm regarded as pretty darn good. What say we have a little bet?'

Rafferty was willing, though he was sure Abra wouldn't like him taking Cyrus's money.

In the event, he didn't have to take the American's cash, as Cyrus thrashed him. Cyrus was ultra competitive, he discovered, and there was not a sign of Christian charity in the way he played and the pleasure he expressed each time he won another game. Rafferty accepted defeat with as much grace as he could muster and paid up, though he backed out of playing any more games with Cyrus. His brother, Mickey, had been watching the game. He had thought Rafferty's thrashing at darts at the hands of an American, the funniest thing he had ever seen, but having watched the game he demurred when Cyrus offered to take him on, too. Nigel didn't play. Darts were beneath him. He thought the game 'common', full of belching and beer bellies. Too much of the underclass about it altogether. Cyrus was forced to retire as reigning champion, so he went and got more drinks in.

Rafferty, Cyrus and Louis staggered down the main road from Elmhurst's centre, arms around each other, as much for mutual support as for camaraderie, bellowing out *The Battle Hymn of the Republic* for all their worth. Cyrus and Louis had been teaching it to them during the latter part of the evening. It was stirring stuff. Rafferty's pleasure in their poor man's 'Three Tenors' rendition was spoiled only by Abra who, when he had eventually managed to make the stairs to their bedroom, complained she could hear them coming from half a mile away.

'I'll have the neighbours complaining to me tomorrow. And we've only lived here for five minutes.'

'Stuff the neighbours,' said Rafferty, in the glories of intoxication. 'Complain who dare. I'm heading for the stars.'

'You're heading for a hangover, anyway,' said Abra. 'Get into bed and shut up, why don't you?'

'None shall silence me,' Rafferty declared, in a valiant attempt at some quotation or other. 'The landlords of three pubs tried, but we walked out those doors with our heads held high, singing our contempt for their petty rules. They hadn't got a music licence, they said, when Louis brought out a penny whistle to accompany us.'

'You mean you got chucked out of three pubs?'

'And barred. One of them doing the barring was our new local, so you can forget about enjoying their hospitality any time in the near future. Some people have no soul.' Thus saying, Rafferty fell into bed on his back and started snoring.

In vain, did Abra push at him and shout, 'Turn over. I don't want to have to listen to that noise all night.'

Failing to either wake or move him, Abra, unlike the fighting republicans, rolled over, pulled the pillow over her head, and admitted defeat.

Gerry Hanks's and the team's further questioning of Adam Ainsley's other schoolmates was gradually bringing in more information. But, so far, only one ex-pupil had been cajoled into admitting that Ainsley had subjected any of the younger boys to sexual bullying and even he refused to come out and say the word 'rape'. To make admissions more likely Rafferty had instructed his team to make sure they interviewed their witnesses in circumstances conducive to confessions and to avoid questioning anyone in the bosom of his family.

When the results were slow to trickle in, Rafferty had everyone in the incident room in order to give them a moral-boosting pep talk. Having been subjected to Cyrus's conversational style for the best part of two weeks, Rafferty felt he had learned something about public speaking and his rip-roaring team talk brought a new verve and they went back to their phones and their paperwork with greater vigour.

'Is there really going to be plenty of overtime?' Llewellyn asked afterwards. 'I didn't think Superintendent Bradley would sanction more outlay.'

'He didn't. I've gone over his head, haven't I?' said Rafferty. 'I've gone to Jack Mulcahy and he's OK'd some more money.' Jack Mulcahy was the Deputy Assistant Chief Constable for the county.

'How has that gone down with the superintendent?'

'About how you'd expect. I'm even less flavour of the month than I usually am. You watch, when we put in our expenses, he'll query every item. Anyway, let's get off. We've got three more suspect interviews to fit in today, so we'd better get a move on.'

Their re-interviewing of the other reunees was a time-consuming business, involving, as it did, many miles on the country's motorways to all points of the compass. But at least it got them away from the office and Bradley.

They went out to the car. The weather had turned cool and grey clouds, pregnant with rain, stretched from horizon to horizon. 'Driving'll be fun when that lot starts chucking it down,' Rafferty observed as he did up his seatbelt.

'I'll drive, if you like,' Llewellyn quickly offered. Never one to admire Rafferty's gung-ho style of driving, the Welshman always preferred to take the wheel when he could. But this wasn't one of those occasions.

'We'll never get round Harmsworth, Sadiq and Fairweather if you're behind the wheel,' Rafferty told him. 'As it is, we're lucky that Gary Sadiq had business in London today; we can get him and Harmsworth done before we see the mandarin.'

The rain started in earnest as Rafferty nosed out of the Bacon Lane car park. Soon it was hissing against the windscreen like so many biblical locusts proving almost too much for the wipers and he had to hunch forward over the wheel and peer through the screen with all his concentration. Beside him, Llewellyn was tense, the combination of his inspector behind the wheel and atrocious weather made him nervous. But even Rafferty had to go slowly in such conditions and soon Llewellyn gave up applying an imaginary brake and sat back and relaxed.

The journey into London was stop-start and frustrating. Even more so when they hit the M25, the so-called London orbital that Londoners had nicknamed the Giant Car Park. But eventually they arrived at the family home where Gary Sadiq was staying – the occupants of which seemed to have imposed some sort of code of silence because Sadiq had had nothing to add to what he'd already said and, eventually, Rafferty gave up his attempts to squeeze information out of him.

Back in the car, he made for Giles Harmsworth's home. Harmsworth lived in Canary Wharf, in a Thames-side apartment. Rafferty envied him the outlook if not the traffic.

Harmsworth was every bit as organizing and officious as he'd been at Griffin. He sat them down, decided that, as they were policemen, they'd want tea, and had it made and poured before Rafferty could be contrary and say he'd prefer coffee.

'Remember me telling you that Alice Douglas had a baby?' Rafferty began. 'Remember me asking if the kid might have been yours?'

'Yes. Of course I remember. You never did tell me why you thought it a possibility.'

On the basis of you and Alice both being swots, he might have said. But he didn't. 'Don't worry, sir. We've now discovered who was the father.'

'That's a relief. I wouldn't like the possibility that I'd fathered an illegitimate child bandied about. My wife wouldn't like it.' He paused. 'So, as you say you've now discovered the identity of the real father, why are you here? I really don't know that I can tell you any more than I've already done.' He glanced at his watch. 'I've a few deals on the go, Inspector, and need to get back to work, so can we make this short?'

Rafferty said he'd do his best to oblige him. But as, one after one, he revealed Adam Ainsley's homosexuality, his pursuit of young boys at Griffin and the possibility of blackmail, he saw that Harmsworth wasn't shocked by any of it.

'I was Head Boy, Inspector. It was my job to know all this, though of course I didn't know about the blackmail.' He paused, then added, 'Or Alice's pregnancy.'

Rafferty admitted that blackmail was just a possibility and only one amongst several that they were considering.

'You say you knew about Ainsley's homosexuality and his pursuit of young boys at the school. Did you do nothing to stop it?'

'I tried to get evidence – Mr Barmforth, the then headmaster, was hot on evidence of wrong-doing. He didn't like to be told what he called tittle-tattle. But I never managed to get any. I caught Ainsley in the toilets with one of the younger boys once, but if he had been intending to assault the boy, it hadn't gone very far. Certainly the child still had his trousers on, so there was nothing I could take to the headmaster.'

'Did you feel he was making a fool of you?'

Giles Harmsworth coloured up at this. He didn't answer immediately, but after a few seconds, he said, 'There were always boys who liked to test authority, to buck against the system. Sebastian Kennedy was the same. Adam resented me, of course. He seemed to think he should have been Head Boy, given his superiority on the sports field, but I believe Mr Barmforth thought he had enough glory. Besides, he wasn't good at rules. He thought they didn't apply to him, only to lesser mortals. I had to disabuse him of that idea several times.'

This was getting them nowhere. He'd thrown all he had at Harmsworth and hadn't shaken anything from the man. It was time to head for the Home Office and Simon Fairweather.

FOURTEEN

Simon Fairweather's office was on the first floor of the new architect-designed Home Office. The Department had moved from the brutal, old Sir Basil Spence monstrosity near St James's Park and was now situated in an ultra-modern building at Marsham Street. As they passed under the multi-coloured glass roof canopy designed, so Rafferty understood from Llewellyn, by a Turner Prize-winner, which said it all for Rafferty, he elected to use the stairs so as to stretch his legs.

Alerted by reception, Simon Fairweather was waiting for them. 'Inspector.' He held out his hand and Rafferty shook it. 'How can I help you this time?'

Rafferty waited until Fairweather had led them along the corridor to his own room and settled them in chairs facing his desk. There were as many pictures adorning the walls here as there had been in Sebastian Kennedy's apartment in Hampstead, but none of them featured naked ladies. Here was displayed original art borrowed from the London galleries. Most were boring landscapes featuring the usual munching cattle, sheep and sheepdogs that showed what a steady civil servant Fairweather was, but there was also a series of political cartoons that lightened the atmosphere and reminded Rafferty of the impish quality to Fairweather's mandarin-bland appearance.

'I was hoping you might have remembered something more since I last spoke to you,' Rafferty told him.

'I'm afraid not. I have been thinking about the lunchtime that Adam was poisoned and I really can't say that I noticed anything untoward. But I'm forgetting my manners. I'm sure you'd like something warming to drink after driving all the way here in such atrocious conditions. And to think the weathermen promised us a golden summer. That promise seems to have followed the examples of the promises of most of our political masters.'

Rafferty was surprised and pleased when instead of ringing his secretary and ordering tea, Fairweather pulled open the door of a cupboard behind his desk and revealed a well-stocked drinks cabinet.

'I can offer you whisky, gin, brandy, vodka. I've even got some tequila somewhere.'

'Whisky's fine.'

'Sergeant?

'Perhaps a mineral water.'

Fairweather served the drinks and Rafferty was glad to see that the Home Office man didn't believe in short measures. The heater on their car only worked when it wanted to and he was chilled, so he soon knocked the whisky back and Fairweather offered to top up his glass – an offer that Rafferty accepted with alacrity.

Fairweather seemed to have a relaxed attitude to drinking on duty, though Rafferty noted that the mandarin followed Llewellyn's example and opted for mineral water. Perhaps he had important meetings later for which he had to keep a clear head? Or perhaps it was this meeting that required clarity? As the Home Office man had claimed he had nothing new to tell them, Rafferty decided he would stir the waters and see what struggled to shore.

'Did you know that Adam Ainsley was a closet homosexual?'

'One did hear rumours. Nothing more. I wasn't importuned myself.'

'Do you know the identity of those who were?' Although Rafferty had names from a number of sources, he was always pleased to add to them. He couldn't know which piece of information would lead him to the truth. Certainly, so far, not one of the suspects had been named as one of Ainsley's sexual conquests.

Fairweather offered a couple of names, but they were ones already in their possession, so they were no further forward.

Rafferty decided on another stir. 'Were you aware that Jeremy Paxton's half nephew had a love affair with Ainsley and killed himself as a result?'

'Paxton? Paxton? I'm afraid you'll have to refresh my memory.'

'The new headmaster of Griffin School.'

'Ah. Yes, of course. I'm afraid the only headmaster I think of in relation to Griffin is Mr Barmforth. He knew how to instil the fear of a God of retribution into us all. I'm sure

Mr Paxton will be a very good headmaster and will grow into the role. But in these days of health and safety and "protect little children", he won't have the opportunity to make such an impression on his pupils as old B did on us.' Fairweather took a sip of his mineral water. 'And his half nephew killed himself, you say?'

Rafferty nodded.

'Any grounds for suspecting Mr Paxton intended any harm to Adam?'

Rafferty shrugged. If this had been a normal interview, he would have said nothing further. But Fairweather was a Home Office mandarin, so he added, 'It doesn't seem likely. He said he hardly knew the boy and his parents confirmed that that was so. No, I think we must look elsewhere for our culprit.'

'I'm only sorry I can't be more help.' Fairweather finished the water in his crystal glass and stood up. It was a signal the interview was over. But, Rafferty said to himself, *I* decide when an interview's finished, whether the witness is a mandarin or a tea-leaf. 'Have you always worked as a civil servant, sir?' he asked, going off on a tangent in the hope it would reveal something – anything – new.

'Good Lord, no.' Fairweather glanced at his watch and sat down again. 'I had a life, quite an interesting one, before I started here. I used to work as a chemist.'

Chemistry. Drugs. Poisons. The words reverberated around Rafferty's brain and he gave Fairweather a sharp glance. Didn't most drugs originate from plants? *Digitalis* from foxgloves, for instance, and datura from the Jimsonweed that was used to treat asthma at one time, and opium from poppies. Who better than a chemist to get his hands on the poison that killed Ainsley? Who better than a chemist to know where and how to get hold of it?

It seemed Rafferty's too open face had revealed the texture of his thoughts for Fairweather laughed and said, 'Don't bother, Inspector, to think that my old career is pertinent to your investigation. I used to work in the petrochemical industry and even if I was in the right branch of the profession, it's a decade since I worked in the industry and things – and people – have moved on. I really don't know anyone in that sphere now. I wouldn't be able to get hold of the poison that killed Adam even if I wanted to.'

Maybe not, Rafferty thought. But, in spite of your protests to the contrary, I bet you'd know who would. You might even know, or be able to find out, where to look for the plant that hemlock comes from. You might even be able to recognize it or have the relevant reference books to help you find it, more easily, anyway, than the average layman. Or woman.

It seemed that just as he was about to accept that Simon Fairweather should no longer be numbered amongst the suspects, he suddenly rose to the top of the list.

Rafferty made to head back to the office. As he'd been about to get behind the wheel, Llewellyn reminded him he'd been drinking and he handed the keys to his sergeant. He wanted to ring Sam Dally and check something out, but rather than use his mobile, he wanted to be at his desk and easily able to make notes. The rain had eased off and he told Llewellyn to put his foot down. As expected, the Welshman ignored this instruction.

'Why can't you be a hare rather than a tortoise for a change?' Rafferty asked. 'Just once?'

'If you remember the story, it was the tortoise that won the race in the end.' Llewellyn paused. 'I was wondering whether it might not be a good idea to investigate the previous careers of our other suspects, given Mr Fairweather's admission of his past life as a chemist.'

Though as to Fairweather's mention of the bullying of which he had himself been a victim, Rafferty was now beginning to think he should be no hastier than the tortoise. Did such an admission really have any value? It would be a different thing if he'd tried to conceal his past as a chemist, but to be so up front about it rather took away some of his previous suspicion. Still, that notwithstanding, Llewellyn's suggestion was a good one and he told him so, thereby earning himself the reward of a tiny increase in the car's speed. It didn't last long.

In spite of the Welshman being behind the wheel, they made good time and the journey back to Elmhurst was done in half the time of the outward trip.

As soon as he reached his office, Rafferty had Sam on the phone. 'What was the Latin name of the plant that hemlock comes from?' he asked immediately Sam came on the line. 'And where does it grow?'

'Good afternoon, Sam. How are you keeping? Got many corpses to cut up today?'

'Sorry, Sam. You sound pretty chipper to me, so I'll take it as read that you're well. But good afternoon, anyway. Now, about that plant.'

'*Conium Maculatum*. And how do I know where it grows? I'm not a botanist or a gardener. It's Alan Titchmarsh you want, not me.'

'I don't know Alan Titchmarsh. Can you find out?'

'You mean you want me to consult my tame plant expert?'

'Yes please.'

'He's not my favourite person, so it'll cost you. A large malt next time we meet up in a local hostelry.'

'You're on.'

'Leave it with me. I'll get back to you.'

Sam was as good as his word and came back to him at the gut-end of the afternoon, when Rafferty had about given up on him and was thinking about going home before Bradley caught him for another update.

'You can find *Conium Maculatum* all over Europe,' said Sam. 'It's a native plant to Britain. Every part is deadly, especially the fruits at flowering time. The root is pretty harmless in spring, but deadly at any other time.'

'So if the killer knew where to find it and knew how to recognize it—'

'Then he's presented with a marvellous murdering opportunity. Why? Got someone in mind?'

'Could be. Thanks, Sam. Let's arrange for that drink very soon. I'll give you a ring.'

Rafferty turned thoughtfully to Llewellyn. 'Can you find out – discreetly – if Simon Fairweather worked in another branch of chemistry before he joined the petrochemical industry?'

Llewellyn nodded. 'I know someone in the Home Office who can check Fairweather's personnel record. It should reveal the names of the firms who employed him. I also know someone at the chemists' professional body who can check out his qualifications.'

Rafferty was reluctantly impressed. 'Your Welsh Mafia seems to have its tentacles all over the place,' he observed. 'You'll be checking up on me next.' He hoped not, because one good root around in his family history would reveal plenty.

'It's not the Welsh Mafia,' Llewellyn protested, 'Merely old friends from my Cambridge days.'

'I wish I had a network of pals in high places,' Rafferty commented. 'I might be able to get Bradley promoted out of my hair. Maybe you could try?'

'I don't believe in promoting a person beyond their competence. There are enough people at the top already who are politicians rather than policemen.'

'Ain't that the truth.'

'Maybe if you placated Superintendent Bradley rather than deliberately antagonized him, you'd have a better relationship.'

It was what Nigel had suggested. The thought wasn't any more palatable from the Welshman's mouth. 'I doubt it. We just rub one another up the wrong way. And seeing as I'm stuck with him, I might as well have the occasional bit of fun at his expense.'

'Expenses. That's another area where you deliberately flout his wishes. You know what importance he places on keeping within the budget. Perhaps the rump steak you insisted on the other day wasn't such a good idea.'

'OK, Dafyd, give it a rest. I'll try to be good and kiss arse in future.'

'I don't think "kissing arse", as you call it, is necessary. Just behave towards him as you would towards any other senior officer whom you respect.'

'Ah. There's the rub. I don't respect him. He should never have risen beyond inspector.'

'Well he has, and you have to deal with it.'

Rafferty nodded and sighed. 'Go and check on your Taffy Maffy and leave me to practise puckering.'

But Llewellyn's investigation of Fairweather revealed that the mandarin had been telling the truth when he had said he had worked in the petrochemical industry.

Rafferty was disappointed, but, he reminded himself, Fairweather could still have the knowledge required to find out what he needed to know. He'd be one up on most people when it came to doing the appropriate research. So Under Secretary Simon Fairweather wasn't out of the woods yet, not by a long way. Although Llewellyn's research indicated that Fairweather had spent just under ten years working for British Petroleum as was, that only took him back to his mid-twenties or thereabouts. It was possible he had worked in – what would it be – organic chemistry? He wasn't sure. But Llewellyn's Home Office pal could certainly find out what aspects of chemistry Fairweather had studied for his degree and find out if he had worked in any other area before he joined BP and the Home Office. He just wished he'd hurry up. Although the Welshman was efficient and thorough, he could be painstakingly slow.

But Rafferty curbed his impatience and just waited for whatever information Llewellyn managed to extract from what he still insisted on calling the Taffy Maffy.

FIFTEEN

Adam Ainsley's agent had been right in his guess where the grand a month that Ainsley had received was from. The new month had brought another payment and this time, Mr Jarvis, the bank manager, had instructed his staff to keep the tapes. Ainsley's generous benefactor turned out to be a customer of the bank and well known to the staff. He was quickly traced and had admitted he had paid the money into Ainsley's account. When asked 'why?' he had simply said, 'He was the best. Many's the time I've watched Adam score a try when we thought the game was lost. I heard he was down on his luck and decided to help him out. I've been in the Far East and only heard he was dead after I made this last payment. A grand a month's not much to me, but his player's earnings wouldn't go far, not the way he behaved off the pitch, his two divorces and his squiring of high maintenance women about town. He's given me a lot of pleasure. I just thought I'd reciprocate.'

So at least that was one mystery solved.

At last the night of the family reunion came round. Rafferty found he was rather sorry that his visitors were all going home. Now that Cyrus had given up the religious preaching, it was pretty good to have an in-house drinking buddy who could match him, drink for drink. Even better, he had taken to regaling him with tales of his ma's youth after Abra went to bed. Rafferty was sure one or two of these titbits would come in useful in the future. He was surprised that Cyrus seemed to have such an affinity with drink, especially given his religion and he asked him about it once.

But Cyrus had said, 'Even Baptists have vices they shouldn't have, much like everyone else, Joe. I might have taken a vow to abstain from alcohol, but didn't you take a vow at your wedding to bring up your children Catholic? And how likely is it that you will?'

Rafferty had nodded. It was a low blow, but an accurate one. As Cyrus had intimated, it was likely to be a vow more observed in its neglect than anything else. Much like Cyrus and booze.

Somehow, in spite of his murder investigation, in spite of Bradley and his ever-increasing complaints about results and budgets, Rafferty had found the time, with his two brothers, to put up the multi-nation flags that Ma had decreed were essential to make the evening go with a swing. As he came into the hall with Abra, he admired his handiwork and had to admit they made an effective backdrop to such an evening. Ma had also decreed that everyone should dress in the colours of their national flags, with the result that there was a preponderance of red, white and blue. The Irish, Canadian and South African contingent were the only exceptions to this patriotic colour scheme.

Ma was already there. She had come over during the afternoon to supervise the placing of the chairs and tables and generally chivvy up the caterers. She was still bustling around on Rafferty's arrival. He and Abra had come a little early to help make sure everything was ready and most of the far-flung Rafferty and Kelly families had yet to arrive. Cyrus and Wendy had also elected to come early and had accompanied Rafferty and Abra in the car. Wendy was a bit shy and was soon taken under Ma's wing. Not so Cyrus, he was off across the hall, introducing himself here and introducing himself there. No shrinking violet him.

Rafferty was beginning to feel a bit like a spare groom at a wedding as everything looked set for the evening and there didn't seem to be anything for him to do. That being the case, he was glad to see the bar was open and he headed over there and had just got himself outside a large Jameson's when Cyrus bustled up.

'You'll have a drink with me, Joe? You and Abra?' He eyed their glasses, accurately concluded what their contents were and gave the order to the barman. He drank his own Jameson's as swiftly as most people down nasty medicine and would have been off on another round of circulating but for Father Kelly, who chose that moment to appear beside them. Rafferty introduced them.

'So you're Cyrus Rafferty.' Father Kelly positively bristled and Rafferty gazed at him with interest. 'I've heard a lot about you.'

'Oh really?' said Cyrus with a pleased smile. 'Who from?'

'My cousin, Kitty.'

'Mighty fine woman, Kitty.' Cyrus's chin went up as he caught the unfriendly cut of Father Kelly's jib.

'Isn't she?'

Rafferty wasn't sure he could believe what he was seeing. Surely they couldn't be squaring up to each other? Not over Ma?

Fascinated, he watched as Father Kelly, celibate Catholic priest, and Cyrus, another of those with a hotline to God and with a wife of over forty years, danced round one another like two heavyweight boxers.

'Is it right that you're not staying with Kitty while you're over here? I thought you would be. I thought that was the plan.' It was clear that such a plan had not met with Father Kelly's approval.

'It was, sir, but Kitty changed it at the last minute. Ah don't really know why.'

Rafferty did. He also now knew the real reason why Father Kelly had pushed her into the change. Ma had wanted Cyrus to bring religion back into her errant son's life and Father Kelly, pragmatist to the last, hadn't given a damn about his mortal soul and was more concerned about Cyrus staying in Ma's home. He was astonished to discover that Father Kelly seemed to think his ma was a delicate, vulnerable soul who needed protecting from predatory males. Rafferty almost laughed out loud.

Father Kelly's cross-questioning continued. 'I hear you're a preacher back in America?'

'That's right, sir,' said Cyrus, puffing out his chest like a bantam cock as if he was anticipating a fight. 'Ah'm a lay preacher and Ah've been told Ah'm a mighty fine orator and—'

'But sure, and you're not the real McCoy, are you? You haven't taken vows of any sort?'

'No, sir. That Ah haven't. But there's a fine tradition in ma country that any man with something worth saying and with an audience willing to listen can stand up and preach the word of the Lord. The sweet, sacred Jesus belongs to all of us, after all.'

Father Kelly's slight inclination of the head acknowledged the truth of this, before he leant forward and put the boot in. 'Personally, I don't agree with lay preachers. I think they can lead people astray through ignorance. A Catholic priest has a rigorous training. Eight years of study beyond High School, including a college degree, followed by four or more years study at a seminary. You can't just walk off the street and start preaching.'

'Is that so? But Ah've studied the Gospels, like you. I know the Holy Bible from beginning to end, in all its glory. Ah preach every opportunity Ah get and folks seems to appreciate it. Ah've had more than a few standing ovations.'

'Standing ovations?' Father Kelly's whiskey-red face looked outraged. 'Preaching shouldn't be part of the entertainment industry. It's a sacred trust and should be treated with reverence.' Father Kelly leant forward and stared at him. 'What denomination are you?'

'Ah'm a member of the Church of the Lord of Savannah, Georgia,' Cyrus proudly proclaimed. 'Ah guess we're non-denominational, though Ah have Baptist leanings, and some of our members are strayed Methodists.' Cyrus grinned, still trying hard to be friendly. 'Ah guess you could say we're a pretty catholic bunch and—'

He didn't get a chance to finish his explanation for Father Kelly pounced. 'The Church of the Lord? And you say that you're not even a proper denomination, like Methodist or Baptist? Not a proper church at all. Ha. I rest my case.' With that, Father Kelly stalked off as if he'd just been talking to the devil incarnate.

Cyrus looked upset and turned to Rafferty. 'It *is* a proper church, Joseph. It's as holy a place as Ah know.'

'I'm sure it is,' said Rafferty who knew little about the place. 'Take no notice of Father Kelly. He's one of the old school Catholics, who believe that every other church, every other religion, is bogus and the only way to the Lord is with the aid of the Pope and the Holy Catholic Church.'

'Ah guess so.' Cyrus perked up a bit. 'Ah bet he's a mighty fiery preacher.'

'He is that,' said Rafferty. 'Though the fire he mostly calls up consists of the Hellish sort, with devils and demons to torment the dear departed.'

'Not a kindly preacher, then? Not one who sees good in the soul of the worst sinner.'

'That's right. Sometimes, I think the good Father would question the purity of the soul of JC himself. Give me the Church of the Lord every time. I bet you have some great tunes to sing along with.'

'That we do. Although we're only a small church, we're hooked up to the whole of Georgia and our services go out over the air. We had an orchestra in the week before I left.'

'Your Church sounds a hell of a lot more fun than St Boniface. A hell of a lot more forgiving as well,' said Rafferty as he clapped Cyrus on the back, 'Though I thought we'd agreed not to talk about religion. Let's get a drink instead.'

'Good ahdea, Joe. Your round, Ah think.'

Rafferty turned for the bar and as he did so he caught his ma's eye and in the split second before she changed it, he caught an expression of pleased satisfaction on her face.

'Still got it, Ma,' Rafferty murmured to himself as he fell in behind Cyrus and headed for some alcoholic refreshment.

In dribs and drabs, the other members of the extended family arrived. Rafferty's hand was sore from all the enthusiastic pumping, his head a whirl of instantly forgotten names. He was thankful when his ma called for a bit of hush and asked everyone to their tables. In deference to the assorted national food preferences, Ma had plumped for an innocuous chicken dish with a salad for the vegetarians. The meals were soon served and the noise level in the room went down as everyone concentrated on their food. But drink had been taken and soon the hall was a noisy hubbub again as people exchanged life histories and explained their particular branch of the two family trees.

'Look at Cyrus,' said Rafferty's mother who was seated next to him on the top table as the proud organizer of it all. 'You'd think he'd come and sit down. I saved him a place beside me specially.'

Rafferty hid a smile. He bet that hadn't gone down too well with St Boniface's own hellfire preacher. And as for Cyrus, ever keen on new members to swell the church's coffers and soul-salvers, he was still going around glad-handing everyone, particularly his fellow Americans.

'His meal's getting cold. Why doesn't he come and sit down?' she said again. 'He can carry on saying hello to everyone afterwards.'

But when he came near enough for Ma to shout at him, Cyrus said he wasn't hungry. The prospect of gaining so many potential souls apparently fed his appetite better than any food. Father Kelly was a bit of a backslider in this regard; he was sitting down, stuffing his face with the best of them.

'Now there's a man to be admired,' said Ma to her lapsed Catholic eldest son as she nodded in Cyrus's direction. 'You could do worse than take a leaf out of his book.'

'You know, Ma,' said Rafferty, who had also been watching Cyrus, 'you could well be right.' He pulled out his mobile and dialled Llewellyn, got a couple of phone numbers and crossed his fingers that he was on the right track at last.

'Can't you put that thing away,' his ma said. 'This is supposed to be a night for family. Cyrus told me how hard you've been working, but tonight's not a night for wicked murders.'

Rafferty snapped his phone shut, put it in his pocket and said, 'You're right, Ma. As usual. Tomorrow will do well enough for that.' He glanced at her plate. 'Have you finished?' She nodded. 'Then let's go and mingle.'

The night had gone with a swing. No one seemed to want to go home and the noise levels were louder than ever as Raffertys and Kellys chatted as if they'd been intimate friends all their lives rather than pen-pals, or unheard of before Ma had got on the internet.

Eventually, with the meal over and a few drinks under his belt, Rafferty had done some more mingling himself. He'd lost Ma and Abra hours ago but was enjoying himself so much that he hadn't stopped to look for either of them. To his horror, he found his new wife eventually, chatting to Father Kelly and Nigel, of all unlikely combinations. Their heads were close together and he couldn't help wondering what they could possibly find to talk about so earnestly. Sure it wasn't to his good, he hurried over and interrupted them.

'You three look as thick as thieves. What are you up to?'

Abra blushed, but said nothing. But he knew what she was like when she'd let her hair down and he was worried that she'd blabbed to Father Kelly about them trying for a baby.

And so it proved as Father Kelly slapped him on the back and said, 'Glad it is I am to hear that you and Abra are trying for another babby after your sad loss.' Abra, like Angie, his late first wife, had lost a baby in the early months of pregnancy. 'And won't your mammy be pleased?'

Rafferty gave a sickly smile and shot an accusing glance at Abra who had the grace to hang her head.

'You'll have the baby baptized, of course. I'll book you in for next year. What names are you thinking of?'

'Hang on, Father. Abra's not even pregnant yet. Give us a chance.'

'Sure and a fine, fecund, Irish Catholic family such as yours, you'll have no trouble at all. You wait, it's my guess that this time next month, you'll have news of a happy event.'

Rafferty could only hope so, because the thought of months of trying, with Ma and Father Kelly egging him on, was too horrible to contemplate.

Nigel chipped in his twopenn'orth. 'You want to cut down on the booze, Joseph, if you're trying for a baby.' He slipped his hand in his inside pocket and pulled out a brochure. 'You want to get yourself some vitamins, too. There's a fine range for would-be daddies. And Milk Thistle's good for raddled livers. It's a new venture of mine. Here, take the brochure. You'll be sure to find something in there to help if you have any problems with the old fertility.'

It was amazing, Rafferty thought as he took the leaflet and stuffed it in his pocket. Trust Nigel to think there could be a profit in his and Abra's hopes for a baby. Was there nothing the man wouldn't look to find the bottom line in?

It seemed not, because as he wandered back to the bar, he noticed several people studying Nigel's cards. Should any of the family decide on a second home in little old England,

Nigel wanted to be sure his was the first office they went to. Rafferty had wondered why Nigel had shown his face at the family reunion. Now he knew. He saw it simply as a marketing opportunity.

SIXTEEN

The next morning, sore head or not, Rafferty made sure he got up early. He had turned the clock radio up so he'd be sure to hear it when it went off. He rang the station to get the troops mobilized and was out the door in fifteen minutes flat, not even stopping to make Abra her tea. He reviewed everything he had found out last night once his ma and her sharp ears had become lost in the throng and after he'd phoned a couple of the reunees. Everything fitted neatly into his latest theory like a size zero model down a drain hole; even the letter they had found in Adam Ainsley's flat. Admittedly, as with the case against Alice Douglas, it was all circumstantial, but he knew a way to make one of the circumstances stick, at least.

Llewellyn was the first to hear his latest theory. And when Rafferty reached the end of the recitation of it, Llewellyn's usually serious and sallow face looked tinged pink with excitement.

'I really think you've got it this time.'

'I have, haven't I?' Rafferty grinned. 'How many of the team have you ordered to accompany us?'

'Just two. I think our suspect will come quietly, don't you?'

Rafferty nodded. 'Oh yes. A well brought up soul like that would do nothing else. Are you all set? Then let's go.'

Rafferty roared out of the car park exit like Lewis Hamilton on speed, causing Llewellyn to grip the dashboard with white-knuckled fingers. 'Why the rush?' he gritted out through clenched teeth. 'If he'd wanted to disappear, he'd have done it by now.'

'Just upping the value of my street cred for the neighbourhood villains.' He eased off the gas. 'But you're right. There's no point in roaring up his drive and giving him warning enough to slip out the back.' The speedo was now at a nice, sedate, thirty miles an hour. 'How's that?'

'Lawful.' Llewellyn let go of the dash and sat back, breathing out on a relieved sigh as he did so.

'He wasn't my half nephew. He was my son.'

Jeremy Paxton hunched forward over the table as if anxious for Rafferty to understand.

'I rather guessed that,' said Rafferty. It was an hour later and they were at the police station in one of the interview rooms. He glanced over at the tape to make sure it was still running. He didn't want a technological glitch to miss any of this.

'You did? How?'

Rafferty was only too pleased to reveal how clever he'd been. How he'd managed to outwit such an intelligent, educated man. 'It was something your half brother's wife said. The way she spoke of David as 'my son'. At first I just thought it was the mother punishing her man for not being the father David had needed. She certainly seemed to blame her husband for the lad's suicide, at least in part. But perhaps she was just rubbing salt in the wound of an already festering sore? That in fact David was her son and not his. And then I remembered something else: that David's supposed father never once referred to your half nephew as 'my son'. It was always by 'David', his given name. It set me to wondering who might be the boy's father if it wasn't Andrew Paxton. Taken together with one or two other things it set me thinking. It didn't take me long to come up with your name.' Rafferty had threatened an exhumation order on David Paxton, so that he could test out his theory of paternity, but it hadn't been necessary to go so far. He had, anyway, been pretty sure that Jeremy wouldn't want the boy's body disturbed. And so it had proved. Faced with the few pieces of evidence that Rafferty possessed, plus the threat of exhumation, he had quickly admitted his guilt. Indeed, he had seemed almost pleased to have the opportunity to confess.

Rafferty continued his explanation of how clever he'd been at unravelling Jeremy Paxton's murder plot. 'You sent Adam Ainsley a letter inviting him to the reunion that purported to be a round robin, yet as I've discovered, the other invitations were pretty standard with none of the gush of the letter Ainsley received. You were determined to get him to this reunion, weren't you?'

Jeremy Paxton nodded. 'I didn't know David was my son until my sister-in-law split up from my half brother, permanently, as she thought and then she told me. I didn't believe her at first, thought she was looking to use me for child support – our affair had ended acrimoniously. But when she reminded me of the dates of our affair and the date of David's birthday, the timings worked out.' His face flamed red for a few seconds. 'All those years and I never knew. All the years I missed.' He shook his head and his eyes shadowed with sadness and regret. 'But, even then, I wasn't completely convinced. I think I was scared to believe her, my longing for a son was so great. So, under the pretext of having another chat to her about it, I went round to see my sister-in-law. I didn't even have to sneak into David's bedroom on my way to the bathroom as I had intended as she insisted on taking me up there herself and handing me David's hairbrush so I could help myself to some hairs. She even told me to be sure and get ones with roots attached. She was that convinced that she was right and that David was my son.

'You can imagine how I felt when the test results came back. I felt so pleased, so proud I thought I would burst. I wanted to contact David immediately and tell him I was his dad, but how could I? His parents' separation had been traumatic. I didn't feel I could just blurt out that his mother and I had had an affair and that the man he had thought of as his father all his life wasn't and that, actually, I was. So I decided to wait a while. Maybe visit more often. Get to know him better. But in the meantime, my half brother moved back in with his wife and they patched up their differences. Then Ainsley got his claws into him and before I even knew about their relationship, before I could let him know about ours, my son was dead.'

Jeremy Paxton bowed his head. When he raised it again, his eyes were damp. 'I was angry enough that Ainsley had buggered my half nephew and then broken his heart sufficient for the boy to kill himself. But then to learn he'd actually done that to my *son*. The son I've always wanted and never had. The son I'd never had a chance to get to know. The son who killed himself because of that bastard. You bet I wanted revenge. You bet I wanted him dead and not too slowly, either. I knew from

Who's Who that he had attended Griffin School and I thought my best opportunity to get close enough to kill him good and slow was through a school reunion. I'd heard on the grapevine that Cedric Barmforth, the old headmaster, was retiring early, so I wrote to the Board of Governors, asking if there would be any teaching vacancies in the new autumn term and was invited to apply for the headship after they'd seen my emailed CV.

'The competition was fierce, but I was determined to get the post and I did. It helped that the old headmaster, Mr Barmforth, took to me and pushed my name forward with the Board. Anyway, as I said, I got the post. It was when the Board of Governors asked me to take over the organization of the school reunion that I discovered Adam Ainsley had never attended the annual get-togethers and it was important that he attend if I was to give the impression that the reason for his murder was buried in the past. I was stymied for a while, but then I hit on the idea of writing him a very special fan letter, one his ego would make sure he responded to. So I wrote him a very non-standard invitation letter, full of little touches to appeal to his ego. I laid it on a bit thick, but it clearly struck a chord, because he accepted my invitation by return of post.

'It was then that I started researching the best way to kill him to meet my requirements. It took me a while, but eventually I found out about hemlock and what it does to the limbs. I thought it an apt retribution that the school sporting hero should suffer paralysis – that the legs and arms that had been his friends all his life would become his enemies and prevent him walking out of the wood to the road. Or even – if he somehow managed to crawl his way out and find a phone, that his hands wouldn't be able to punch nine nine nine for help.'

'Surely he had a mobile?' It was one of the things he had neglected to check, Rafferty now realized. There was always something.

'Of course. He was the sort of man who would have to have all the latest gadgets, all the boys' toys, to go with his famous name. I took care to check out his room before I went in to lunch that first day and I removed the battery.

'But I didn't think for a moment that he'd manage to overcome the panic when he found his legs wouldn't do what he wanted. Adam Ainsley was a person who had it easy all his life: all the girls he wanted – which is a bit ironic when you think about it – good looks, sporting success, popularity. But none of it was enough for him. He had to treat my only son so badly that he killed himself.'

'And what about Sophie Diaz? I suppose she saw you do the hemlock trick?'

'Yes. I was sorry about that. She told me plainly that she'd hated Ainsley for years. She told me he had humiliated her when they were at school together and that she wasn't sorry he was dead. But she just wanted to know why I had killed him. Funny, she didn't seem to think she was in any danger. I was a respectable headmaster, albeit with poisonous tendencies. But she seemed to have convinced herself that my murderous bent was strictly limited. It would have been, too, but I couldn't risk leaving her alive. I had my family to think of.'

He sat back and stared intently at Rafferty. 'But Ainsley's dead now. And you know what? Suddenly I don't care any more what happens to me. You can charge me. What are you waiting for?'

'Nothing.' Rafferty read Paxton the statutory caution for the second time, got up and walked to the door and gestured to the uniform standing outside the door to lead him away. At least this time, unlike at his house earlier, he didn't have to be led past his distraught family, his wife and three young daughters.

But still, he didn't feel good about the arrest. Why was it, he wondered, that, so often in his career, the killer turned out to be a better human being than the victims? With motives for murder that were understandable, maybe even laudable.

He said as much to Llewellyn and got some Latin claptrap back.

But whatever he felt, the case was over now. And he owed Cyrus a big thank you. Without him it would never have occurred to him that Jeremy Paxton would make his way around each table at lunch that first day of the reunion and greet everyone personally – all so that he could get the opportunity to slip the hemlock in Ainsley's meal. It was that and his memory of the discordant way David's parents had spoken of him. It was unsurprising that none of the reunees had thought to mention Jeremy Paxton's personal greetings. After all, they had thought, just like Rafferty, that this murder must be rooted in the past, in their youth spent together at Griffin School. How could the new headmaster figure in such a scenario? Jeremy Paxton didn't even know any of them. What possible reason could he have for wanting to kill Ainsley?

It was seeing Cyrus glad-handing around the tables at the family reunion that made him think outside the box; think that maybe he hadn't been the only one to do a bit of glad-handing at a reunion. And if his ma hadn't organized her own reunion, he might never have got the answer, the same as he would never hear the end of it if Ma ever got to know about it. She'd adopt it as 'my murder' and for the foreseeable future proclaim to the neighbours that she'd had a big part in its solution. So, once again, to avoid that, he had sworn Cyrus to secrecy. The American was turning out to know more of his secrets than Father Kelly had learned in the confessional in his youth. But, for all of his talk, Cyrus had proved far less of a blabbermouth. And, unlike Nigel, he was confident that this was one cousin who would keep his secrets safe without the need for bribery.